AF254580

Take Me Home to Woodstock
A Novel

By
Sally Cissna

SuLu Press
Oshkosh, Wisconsin
2019

SuLu Press

3145D White Tail Lane

Oshkosh, Wisconsin 54904

sallycissna@sulupress.org

Publisher's Cataloging-in-Publication data

Cissna, Sally.

Take Me Home to Woodstock: A Novel / Sally Cissna.

p. cm.

ISBN 978-1-64633-160-4

1. HIS054000 HISTORY/Social History 2. FIC008000 FICTION/Sagas/Family Sagas 3. SOC026000 SOCIAL SCIENCE/Sociology/Women/Religion.

I. Cissna, Sally. II. Take Me Home to Woodstock.

Library of Congress CN: 2019911303

While people, places, and events in these stories are real, the details of their lives and experiences have been changed for narrative purposes. Accounts herein are meant to reflect the mores of the era, and while sometimes jarring, are not meant to disrespect any person or group, past or present.

Cover design is a Wienke family photograph of Lincoln Avenue, Woodstock, Illinois, circa 1904.

Printed in the USA by Lighting Source/IngramSpark Publishing

First Edition

Dedication

This book is dedicated to the family of
John Wienke and Ida Doering.
May Ida and John's legacy forever be preserved
in the generations to come.

And to the people of Woodstock, Illinois,
the pretty little village where
John and Ida made their home in 1902.

Peace and rain.

Thanks

Without the time and support of the following individuals, this book would never have come to fruition.

Thank you to my friend, Liz, for being my cultural reader and unofficial counselor. Your ear for writer-truth and reader-reaction for the controversial areas of this enterprise was greatly valued – along with the lively discussions over our two-margarita lunches.

Thank you, Shari, my friend and most enthusiastic reader. Your constant encouragement kept me productive and our long friendship makes me happy.

Thank you to my niece Becky who proofread as she read the first draft of the book aloud to her mother, Marian. Getting a family perspective on the story was so important and finding those infernal typos.

An enthusiastic thank you also to my editor and mentor Juliet, without whom this project would never have gotten off the ground. She was the rational voice calling in the wilderness, who sat me down to develop a timeline to publication.

Thank you to the Carmel Crisp Writers Group, who have over the last year, acted as my sounding board and brainstorming group, as I organized and reorganized my short narratives into a cohesive book. You, my friends, are the best.

Thank you to Sarah who brought her creative ideas and skills to the project.

And finally, without the love and support from my life-partner and spouse, Rebecca, I wouldn't have had the ability nor the time to do the research necessary, or for that matter, write at all. Thank you, for your patience and encouragement, for your knowledge of many things, and for being my primary shareholder in this undertaking.

The Wienke Home
At the edge of Oakland Protestant
Cemetery, Woodstock, Illinois,
circa 1900.

New Year's Eve - 1911

Cold, crisp air greeted John and Ida Wienke as they climbed down from the train to the platform in Woodstock. John looked about for the horse and sled that was to meet them and carry them home. The train was several minutes early, but still, it was too cold to wait long. Then he heard the jingle of far-away bells approaching — and a robust, jolly elf drove his trusty steed off the roadway coming forward for their pickup. The driver had a ruddy face and a winter beard frosted white with his breath. He wore a red stocking cap and scarf over a heavy sheepskin coat. Their dear friend, Roger Kaufman gave a hearty, "Whoa, Gertie!" as he pulled on the reins bringing the sleigh to a skidding stop on the ice-covered surface.

"Guten Abend!" he shouted to those assembled on the platform.

"Guten Abend," John, Ida, and eight-year-old Helen answered in unison.

"Wie geht es?" Roger asked. His voice echoed in the cold air. Then noticing the two sleeping little ones slung over shoulders, he shushed himself laying a finger to his lips.

He sprung from the sleigh and took Dody out of Ida's arms. "Here, my dear. Let me take this burden from you," he said, lowering his voice. "Better that you have just yourself to worry about on this icy night, especially—"

"In my condition," Ida finished his thought, placing her free hand self-consciously on the swelling at her waist. "She's not such a burden, although I'd like it if she would stop growing quite so round." As she transferred the child to him, she noted the transport. "I see you brought the sleigh. We feel like royalty."

"Oh, I've been up to Queen Anne's for service this evening. The station was on my way home," he demurred.

Roger cradled the sleeping five-year-old on his shoulder and gave the other hand to Ida to step down off the wooden planks onto the icy ground. "Here you go then," he said. "Be careful, the footing is less than perfect, and we wouldn't want you to fall."

Ida took his hand and stepped gingerly down. She felt her foot slip, but then it caught on gravel poking through the ice. Roger guided her over to the sleigh and allowed her to pull herself up into the rear seat without assistance and handed Dody up. He turned his attention to John who had one-handedly gathered the luggage to the near side of the platform. Roger loaded the luggage in beside Ida, and Helen climbed up to the middle position in the front. John made his way to the sleigh and climbed up, sheltering seven-year-old Mamie's face from the cold blast with his gloved hand. All they needed was for her to get sick again.

Roger jumped up and took the reins. "I'll have you home in a jiffy. Cold night, aina?"

"Sure is," said John. "The train was warm by comparison even without heat."

"Great way to travel, but certainly not perfected," agreed Roger. "Come on, Gertie. Let's go. Hold tight to your precious cargo!"

As the roan began to pull, the sleigh slid sideways rather than forward, and Gertie had to put her back into it to get the sleigh out onto the street. The Village of Woodstock lay quiet on this night of transition. Tomorrow would begin a new year with its promise of prosperity, but they heard no revelry as was common for such a night. Not a sleigh or sled in sight. As they left the station and headed toward the square, the quick clop of Gertie's feet was the only sound and the moon above the only light.

"Where are all the people?" asked Helen.

"Hunkered down at home in front of the fire, I would guess," answered Roger.

But then they rounded the corner onto the square. The park was lit with hundreds of electric bulbs in all the colors of the rainbow. People, their faces muffled in gayly-colored scarves, bustled here and there. Lively music issued from the speakers at the hardware store and people were happily coming and going from several of the saloons on the square. It was a scene they would all long remember.

"Oh," said Helen, "how beautiful. Do you think there will be fireworks tonight, Papa?" She stood up to get a better view.

"Maybe," said John. "But, I hope, we will all be sound asleep by then."

Bang! Bang! Rata-tat-tat! Firecrackers broke the crystalline silence. Gertie was taken by surprise and shied away from the sound, sending the heavily loaded sleigh into a skid. They spun, and Gertie lost the ability to control the momentum. Bags flew from the rear seat as Ida clung to Dody with one hand and the front seat with the other. John lost purchase on the front seat and slipped one foot out to stand on the right runner, hanging on tightly to Mamie and the front rail. Roger pulled Helen to him as he too clung to the rail. The world slowed – the sleigh turned dragging Gertie in a half-circle.

They came to a stop facing the wrong direction on the one-way street around the central park. Gertie had somehow kept her feet, and they, sleeping children and all, had stayed in the sleigh. A silent moment ticked as everyone remembered to breathe. Mamie opened her sleepy eyes and looked around. "Woodstock," she sighed and laid her cheek against her father's rough wool coat.

John smiled. "Yes, we are home in Woodstock," he whispered to the top of her head. Mamie smiled a little and slipped back into sleep.

Roger clambered down, making comforting sounds to Gertie whose breath came in frosty steam puffing from her nostrils. He retrieved the bags and was back in a flash of good humor.

"We meant to do that," he said, looking at Helen. "Gertie and I have been practicing our skating all week just for you." Helen giggled.

"It's a bit icy," said John.

Roger chuckled. "Yes. Ice storm yesterday, don't cha know. You may not have electricity at your place. The whole town was out. It's certainly back on here on the square," Roger said, as he carefully turned Gertie in a sharp circle to continue the journey. "We best just walk, Gertie. No more skating. We want to get these folks home in one piece."

The horse walked up Cass Street, past the old grocery shop, and turned right on Throop, past Ida's brother's house. They continued left on Judd, past the place where Helen had lost her mittens on the way to visit Papa at his 'tore. Gertie pulled onward turning right on Tyron and then left on Lincoln Avenue. The way was circuitous, but it was always nice going through the square when coming home. Half-way up Lincoln Avenue, Roger gently reined Gertie to a stop in front of 365, the house that John built.

"Here we are!" he announced. "Home Sweet Home!" Helen giggled again. She loved the way Roger talked, often a bit too loud and always cheerful.

Someone had sanded the street and the front walk which gave better footing to both the four-legged and the two-legged. The transfer of children and bags was quickly done, and Roger took his leave, responding to expressions of thanks with a hearty, "Frohes neues Jahr!"

While John checked the fire in the basement furnace, Ida unbundled the children and herself. The house had been standing empty overnight, but the fire was in good shape from an earlier stoking – Roger again.

With the children tucked into bed, John flopped down on the davenport next to Ida. Their eyes met, and he smiled. "How is Mama?" he asked.

"Mama is tired. And Papa?"

Before answering, John glanced around the room with its sturdy walls and large front window looking out onto the wintry night. The Christmas tree was still up, and the room smelled of pine and wet wool, with just a hint of cooking smells from Ida's kitchen. "Well, Papa is glad we're all back safely. I'm always lonely when you and the children are in Racine," admitted John.

"I'm sorry. Maybe next time you can stay for the whole week instead of just taking us to Racine and coming back to retrieve us. Oma would love to have you all week if only to put you to work."

"Maybe. But it's sure good to have Mama back home," and he leaned over and kissed her, his hand resting on her rounded belly. He pulled away slightly, leaving his hand in place. "How is my boy tonight?"

"I think he rather liked the train ride."

A quick punch under his hand took John by surprise. He jumped.

"I think he's telling you himself that he is fine," laughed Ida.

"Three more months," said John.

"Two and a half," Ida corrected.

Off in the distance, church bells began to play the music of the arriving year. The peals echoed from the Catholic belfry at the end of the block and bounced across the village, being joined by the two Lutheran bells, the Presbyterian bell, and the Congregational bell, all ringing the glad tidings of great joy that the world had made it through another year. The distant booms of fireworks added syncopation to the tune, and the rata-tat-tat of close-by firecrackers kept the beat going for long moments before fading away.

"Happy New Year," they said almost as one and pecked a kiss in celebration.

John looked at Ida. "Did I ever tell you about the night that I knew I was going to marry you?"

"Mm, I don't believe so. I'd love to hear how you came to such a precipitous decision."

John chuckled and began, "Well let's see…it was New Year's Eve and Ma threw a party."

"Your mother?"

"Yes, my mother. It was the beginning of the new century, and Ma was not about to be left out. So, she brought the celebration to her."

The Doering family of Racine, Wisconsin, circa 1893. Front: Ida Doering; Second: (L to R) Clara Doering, Emma Ardelt; unknown. Back: Louisa Ardelt Doering, Floyd Fisher and Emma Doering Fisher

The Wienke Brothers from Woodstock, Illinois, circa 1890. Front (L to R): Emil, Charles, William, Ed. Back: Bob, Frank, John, Albert

The Pouring – 1900

John Wienke raised his cup and called out, "Frohes neues Jahr!" And those gathered responded in a shout, "Frohes neues Jahr!!" John imagined all the citizens of Woodstock, Illinois, gathered in groups like this one, counting down the 1800s and welcoming 1900, shouting "Happy New Year!" He watched as couples came together for the first kiss of the new year. No kiss for him again this year, his twenty-ninth, because he was not yet coupled.

The gathering was a small one of about twenty family and friends. The Woodstock fathers had bowed to the national scholars who said that the 1900s started at midnight at the end of the year 1900, not at its beginning. They announced in *The Woodstock Sentinel* that the citywide celebration of the new century, if there would be one, would not commence until December 31, 1900. So, everyone was left to celebrate in private or at church watches.

Protesting the decision of the authorities, John's mother, Sophia, had gathered this company to her parlor to ring in the 1900s. John and two of his seven brothers still dwelt in his mother's house, and they were put to work while she cooked the morning away.

By eight o'clock in the evening when the first guest arrived, the buffet was laden with all good things for Silvester. How silly it was to call New Year's Eve "Silvester" after a fourth-century pope who died on this day, but all the German families in town did just so. John was designated keeper of the Glühwein, red wine warmed all day with cinnamon sticks, orange, and other fruit, and then set theatrically on fire just after the first guests arrived. It was an old-country way of ensuring people would be prompt. Only those to the party on time were privy to the show.

Al, third to youngest of Sophia's sons, was assigned the duty of overseeing the lead pouring. This prophetic enterprise required old teaspoons, a candle, chunks of lead and a bowl of water.

Bob, second youngest of the eight Wienke brothers, was handling the pyrotechnics. The intent of loud fireworks at the dawning of a new year was to scare away the evil spirits for the whole year to come. Sophia insisted that they continue these old traditions brought over the seas from Germany.

Most of the guests were attired in formal Edwardian style with high collars and ties for both men and women. The women wore long skirts in dark colors of grey, green, or burgundy reaching to the floor with tight white or cream bodices covered by short jackets. The bustle, which John had thought was going out of style, was a part of several of the ensembles. Top hats filled the hat rack. The cold had necessitated capes and topcoats, which were piled on his mother's bed down the short hallway.

A tremendous BOOM! knocked John back on his heels. It shook the house and china cups tinkled on their saucers. And then another one…BOOM! The seated guests immediately rose and went to look through the east windows.

Outside the showers of white sparks twinkled against the black sky sending light shimmering across the room, overwhelming the light from the three meager kerosene fixtures. John looked at himself in the dark window glass between fireworks. His face was pleasant, but far from handsome. His hair, what was left of it, was cut short. He was not ashamed of his balding pate, but he wished that it didn't make his head look so pear-shaped. He was strong and tall, second tallest of his family at six foot; only Frank stood taller. His greatest strength was the color of his eyes. His father had had these striking Prussian blue eyes, as did his mother and brothers. He would take no awards at the county fair with his looks, that's for sure. Tonight, he wore a stylish high-collared white shirt with a black waistcoat and continental cross tie. In the pocket of the waistcoat, he had placed a red handkerchief, for just the right dash of color.

Al Wienke walked over to where John was looking out the front window, and laughed, "I think Bob has found his calling – fireworks." BOOM…. sparkle, sparkle, sparkle. The guests peered around each other to see out. Some of the men grabbed their coats from the pile and went out onto the side porch to watch the show.

John looked at his kid brother. Al had grown into a fine-looking man of twenty-five years. He was sporting quite a bit of wavy hair now. Maybe it was the styling. Al had allowed it to grow longer and then combed it forward to cover his receding hairline. It looked good. No wonder the girls were noticing him. Al's eyes were an azure blue, not the paler blue of the older brothers, and tonight, they were attractively accented by his festive blue, single-breasted waistcoat with cloth-covered buttons over a white shirt. His au courant bow tie was black and floppier than what John would wear, but it looked modern and smart on Al. Both he and John were sans formal jackets, a bow to their "positions" as hired help for the party.

John took a sip from his cup. "Glad there is room between here and the cemetery to set them off," he said. "I had considered going out to help him but decided that I'll stay right here where it's warm…and safe."

BOOM…. sparkle, sparkle, sparkle, some red this time. "Ooooooooh," said the appreciative crowd.

"Ja, me too," Al shivered. "This cold snap doesn't seem to want to end, and I spend enough time out in the cold."

John laughed, "Oh, you're painting outside this time of year, are you? What a Kätzchen you are!"

Al tapped him lightly on the shoulder with his fist, careful not to spill the wine. "I'm no kitten!! You work inside all day, you are the Kätzchen!" They chuckled together for a moment.

"So, what are you up to these days at the typewriter factory, brother?" BOOM! Those gathered, sighed with pleasure, "Aaaaaah."

"We were on furlough last week, so I went over to see what trouble I could get into in Rockford. I'm still looking for a girl like yours." They both smiled thinking about pretty Lena from Wisconsin. "Speaking of Lena," said John, "I thought you'd be in Beloit tonight."

"Ah, well. Ma needed me for the pouring, and I must work tomorrow. We are completely engaged with the city hall renovation, don't cha know, and now Wienke and Davis have a new contract to re-paper all the rooms at the Hotel Woodstock starting next week."

"Both city hall and the hotel? At the same time? Need help? I'm free tomorrow."

BOOM BOOM BOOM BOOM! "Ah, the finale!" said John. The commotion in the side yard ceased, and the crowd began clapping and moved away from the windows and back to their seats and conversations.

"Albert?" their mother called out. "Mrs. Ohme vill da pourink do."

"OK, Ma, be right there," Al called. "Sure, come on over – wear old clothes." Then he asked, "Have you done a pouring yet?"

"No…I suppose I should."

"Come on. You can pour after Mrs. Ohme."

John followed Al into the kitchen where the lead pouring was set up. Al broke a small chunk of lead off and put it in the spoon.

"Be careful. Touch only the wooden handle," he said, handing it to Mrs. Ohme.

Mrs. Ohme put the spoon over the candle and watched as the lead quickly melted. She looked at Al who nodded that it was ready to be poured. She carefully poured the molten liquid into the water. While she was doing this, John began melting his own portion of lead.

Al waited until the lead in the water was again solid and then using wooden tongs reached into the water and retrieved the piece of lead now in the form of…. of what? The three examined the shape, and Mrs. Ohme proclaimed, "A fish!" The other's nodded. "A carp!" she modified her answer. Al looked up "carp" on a list that was as old as the old country.

"Karpfen. Unerwartete Gehaltsergogung," Al said, in less than perfect German. Luckily, Mrs. Ohme was looking over his shoulder.

Mrs. Ohme laughed. "Unexpected raise in salary? Oh my, do you think Mr. Ohme is going to give me a ten-times raise? I get paid nuttin' now and ten times nuttin' is still nuttin'." They laughed with her.

"A windfall from an old uncle?"

"Maybe, but I only have old aunts," said Mrs. Ohme.

John's lead was ready to be poured. He poured the melted liquid quickly in a glob. Al waited and then retrieved the lead. "Oh my," said Mrs. Ohme.

"Wow!" said Al. A glob with gossamer wings.

"A bug," said John.

"A beetle," said Al.

"A bee," said Mrs. Ohme.

"Yes…a bee…let's see…." Al looked over the list, trying to remember the German for bee.

"Beine," said Mrs. Ohme, somewhat disapprovingly. These young people were losing the language.

"Ho, ho!" shouted Al. "Perspektive der Ehe! Good news, brother! This is the year! Did you hear that Ma? John's pouring is "Prospect of Marriage!"

The whole crowd burst into spontaneous applause. John reddened. He hoped so; he really hoped so! He raised his cup in salute! "Prost!" he said, and they answered with the same.

Bob burst through the back door into the kitchen, face blackened with soot and smelling a little burnt. "What's all the clapping about?"

"You, my brother, and your fine fireworks display!" John said, raising his cup again. "To my brother, Bob. May he always have a way with fire."

The others responded, "To Bob!" and broke into applause, which Bob accepted with a deep bow and a wide smile on his handsome face. His bright blue eyes sparkled like the exploding caps he had provided for the entertainment. His hair was black and thick with no sign of thinning. As he removed his overcoat, John wasn't surprised at the roguish paisley waistcoat he wore with matching satin tie in reds and golds. Around his upper arm was the gold garter of the player that he was. His perfect white teeth glinted in the gaslight each time he broke into a smile, which was often.

"Any of that Silvester wine left?" Bob asked. He made his way to the buffet, eyed the food, and found the Erbensuppe – Pea Soup – another good luck charm for the new year.

"Ah, soup! I'm freezing!" He ladled a bowl and added pieces of Silvester bread to it and then examined the rest of the buffet. Sauerkraut and schnitzel, and oysters, several kinds! And smoked carp with the scales removed. The scales were displayed nearby for guests to pocket for good luck in the new year. He loaded up a plate with oysters…good for virility! And added pretzels which surrounded a kuchen wreath. Both symbolizing togetherness. He helped himself to portions of each dish and claimed a seat at the kitchen table near the lead pouring. A large stein of hot wine had been set at his place.

He held it up in a toast to his benefactor, John, and said, "Looks like you furnished the food."

John nodded. He seemed to have an eye for quality when it came to foodstuffs. "Looks like you furnished the wine," said John.

Bob nodded. "You should open your own grocery shop. Then we'd always eat like this."

"You just love the oysters," said John, smiling.

"I admit it, I've never met an oyster I didn't like nor a girl," Bob laughed.

John snorted. "Well, I imagine you meet quite a few down at your establishment, girls, not oysters."

"Ja, ve got Madchen und Austern. Aber, I hem not sure vhich ich love mehr," Bob said, with a mock German accent that had a Norwegian lilt.

John had to laugh. The oysters were quite good at Wienke and Schneider's Saloon. "We haven't crossed paths at the Pleasure Club lately," John changed the subject. "You still working hard on the weights?"

Bob dropped his fork and stretched out his arms making muscles with each. "You bet I am! What do you think?"

John looked at the bulging sleeves of his twenty-three-year-old brother and took in his slim build and handsome face under a mop of dark hair. He was without a doubt the best looking of all the brothers, and he knew it. The Wienke boys all had tall slim bodies, except for Emil whose body was more compact and athletic. At nineteen years, Emil was the shortest

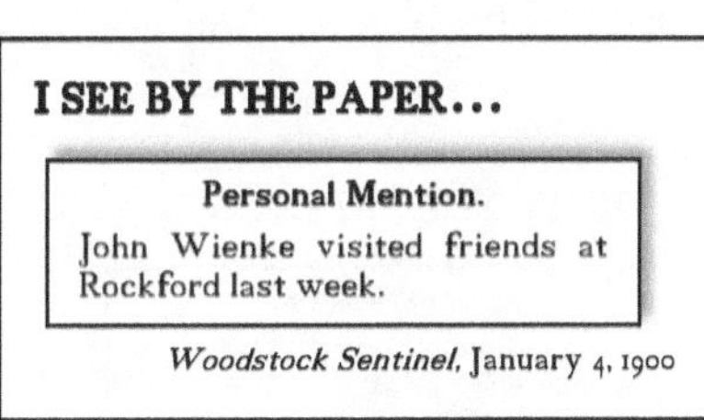

I SEE BY THE PAPER...

Personal Mention.

John Wienke visited friends at Rockford last week.

Woodstock Sentinel, January 4, 1900

at five foot ten, but with those piercing blue eyes, he was good-looking on his own account, especially in a baseball uniform. But, except for Bob, the rest were losing or had lost their hair. Bob, of course, with his good looks was rakish even with soot smeared on his face.

"Hm…better work harder, I'd say," John said, sober faced.

Bob lowered his arms and did his best to look hurt. "Heck, and I thought I was surely making progress."

John laughed, shaking his head, "You are such a Mensch. How is business?" He thought a change of topic was in order.

"Not bad; not great. Enough to keep the place running with a bit of cash for the proprietors. I love the hours and the freedom with both of us serving. Albert Schneider is easy to work with, and we both try to be flexible. So, I'm happy enough. I might have to change professions if I meet the oyster of my dreams."

John laughed. "You do have a way with words, Bob Wienke. No wonder people like to drop in for a snort at your place."

"You should come down sometime," said Bob, "on a day I'm serving, and I'll give you a snort on the house."

"Not much for the hard stuff," admitted John. "A little wine is about all I take. Well, and beer, of course."

"Unt ve got wine unt bier!" Bob shouted. He stood, raised his cup and called out, "To Glühwein unt Bier! Happy New Year!" And the crowd raised their cups saying, "Happy New Year!"

Bob continued, now the center of attention, "My friends, here's to the 1900s. May we spend it in as good company as this night finds us. May our houses always be too small to hold all our friends."

"Zum Wohl!" called out those gathered, the German equivalent of "Here, here!" It seemed an appropriate end to a very pleasant evening.

I SEE BY THE PAPER...

Personal Mention.

John Wienke visited friends at Madison last week.

Woodstock Sentinel, January 11, 1900

Later, after the last visitor was hugged, after that last sleigh had slid away into the darkness, after the booming of the fireworks across town had diminished into a few rifle shots in the air, after the food was packed up and stored in the back-porch locker where it would freeze for another day, after Ma and his brothers headed for bed — John sat at the kitchen table and thought about the coming year. He had always looked forward to 1900. He would be thirty years old this year, and it was time to settle down. He was making good wages at the Oliver Typewriter factory. With his salary and investments, he could start thinking about opening a business, most probably a grocery shop or a café or a bakery. But most of all, he wanted to find a wife. Not quite yet, but soon. He hoped this would be a year filled with Wohlstand und Liebe…with prosperity and love.

> *January 15, 1900*
> *936 Huron Street*
> *Racine, Wisconsin*

Dear Lena,

I was distressed to hear that you were not able to see Albert for New Year's Eve. Has he asked you yet? How long will you wait before you ask him? Have you thought about the wedding? Where you'll have it? When? Ha. So many questions and your answers not coming for weeks. You must write soon!

You say that Al has an eligible brother — even for an old maid like me. I know we are the same age, but you have all the looks, and I have all the talent! Ha! That is if handiwork is a talent. At least I can embroider pillowcases for your nuptial bed. I like the thought of a nuptial bed, but I wonder if all couples share them. My Papa and Mama did — I shouldn't tell secrets like that, should I. I am so naughty.

My "just-friends" Julian said that he will take me to dances to meet a beau. Isn't that sweet of him? I wish I could get interested in him, but he's just not my type, too particular, too natty a dresser, kind of a dandy. My homely self cannot measure up to his standards. He says he doesn't mind that I'm homely — isn't that adorable — that he would still marry me. But no, he is not the one. I will know when I meet the one, just as you knew with Al, don't you agree?

Racine has also put their new century celebration at the end of 1900. I don't quite understand. Why wouldn't 1900 be the first year of the 1900s? I wonder where I'll be on December 31, 1900, when the new century begins?

I'm making myself — in my leisure time — a new spring frock. Maybe it will entice the boys when they see what a good seamstress I am. I also crocheted hats for everyone in my family for Christmas, even Mr. Stoffel who has become a fixture in our house and who has escorted my mother out on the town several times now. I can't really see them in a nuptial bed, but one never knows! Herman took to the hat right away, but it wasn't brotherly kindness but rather the cold temperatures. Clara didn't like the color of hers, which was a pretty lavender, so I will redo it in pink, and I will have the lavender. Emma, Frank and the little ones also got hats, and Emma says they all love them. She has three children already. Can you believe it? I'd be jealous but I'm above it. Ha!

Mama and I have been working on a gown for Mabelle Horlick here in Racine. Her father is the malted milk fellow. Have you tried malted milk? It's wonderful especially with ice and cream added. The gown is for the Spring Fling. I'm doing the dress in blues and yellows, and Mama is working on the petticoat. It will be gorgeous. We also have had a lot of darning to do this winter – socks mostly – and letting out of dresses. Too many malted milks? Ha!

Oh! I must report on a strange event that happened a few days ago. There were these two men who were building a chicken coop for our neighbor to the north. We were surprised by a knocking on the front door and the boy there said that Mr. Jones had been taken ill and could Mama come and see if she could nurse him. We ran out just in time to see the man, Mr. Jones, take his last breath. That was the first time I've seen a man die, breathing one moment not breathing the next. There was nothing Mama could do for him. We waited until the authorities arrived, and they just picked him up and put him in the back of the paddy wagon and were gone. It made the paper. I shall include the clipping. Shows how quickly any of us can just pass over. They said in the paper that Mr. Jones was fifty-eight which is just about the same age as Mama. It makes me satisfied if my fate is just to stay here and watch over her. On the other hand, if I found a nice boy to marry, I would be truly happy.

Well, back to the needle as they say, ha. I'm looking forward to seeing you soon as I hear you and your mother will be visiting sometime after the snow melts. I will hold my breath!

Greetings to all,
Ida

"Clara! Did you hear? Lena is coming next weekend," Ida Doering was breathless with excitement as she read Lena's letter for the third time.

"How wonderful! What shall we do? And don't, please, say *'walk by the lake.'* I am so tired of walking by the lake. Besides now with the ice gone it is disgusting, fish and flotsam up on shore. One has to wear high boots just to stay out of the muck."

"Oh, you are such a baby. Maybe we'll go shopping downtown. What would you think of that?"

"Oh, I would love it!" she exclaimed. Then her face fell, "Unless we have no Geld to spend. I hate shopping and then finding something and not being able to buy it."

"Well," shrugged Ida, "do you have any money?"

A small voice, "A little."

"We shall have to see what we see. Mama is pleased with their coming. I might be able to get some luncheon Geld at the least."

"Oh! Can we go to the Hotel Racine for lunch? Maybe Mama and Mr. Stoffel and Mrs. Steinke will join us."

Ida was impressed. "That is a splendid idea. You are turning out to be quite a bright girl."

Clara flounced a bit. Of course, she was quite bright! She was seventeen and ready to go out into the world to find her beloved. Everyone could see that. And what adventures awaited her! But she must get Ida married off first. She just couldn't bear the thought of her spirited sister being an old maid and living out her life with their mother, sewing for other people. If I am ever twenty-six and not married, I shall just kill myself, thought Clara. Oh heavens! Was Ida thinking about killing herself? Clara's mood shifted, and she looked at her sister with concern.

Ida was, thought Clara, the prettiest of the sisters. Their older sister, Emma, was round of face looking very much like a Wisconsin milkmaid. And my face looks like a baby yet, too chubby to be pretty, she thought, glancing in the mirror. But I have personality! Ida had their father's face with a shapely, if somewhat pointed, nose and just slightly too-thin lips. But when she smiled, the whole room lit up, and when she laughed with her merry hazel-green eyes, she was a sight to behold. That she hadn't yet landed a man was a mystery to Clara. Was she too straitlaced for these modern times? Women were starting to stand up for themselves, but Ida was satisfied to sit down, sew, and wait.

Ida, feeling her sister's gaze, looked up. "What?"

Clara shrugged.

"WHAT?"

"You aren't going to kill yourself over being an old maid, are you?"

Ida was taken aback but then burst out laughing. "No, Clara," she said. "I'm not going to kill myself. I shall just wither away on the vine here in Racine."

Still chuckling, Ida went back to her sewing. Did women truly kill themselves over not finding a suitable mate? No. That was absurd. She would find someone, and if not, she'd be the best seamstress in Racine.

May 31, 1900
936 Huron Street
Racine, Wisconsin

Dear Lena,

Thank you for the kind letter of gratitude — you are most welcome. We also had a wonderful time. It isn't often that we all get to go out on the town and with Mr. Stoffel footing the bill! I think he may be getting close to asking for Mama's hand.

We were so glad to see you and your mother and to learn all the news from Beloit. I'm glad you took the new evening train, so you had the extra night here. Herman was very happy to pick you up. The streetlights are such a boon — extending the day easily to eleven o'clock or even after. It was such a joy to see your face after all the months of only writing. You are such a good friend, and I was glad to have time to catch up with all the news of your engagement and hopes for the future.

Wasn't the lunch at the Hotel Racine marvelous!! I just loved the little sandwiches with tuna and salmon and cucumbers. And the cakes!! I'll never forget those cakes. If that is the only time I get to go out for luncheon, I will die a happy girl.

I think your talk of marriage inspired my mother because as we walked to church last Sunday, she asked me what my plans were. "What plans?" I asked. She said that there are several eligible older men at church who might be potential mates. OLDER? I think the youngest is forty-five. Can you imagine? I asked if she was trying to marry me off to the highest bidder. I shouldn't have said that, of course, because she got a little miffed and said she was just thinking about my best interests. So, do you think my lot in life has come to this? Marrying an old bachelor to save myself? Bah.

I am, however, very interested in meeting your fiancé's brother. How nice it would be to find someone mature and about my age to make a life with. Let me know what Al finds out, and we can make plans.

I best be off before mother says that I am not only an old maid but a lazy old maid.

Regards to all,
Ida

"John?" Al called out as he burst in through the kitchen door. He remembered to wipe his feet and then continued into the parlor with his bowler in hand calling again, "John?"

"Shhh," John admonished looking up from the paper. "Ma's already abed. Well, look at that – a new bowler! Aren't you the dashing bachelor? At least for a while."

"You heard! Ma never could keep a secret."

"Yes, I heard," John rose and stretched out his hand. "Congratulations, brother."

"Thanks, I'm very glad. But that's not why I ran all the way from the train station."

"No?"

"No. I just got off the train from Beloit, and Lena's friend wants to take a look at you."

"What?" John sat back down and motioned for Al to take a seat also. "Take a look at me?"

Al sat down catching his breath. "Sorry, I am so excited to tell you, it's all muddled. Let me start from the beginning. Lena has a friend that she met in the Wisconsin German community. This girl grew up in Whitewater. Ida is her name. Ida's father died a few years ago, and they moved to Racine where they all live."

"All?"

"Yes, her family, I mean. Anyway, she moved, and so Lena hasn't seen her much for a few years, but they write letters, and so she suggested, or I guess I suggested, that she suggest that my brother might want to meet her as they were both getting older and needed…," he paused, "um… company."

John laughed out loud. "Company?"

Al rushed on. "Yes, company and a family and comfort."

John still chuckling, "Comfort?"

Al was now red in the face. "You know what I mean! Wisenheimer!"

"So, little Ida wants to meet big bad John."

"Oh, she's not so little…I mean…young. I don't mean she's fat. At least I don't think so. The picture I saw, she was…well…pretty. She's the same age as Lena, twenty-six. And you need to be bad more often." Al stopped and smiled.

"Oh, I don't know, Al. I'm becoming rather set in my ways. I always thought I'd find a Woodstock girl through church; someone who already knew me. Racine is a long way off for courting."

"It's a brief two-hour train ride. You can go up and back in one day if you must."

"Well," said John, considering, "you've certainly pulled off courting long-distance to Beloit. How are Lena and her family?"

As Al lapsed into events of the weekend in Beloit, John's mind wandered. A girl wants to meet him. Can it be true?

"So how are we going to make this happen?" John interrupted Al midsentence.

"Make what happen?" Al looked at him confused.

"Meeting this girl, Ida." John was looking down at the paper.

"Ohhhh…," said Al, an understanding smirk on his face. "Well…Lena said that you should just go up to Racine and visit. Lena could write you a letter of introduction."

"I don't think so. I couldn't do that…too humiliating if she takes one look and leaves me on the doorstep. When will Lena be down here? Will she move before the wedding or after?"

"Did Ma tell you we won't be tying the knot until next February. I wanted it sooner, but some cousins are coming over from the fatherland around that time, so our wedding will be the main attraction at the circus. Looks like they'll move her goods down sometime in the fall before the roads get impassable. We'll find a big enough place at that time, and I'll take up residence, and then she'll move down after the wedding. But I'm sure she'll be down during the fall. What are you thinking?"

"Let's wait until Lena will be here, and she can invite Ida down for the day, and we can get together, or I suppose we could all go to Racine?"

"OK, I'll write Lena tonight. Ma went to bed early, aina?"

"Ja, day of rest and all. I sure wish they would add an English service at church. I'm to the point that I can

> **I SEE BY THE PAPER…**
>
> **Over 15,000 on Strike.**
>
> Chicago, May 2. — More than 15,000 men went on strike Tuesday in various cities of the country, the demands in most instances being for an eight-hour day and higher wages. In some cases, recognition of unions is the issue. The building trades are most seriously affected, particularly in the east, although the railroads centering in Buffalo are threatened with general strikes. A conference will be held at Buffalo to-day, at which it is hoped a settlement can be reached. In some cities the demands of the labor unions are still pending, while in others sympathy strikes are being discussed.
>
> *Woodstock Sentinel*, May 3, 1900.

understand about one-fifth of what they are saying. If it wasn't so much repetition in the service time and again, I'd be lost. Ma doesn't struggle, but a lot of younger people are not coming as often."

"Hm…let's think on that," Al mused. "Seems like adding an English service would be easy to do. Well, except finding the English-speaking pastor who will work for a pittance. I don't go that often anymore."

"Ja, I know. Well, you should go write that letter! I haven't a moment to waste!"

Al smiled and gathered himself up putting on his bowler slightly askew. "Dashing, aina? Lena thought so."

John rubbed his forehead, "Ja, dashing catches the girl, aina? Not sure how I'm going to accomplish dashing, except that I can run pretty fast."

"Just so you are running toward her, not away, you'll be alright," Al patted John on the arm and took his leave.

July 10, 1900
205 Mill Street
Beloit, Wisconsin

Dear Ida,

He wants to meet you! John Wienke wants to meet you. I am so excited because if this would come true, we would be sisters-in-law. How fun! And probably both live in Woodstock. Can good Wisconsin girls stand to live so close to Chicago? Of course, you are used to the large city, but I'm just a country maiden. Al and I will try to get a meeting set up later on in the fall if you can wait that long. I'll be going down to start preparing the house or apartment…I do hope it's a house…it will need cleaning, polishing, painting, and furniture. I'm not sure how much we will have. Al may have to make some of the furniture at least at first.

I will write when we have found an agreeable day. We might make it a bit more of a party with other friends, so it isn't so uncomfortable if you take one look and decide not to pursue him. He is, I know, a hard worker, has good common sense, and can fix anything according to you-

know-who. I'm not sure how that blends into a man you would want or not, but that's what I hear. So, from one friend to another, it's worth taking the chance.

Can't wait to see you in the fall. I will post a letter as soon as I know something for certain.

Love to your mother and Clara,
Lena

Clara Doering modeled a new gown being sewn for a Racine debutant's coming-out party. She posed in the middle of the room and then walked one way and back saying in a slightly mocking voice, "Well, thank you. Thank you! You must have some champagne. Why hello, Mr. Mayor, so glad you could come. Do try the canapes—they are marvelous."

"OK, that's fine, Clara. Thank you for your great showmanship," her sister said, trying to stop the show before too many straight pins fell out. "It flows nicely and exaggerates what needs to be exaggerated."

"Exaggerates? What these?" She cupped her bosom in both hands. "I don't believe these need any exaggeration."

"Clara!! Goodness. Do not let Mama hear you saying such things," Ida shot back, but there was a bit of a smile on her face.

Ida unpinned the back of the dress, and Clara stepped out of character and back into her own restless self and pulled on her blouse and long skirt. "Did I tell you that I met a boy?" she asked.

Ida busied herself with needle and thread. "Yes, you did."

"And we danced every dance – more than just danced."

"Yes, you did."

"Goodness, Ida. Does nothing ever shock you?"

"Well, yes, it shocks me that you are expecting to live here, have food on the table and a roof over your head, while you continue to be a lazy girl about work. Sit down and get busy. That petticoat isn't going to finish itself."

"You sound just like – Mama."

"No, she would say, 'Dieser Petticoat wird sich nicht selbst machen.'"

"And I would say, 'Ich bin nicht faul, ich langweile mich.'"

"You're bored?" Ida shook her head. "I've never been bored a moment of my life. Tired, but never bored. Remember the stitching hanging downstairs? 'Let not the setting sun find at your hand no worthy labor done.'"

"And again, you sound just like Mama. You will make a good mother someday."

"Well, thank you. I'll take that as a compliment. And Miss Nosey, just so you know, I'm going to meet the man of my dreams soon. He will be kind, tall, and handsome. He will want many children and be a good father. He will be a shop keeper and a Christian leader in his church. He will be—"

"What did you do?" Clara's eyes grew large. "Did you go to a soothsayer?"

"No such nonsense. Lena is going to introduce me to her fiancé's brother."

"OH Ida!....what's his name!!?"

"John."

"John?" Clara wrinkled her nose. "But that is Mr. Stoffel's first name. He doesn't even like it; he uses J. Nicholas. You need someone with a unique name. Like James or Joseph or Raymond. Something you can shorten into sweet names like Jimmy or Joey or Ray baby darling!"

"I'm sorry, but I cannot change the name of a man I may admire. Nor do I have the luxury of rejecting a man based on his name. John is a perfectly good name. It is neither hated nor loved."

"I'm going to look for a man with a unique name, so he will always know when I am talking to him. He won't say, 'Are you talking to me or that John over there?'"

"If you don't get back to your sewing, I'm going to talk to Mama again, and you might not get out of this house for the next decade."

"Oh, alright. You are so pushy, Miss Ida. You just wait until you and JOHN have ten children and need a nanny. I will be nowhere to be found." She flounced down on the hassock and picked up the petticoat and began making fine small stitches. Someday, she thought, she'd wear dresses like this instead of making them. Yes, someday.

"I'm going to look for a real job soon," said Clara.

"Sure, you are." Ida smiled.

"Well, that was quite a lot of fun!" declared Al as he, John, and Bob headed home after cleaning up the theater from the Pleasure Club's minstrel show. "I hope we do it again next year."

> **I SEE BY THE PAPER...**
>
> **Old Custom Resumed.**
> The early-closing agreement expired by limitations last week Wednesday evening, and the business houses are again open until any hour of the night they see fit. The clerks and some of the proprietors are anxious to close year around. Why not?
>
> . *Woodstock Sentinel,* March 8, 1900.

"Ja, it was fun," agreed John. "But a lot of work. I guess clearing a hundred dollars isn't bad for the first time. What do you think, Bob? What would you do for a hundred?"

"Hmmm…. race someone across Wonder Lake!"

"That's it? How about you Al?"

"Paint and paper a small house," answered Al.

"Oh, you workhorses. I was thinking more as a wager," said Bob.

"Of course, you were," said Al. "How about you John?"

Although he had proposed the original question, John had to think a minute. What would he do for a hundred dollars? "Well…" he began, "I'd ask a girl to a dance and kiss her on her stoop."

"Oh heck," said Bob. "I'd do that for free. Although, I would kiss her on her lips!"

They all laughed. Bob continued, "But why, pray tell, would you need to get paid for that?"

"Because he's scared of girls," said Al, elbowing Bob.

"Only a little," said John, turning red. "Certainly not in general, but the thought that…. oh, never mind."

Al and Bob burst out laughing. They both were aware that he was to meet Lena's friend soon and was a bit nervous about the arrangement. John reddened more deeply thinking about it.

"Not to change the subject," he said, in fact to change the subject, "but where are you off to next, Bob. I think you are quickly becoming the most traveled person in Woodstock."

"I don't know. I sure like watching the ponies," Bob said. "I was thinking of going to the Washington Park track on Derby Day, but I'd need a new suit."

"Isn't that a club track?" asked Al. "How would you get in?"

"I know some people," mumbled Bob.

"That's right! You went down for the Kentucky Derby beginning of May, didn't you?" said Al. "Mixing with the big and bad from Chicago, eh?"

"Yup, hit it big, too. Bet my wad on a horse named, Lieutenant Gibson to win, place or show, and he won the whole caboodle! He was favored so I didn't win as much as I might have, but it was a great day!"

They walked a few minutes in silence considering how much a caboodle was worth.

"Do you have a horse entered in the Elkhorn or McHenry County Fair races this year?" asked John.

"No, haven't seen a horse around here that could run since Marmaduke."

I SEE BY THE PAPER...

Paint and paper are being applied to the store of C.F. Thorne by Wienke & Davis, making a great improvement.

There will be a grand masquerade ball in this city on St. Patrick's Day, Mar. 17. The bills have already been issued.

If you want a really satisfactory smoke buy the Fontella at Austin's grocery.

Railway trains were run at a disadvantage yesterday, and most of them were late on account of the drifting snow. Extra engines were added and still the schedule could not be maintained.

Woodstock Sentinel, March 1, 1900.

"He could really run," agreed Al, "it's been, what, two years since THE RACE?"

"Yes, I miss the excitement of race day when you have an investment in one of the ponies, but then there's finding a jockey and the training, and…," Bob's voice trailed off.

"Marmaduke loved to run," said John. "Still think he was faster than that old Splenda-dope."

"You know," Bob said, reaching in his pocket. "I keep that article from the paper in my wallet along with the carp scale for good luck – the scale not the article. The article is just a reminder. I had so much faith in that horse, but faith doesn't win the race."

He pulled the clipping out and opened it. It looked a lot older than two years, browning but not brittle and still readable. They gathered under the last lamp before the darkness of the cemetery hill. They could make out the date. September 8, 1898 was penciled at the top along with the words The Sentinel.

"Just read it out loud, Bobby," said Al. John and he didn't have a chance of reading it over Bob's shoulder.

"OK, I'll try to do it without crying," said Bob. John and Al chuckled.

Splendoline the Winner

For some time, a good-natured rivalry has existed between John Dennis, the liveryman, and the Wienke brothers as to the speed qualities of Spendoline and Marmaduke, their respective running horses. This rivalry culminated in a matched race at the fairgrounds last Saturday afternoon for a purse of $100 a side, and a large crowd watched Jack's horse gather in the boodle, making the distance in 53-1/2 seconds, fully two lengths ahead of his rival. Splendoline drew the pole, and Judge Donnelly acted as starter. The horses were nose-and-nose when the word was given, Splendoline taking the lead around the turn and holding it the entire distance. Martin Richardson piloted Splendoline and Geo. Mountain was astride of Marmaduke. It was a nice race and Jack is jubilant over his victory.

"One hundred dollars! I had forgotten that's how much we lost," said Al. "So where is old Marmaduke now?"

"Sold him to Bill Quinlan in Elgin for a surrey horse. I see him now and again." He gently folded the clipping and slipped it back in his wallet. "My almost claim to fame."

"We all thought he'd win," said Al, considering his brother's downcast face.

They walked up the hill in silence, contemplating a hundred dollars gained and lost and the running of the ponies. Marmaduke's race was the one time that John and Al had bet on a race, and for John, at least, it was the last time. But something had clicked with Bob, and now he was willing to pursue a wager of almost any kind.

What would I do for a hundred dollars, thought John? The only good answer he could come up with was work at the factory for two months. He was not a betting man.

Al spoke up as they reached the top of the hill and rounded the corner almost home. "Are you going to the first ball game a week from Thursday."

"You bet!" Bob exclaimed.

"Hadn't planned on it," said John. "Why?"

"Woodstock is playing Beloit," Al and Bob replied in unison.

"I'll be there!"

> *Wednesday 6:05 a.m.*
>
> *Ma, I didn't want to wake you, but I forgot to tell you that Emil will be here for the baseball game tomorrow afternoon. If you want a ride down to the park, tell me at supper.*
>
> *Al*

"Hi, John! Good to see you here!" Bob slid onto the bench beside John. The bleachers were filling fast with Olivers from the typewriter factory just getting off work. "I have

Woodstock, two to one over Beloit, and Beloit eight to one over Woodstock. If Emil can pull this off, I'll win big! You in?"

"Robert, how many times do I have to tell you, I am not a gambler!" replied John with a bit too much sting to his tone.

"Oh, big brother, so serious! I withdraw the offer. Al should be coming soon, right?"

"Yes, he went to pick up Ma, so she didn't have to walk."

"What did he do, take the cart to work this morning?"

"I'm not sure, but I think he took off a bit early to accomplish it. My assignment was to save good seats."

"Ma might want a piece of the action," Bob mused, not looking at John.

"Bob…"

"Okay, okay. I have to circulate." And off he went to find other fellows more likely to have money to waste.

John watched the cart pull up with Al and his mother. They waved that they saw where he had saved seats in the hometown bleachers. Al secured the horse and then gave his mother a hand down. Together John and Al lifted their sturdy mother up to the seats, high enough to see well.

Just as they settled in, the field umpire Billy Magill called out, "Play ball."

The first two batters from Beloit struck out, and then Emil came to the plate. He let the count go to three balls and two strikes and then swung away for a hit! Sophia and her boys jumped for joy, forgetting that they were cheering for the visiting team.

A snide voice behind them said, "What are you, Beloiters? You best be moving to the other side."

Sophia stood slowly, turned around, and faced the man. He had a Bollman hat on his head, a cigar clenched in his teeth, and a smug smile on his face. Sophia looked him straight in the eye and said, "Das ist mein sohn!" She was not a tall woman and was dressed in a black walking dress that just skimmed the rough wood of the bleacher step below her. She was hatless, and her hair was pulled back into a severe bun. She could have stepped off the streets of Berlin. Her milky blue eyes blazed as she looked up at the man in a white shirt, a blue garter on the sleeve. His black waistcoat, gray and white striped pants and brimmed hat made him look like he had just stepped off the stage from Dodge City.

Al mumbled, "Ma." But John stood up, turned and faced the man. John was a foot taller than Sophia, so he was nearly eye-to-eye with the man. His strength was obvious in his Oliver work clothes, but it was from Sophia the man heard.

"Ich habe acht Sohne!"

"She has eight sons," John translated.

Sophia looked at John, nodded, and then back to the man, "Ja, acht Söhne, und dieser ist das jüngste."

"This batter is her youngest."

"Ja, und ich werde ihn anfeuern, wenn ich es wünsche! Und auch seine Brüder!"

"She says that she will cheer for him if she wants to and so will his brothers."

"Ja!" said Sophia.

The man stared at her and then tipped his gambler hat. In a milder voice said, "Sorry, ma'am. You go right ahead!"

John smiled at the man who tipped his hat to John also. John nodded, and then he and Sophia turned back to the field and sat down.

John leaned close to Al and whispered, "Never underestimate the power of the Mama!"

Al smiled, "You said it!"

The game continued with the Woodstock fans cheering often. But every time, Emil came to bat or had a successful play behind the plate, they boldly cheered. By the end, several others were clapping for his skill with the bat and catcher's mitt. Around 6:00 p.m., the last out was made, and the Woodstock team prevailed 16 to 3. All three of the Beloit runs had come with the aid of Emil's bat.

As they were climbing down out of the bleachers, the man in the black hat gave Sophia his hand to guide her to the ground. "Quite a son you have there, ma'am. You have a right to be proud of him."

"Tank you," said Sophia. "I am."

The next day the paper would hail the conquering Oliver heroes, but it also wrote, "A feature of the game was the perfect work of Emil Wienke behind the plate for the Beloiters. He is a ballplayer from the ground up, but his support was hardly up to the standard that he set."

John was awakened by a sound. Without moving, he listened. He heard a giggle…a giggle? And a shush. Then Bob's bedroom door opened and closed. John thought about what he should do. Should he go right now and throw her out in the cold, throw them both out? No, the ruckus would wake Ma, and tomorrow was a workday. He needed his sleep also. But tomorrow, he would put a quick end to this. He turned over and closed his eyes. A strange heat had come over him and a yearning that he hadn't experienced since his youth. No, this could not go on under Ma's roof.

At first light, John again awoke to the sound of footfalls in the hall. He rose, washed up with the tepid water on the nightstand, relieved himself in the chamber pot and dressed for work. That should have given them time to say their good-byes.

As he came into the kitchen, he found Bob sitting at the table, eyes dazzling with the craziness of what he had just done.

"How often have you done that?" asked John, abruptly. He busied himself with stoking the wood stove and pumping water for the coffee pot, his back to Bob.

Bob's head jerked up, and he looked at John but was silent.

"How often?" John allowed anger to seep into his voice, still busying himself at the stove.

"First time," was Bob's soft answer.

"Last time," John replied. He turned to look Bob straight in the eyes. "Last time, understand?"

"Who are you to—"

"I am the older brother who lives with his mother, who is a good Christian woman. I am a good Christian man, and you are not going to be bringing hussies and prostitutes under this roof."

"She's not a—"

"I don't care who she is or what she is to you, not here! Understand?" John let the silence ride out a while, and then said, "If you need to do that kind of thing, go to her place or—"

"She lives at home."

"…or find a place of your own. Use some of the money you are wagering away to stand up and be a man."

"I'd talk. You are still living with your Mama."

John turned to face him. "I have never desecrated this house with such debauchery."

"OK. But we might be getting marr—"

"Married? Do it then. Get a job that pays more than gambling money and get your own place!" John felt disdain for his little brother and his shiftlessness.

Bob stood up fast, knocking over the chair. They stood face to face, less than two feet apart. Bob's face was red, and his blue eyes sparked with anger. John readied himself for a punch, but instead, Bob turned abruptly and stalked from the room. Disappearing down the hallway, he slammed the bedroom door.

John put the chair aright and found the frypan. He placed it on the woodstove and broke two eggs into it. As the eggs turned from clear to white, he cut two slices of homemade bread, and after turning the eggs over, laid the bread atop them to warm.

Sophia came into the room in her headscarf and housecoat. "What vas yellink about."

John pulled out a chair. "Want some eggs?"

The coffee had started to boil and would be ready soon. He found two cups and placed them on the table along with sugar, milk and butter.

"John?"

John dished the eggs and the warm bread onto a plate and put it down in front of her.

"I think Bob needs to find a place of his own," he said, at last making eye contact. "His behavior is unseemly, and it will sully your reputation… and mine…if he continues to live here." He turned and began the egg preparation anew. He took the coffee off the stove and set it on the sideboard to settle.

"Vat happens?" Ma asked. Appreciating the eggs, she picked up her knife to butter the bread before it cooled.

"I'd rather not tell you, but I asked him to stop his carousing till all hours of the night, coming home half in the bag, and waking up the whole house. Either that or out."

"Vhat didst he say 'bout dat?" Sophia asked. She took her first bite of the breakfast.

John paused, fussing with the bread and eggs, and then picked up the coffee pot and carefully poured the coffee from the top trying to avoid the grounds. If there were any, they would settle to the bottom of the cup. He looked at her, "He said they might be getting married."

"O meine!" Sophia's continence had been somewhat befuddled, but now it took on an understanding look. John went back to nursing his eggs. She looked at his stiff, upright back.

"Vell den," she said, her gaze back on her plate. "Maybe he movink out ist best."

John turned with his own breakfast and sat down across from his mother. "Yes, I think so unless he makes some promises about his behavior."

As they ate in silence, John thought about his father, dead now fifteen years. It had been a sudden and unexpected death at the young age of fifty-three. His grave was not more than 200 yards away, just over a small rise in Oakland

Cemetery. His mother visited it often. He had heard her talking to Pa in German as she planted blue cornflowers; he had loved the color blue.

When pneumonia had taken Carl Wienke in January of 1885, Sophia was left in bad financial straits. His oldest brothers, William at twenty-two and Ed at twenty-one had bowed to the duty left by their father and began funneling support to their mother and younger siblings. Charles, at sixteen found die Lehre, an apprenticeship, at C. T. Andrew's blacksmith shop. Charles had turned out to be a well-respected smithy for his age. Eventually, the three had married and started families, William and Ed here in Woodstock and Charles in Beloit. In fact, William was the city engineer now. Ed was foreman of typebar fitters at the typewriter factory.

John himself had been fifteen. He stayed in school until year's end, and at sixteen he found work, mostly odd jobs chopping wood for twenty cents a cord, laboring on road construction crews and working at the courthouse when they needed a runner. That was a job he had most enjoyed, but it had paid very little. Hanging out at the courthouse had given him a taste for politics. Then he landed his own Lehre with a groceryman, B. S. Austin. He had started sweeping up and doing deliveries and had learned the grocery trade from the bottom up. In 1896, the new Oliver Typewriter factory opened, he had applied and was taken on that very day. There he had worked his way up to a materials foreman in just four years.

Frank was eleven when Pa died. Albert was nine, Bob was eight, and Emil was four. Between the older boys' jobs and Ma taking in laundry and selling produce from an acre of garden

---

I SEE BY THE PAPER...

Told in a Few Lines.

T. J. Selby, of Calhoun County was nominated for congress on the two thousand four hundred and fifty-second ballot by the democrats of the Sixteenth district.

Chicago physicians are elated over the successful use of a discovery for cure of typhoid, scarlet and malarial fevers.

Woodstock Sentinel, August 16, 1900.

that the younger boys tended, the family had made it, and now all the brothers were responsible citizens…well, except for the saloon keeper, he thought, still irritated.

"You vill verk today?" Ma asked, breaking into his thoughts.

"Yes. No rest for the wicked, you know. Will you talk to Bob so it's not just my say so? He'll listen to you," John asked.

"Uf course. I will speaken mit him. Don't vorry. Ve vill be fine. He ist my boy."

That is exactly what I'm worried about, thought John.

Al was sitting with his mother eating breakfast at the kitchen table when he noticed the brief personal ad in *The Woodstock Sentinel.* "Messrs. F. N. Blakeslee, J. P. Brink, F. L. Kappler, Frank Kniebrush, L. W. Richards, Amos Stevenson, C. N. Wright, and Albert and Robert Wienke were at Lake Geneva, Sunday, going and coming via the electric railway from Harvard." Bob or one of the other boys must have dropped it off at the paper. Best he say something before his mother noticed it. "Did I tell you that Bob and I went to Lake Geneva last Sunday?"

> **I SEE BY THE PAPER…**
>
> The Hoy Block is in the hands of Wienke & Davis, the painters, assisted by Fred Eiklor, and will soon shine in a new dress of color.
> Try Maple City Self-washing Soap for washing woolens or lace curtains. It is unequalled for washing ladies shirt waists.
> The Oliver Typewriter band gave its first summer concert in the park last Thursday evening, and there was a large crowd out, regardless of the coolness of the evening.
>
> *Woodstock Sentinel,* March 1, 1900.

"Ist dat vhy you not here for church?" asked Sophia.

"Partly, but also because I can't understand the service anymore."

"Humph. Es ist nicht schlecht, en der Kirche Deutsch zu sprecken. Gott Deutsch verstehen."

"Of course, it isn't bad to speak German in church. I'm sure God does understand, but what I'm worried about is my understanding. Anyway, we went over to Harvard and up on that new electric railroad. So easy."

"Was in Lake Geneva was?"

"The lake, the beer, the girls," he teased her.

"Ach, pshht. Dats all youse boyz tink 'bout? Unt du almost married," Sophia said, shaking a drying towel in his general direction in a shooing motion, but smiling just the same.

"Well, right now I am thinking about that special girl and finding her a house to live in." He turned to the People's Column of the paper where houses and such were advertised for rent or sale. Let's see…he perused the offerings.

PEOPLE'S COLUMN.

"Ads." in this Column, 25c per week for five lines or less; over five lines, 5c per line.

FOR RENT.—Six-room house. Inquire of A. F. Miller.

FOR RENT.—A 6-room house, $6 per month. Inquire of Emil Arnold.

MONEY TO LOAN.—Inquire of E. H. Waite, J. P., office in Hoy block.

FOR RENT.—A good house on Tryon street. Inquire of Mrs. E. S. Austin.

TEN FINE SHOATS FOR SALE.—Inquire at the office of Wm. H. Cowlin.

"Ma, are you in the market for a shoat?"

"Ein goat?"

"No, you know, a little pig. Spanferkel. Bill Cowlin has some for sale," said Al.

"Nein. Ve haft nutting to celebrate," said Sophia.

"Could raise it until it's ready to be butchered."

"Ach, kleine Zeit…no time."

"You sure?"

"Ja."

"OK," Al relented. Al read on looking for available houses.

FOR RENT.—The Cook house on Jackson street.   D. F. QUINLAN.

WANTED.—A girl to do housework. Will pay $5 per week. Apply to Mrs. Delia Johnson, Woodstock, Ill.

FOR SALE.—Four good square dining tables, one extension table and an Otto buggy. Inquire at Conklin's restaurant.

FOR SALE.—A number of choice farms. Call and see us.
          BLAKESLEE, BRINK & COWLIN.

$400,000 TO LOAN at 4, 4¼ and 4¾ per cent. on good farm security. Inquire of Jackman & Bennett.

FOR SALE CHEAP.—A large Diebold safe, best in McHenry county. Original cost, $600. Address C. P. Barnes, Woodstock, Ill.

FOR SALE.—Some good choice real estate situated in the city of Woodstock. Give us a call.   BLAKESLEE, BRINK & COWLIN.

FOR SALE.—Large list of farm lands and city property.
          EICHELBERGER & MURPHY.

ESTRAY NOTICE.—Strayed into my enclosure about May 1, a yearling bull, black and white, with slim tail. Owner can have same by paying for this notice and costs.
          W. B. SULLIVAN, Seneca.

Not many houses, and for the most part, they were for rent rather than for sale or they were available so soon. Originally, he had thought they would build the house of Lena's dreams, but a wedding in the winter had thrown the brush in that paint!

FOR SALE.—8-room modern house, fitted complete for furnace, city water and electric light, large cellar and attic; high, desirable lot. House will be finished about July 25.
          F. W. STREETS, Owner.

FOR SALE.—Republican newspaper for sale, in a thriving town of 800 inhabitants in Illinois. The only paper in town. Good location for wide-awake and up-to-date man. Will sell cheap for cash. Address Printer, SENTINEL, Woodstock, Ill.   2285

Oh, here's one. Nope. Too soon. Wait, that last ad? A Republican newspaper is for sale? Cheap? Maybe he should go into the newspaper business instead of the wall-paper business. He laughed aloud.

"Vas?" his mother asked. She had finished drying the dishes and now sat down at the table with him where they still had cups of black boiled coffee and kuchen left over from supper last night. Sun streamed in the windows revealing dust motes floating in the air. The room smelled of schnitzel kraut. Al looked at his mother, hand poised to dunk her coffeecake into her cup. Here I am looking for a modern house and Ma is still pumping water at the sink and carrying out chamber pots every day. My brothers and I need to have a talk about this.

"Oh nothing," he answered. "A newspaper is for sale cheap. Should I buy it and go into a different kind of paper business?"

"Ach, nein," Sophia took his question as serious. "No Geld in dat business. Du need new biznis?"

"No, no, no. I like my business. I'm looking at the houses for rent, not at new businesses. There are quite a few available just now. I suppose I don't need to rush into anything. The wedding is still six months away."

"Vell, if du mus' da haus let, do. Move you now in da let haus unt finden da dauerhaftes haus ven Lena with her mind here ist."

"Are you trying to get rid of me?" Al laughed. Sophia shook her head, her mouth full of cake. "But that's a good idea, Ma. If I rent now, I could live there and paint it inside, and Lena would have time to get it shipshape before the wedding. I'll go take a look at these and see if they

I SEE BY THE PAPER...

Eight-Hour Day in Toledo.

Toledo, O., August 15. — Under instructions from Mayor Jones and the city council, City Engineer W. F. Brown issued a mandate that after August 16 eight hours shall in every department constitute a day's work. Penalty will be inflicted for violation. Contractors purpose to test the constitutionality of the law in court.

Woodstock Sentinel, August 17, 1900.

have potential. Lena wants a house not a flat, so what Lena wants, Lena gets."

"Dat's a gut husbant," his mother encouraged.

> *October 1, 1900*
> *936 Huron Street*
> *Racine, Wisconsin*

Dear Lena,

Just a quick note to say, YES, I would love to come to Woodstock on Sunday, October 16th to see your new house and meet your fiancé and your Woodstock friends. I will be able to catch the 7:00 a.m. which will get me there by 10:00 a.m., and then I will have to meet the 5:30 p.m. coming back, but that should be fine, I hope? It isn't a lot of time but should be enough for a good look…at Woodstock that is.

Got to hurry off. Today, I am clerking at the laundry. I'm doing that more now than sewing.

> *Highest regards,*
> *Ida*

John strode into the parlor with a big smile on his face. His hair had recently been cut, and he had on his church suit and two-tone shoes. His wide black tie had been carefully knotted so that it lay neatly on the front of his white shirt with the tall, stiff-starched collar.

"Mein, sehr gutaussehend…very handsome," his mother said, as she looked up from her mending. "Vhere du go off?"

"To meet the girl of my dreams!" he chortled.

His mother said, "Haft a gut time. Brink her home to meet mir."

"I will, Ma. I will when I know for sure."

John's excitement was palpable. It was like Christmas only better. He loved the anticipation of the moment.

It was a glorious fall day. The large trees of the cemetery across the field from Ma's house were in full color with oranges, reds, and yellows and just a bit of green still showing through. It was his favorite time of the year because fall postponed the advent of winter. As he hurried along on the dirt track passing between the stone walls of the Protestant and Catholic cemeteries, he could smell and even taste the clay in the air, dust from a passing surrey. Al and Lena's rental

> ## I SEE BY THE PAPER...
>
> ### CITY COUNCIL
> Regular Meeting.
> Woodstock, Ill. Sept 7, 1900.
> E. C. Jewett, mayor, presiding.
>
> The following bills, approved by the finance committee, were read:
>
> Wienke & Davis,
> painting City Hall $403.05
>
> *Woodstock Sentinel*, September 13, 1900.

was easy to find, just over the hill on Jackson Street about halfway to the square from Ma's. It had come up for rent in August, and Al had jumped at it. In the intervening months, he had papered and painted it inside and out and had added bits of furniture, but it still needed a woman's touch.

Al was a hard worker and a civicminded soul who was doing well with his business. He had been asked to paint and paper many of the houses, churches and civic buildings in Woodstock. His crew had worked their magic on the City Hall renovation, and the paper said, "a transformation that must be seen to be appreciated." Al was exactly at the right place in his life to take a wife.

But was he? John slowed his pace – suddenly a bit more nervous. He had no house, no business, no great looks to bring to the table. Did he know what he was getting into? What if he disliked how Ida looked, maybe he should have asked for a photograph? He shook himself and picked up his pace again. If anything, she was the one who would be put off by his looks. He was going to have to show off his gregarious side today because his looks were not going to carry him. He stopped. He was standing in front of the house. His stomach lurched, but his excitement and curiosity won the day. He walked up the path worn bare by many feet, and onto the porch. He shuffled his feet on the mat to remove the dust, and then, with a deep breath for courage, turned the knob.

"John!" Al greeted him with exaggerated joviality. "Glad you could make it."

John looked around the interior of the house. A good number of people were already in attendance; after all, this was a housewarming for Al and Lena, not a "meet-Ida" party. He had furnished much of the food and drink for the party – his donation. The house was not totally bare. One huge square, expandable wooden table was covered with a variety of beverages, sweets, and sandwiches. With about twenty people milling around, it looked like a good turnout.

"When do the drapes go up?" John asked, too brightly.

"Lena's brother and father will be bringing her goods in two weekends. She can't wait to start decorating."

"Excellent," said John. "Are you enjoying your last few months of bachelorhood?"

"Not much; I have a pallet on the floor in the bedroom. Lena says she might get a bed from her family. So, I'm on the floor for now. It's OK, but a bed would ease my back after a day of painting."

"I haven't seen you down at the Pleasure Club for a while. Lots of work?"

"Yes, we are busy on houses now…trying to get the outside work done before it gets too cold."

"Good for you!" Out of character, he clapped Al on the back. "Is Bob here?" he asked. He looked around at faces for the first time.

"He said he is coming but isn't here yet. You shouldn't be so hard on him, John. He's just young and feeling his oats…John?"

I SEE BY THE PAPER...

The Woodstock Pleasure Club held its annual meeting last evening, and elected the following officers for the ensuing year:

President——Harry Cross.

Vice-President——A. J. Mullen.

Secretary——Geo. W. Lemmers.

Trustees——Albert Wienke, C.C. Harting, E.A. Wyant and Wm. Gritzbaugh.

The Club is in a very prosperous condition, and its popularity is not waning one iota.

Woodstock Sentinel, October 15, 1900.

But John's mind had stopped working. He heard the words, but the advice was not registering. He was looking at a striking young woman, who was laughing with Lena and a few other women. She stood out in the crowd in a stylish dark green brocade traveling suit, a Gibson girl blouse with a black cross tie. Her brown hair was upswept under a fashionable black hat with a few tastefully applied feathers and a bow that hung down the back. She looked up and locked eyes with him. A small smile played across her lips, but then as if she realized it was rude to stare, she returned to the group.

Al smiled.

"John?" Al's voice broke through the reverie. "Do you want to meet her?"

As John walked with Al across the room that would soon be the parlor, he tried to smile or at least look friendly.

"Excuse me, ladies." The women made the circle wider. Oh no, not in front of all these women, John's inner voice shouted. "Miss Ida Doering of Racine, Wisconsin, I would like you to meet my brother Mr. John Wienke of Woodstock, Illinois. John, this is Lena's friend, Ida."

Ida was first to put out a hand, not like a real handshake, but in a palm-down way that left John not knowing what to do with it. He clasped it in his much larger hand, and they both said, "How do you do?" in unison. He didn't bow to the hand nor did he kiss it which he had heard was at times appropriate. He did lower his eyes and his head as he took her hand, and then he just held it as his eyes slid back up to her pretty face. They held each other's eyes for a long moment. And then as if on cue, Al and Lena both started talking about the house, and the moment was gone, the gaze was broken, and the hand was dropped. John stood there spent. He listened to Lena's plans and tried to relax. Without warning, Ida was at his elbow. "Would you like to buy me a drink, John?"

He started a bit and then smiled back at her smile, "Of course, I would, Ida." He held out his arm to her. She took it, and they moved across the room as one.

November 1, 1900
936 Huron Street
Racine, Wisconsin

Dear Lena,

Oh, what a day you gave me. I am destroyed having to come back here and to not be able to see all of you until – when? – your wedding in February I suppose!

I am now clerking five days a week at the Fisher Laundry. Good clean job, ha! I am also working on a quick baptismal outfit. They didn't want to order it before the little one arrived safe and sound. But now he's here, they want it within two weeks. So, I must apply myself, but I cannot hardly think about hems and stitches to say nothing about embroidery designs.

Have you heard anything about whether John would want to see me again? I know, there's not been time for letters to be sent. I was encouraged that he wanted to walk me to the train. It was such a short time to get to know someone. I'm all sixes and sevens.

Please, please, write soon and let me know what Al said.

Anxiously awaiting your reply,
Ida

Ida looked at the sewing in her lap. She had gotten Lena's letter to the box just as the postman was emptying it. The letter should make today's train. She had to concentrate and embroider on this beautiful little dress. As she stared at her work, needle poised to dip through the fabric, her father's face seemed to appear on the white cloth. Oh, how she still missed him.

Strong, handsome Heinrich Döring was a real Mensch. With black hair and hazel-green eyes, he had turned many a lady's head. Heinrich or Henry, as he would be known in the new world, brought his family to America when Ida was six years old. She remembered the day they stood hand in hand on the top deck of the ship, feeling the salt breeze on their faces, looking westward toward America. He had told her about their new country with its many opportunities. "It is a great land," he had said, "and we are going to be so happy and free in America." When she heard that, little Ida had felt such joy. America.

Then they were in New York City. When they were checked in at the port, the man changed the spelling of their name, and Papa told everyone they were now Doerings. New York was a city very different from the German cities she had seen. For one thing, it was MUCH taller. The buildings looked modern, not old and common as they had in Germany. She loved the streetcars, horses in straw hats, and the bustle of the city.

Too soon they were off again, this time on a train, to the city of Racine in Wisconsin, and then by cart fifty miles west to the small town of Whitewater, Wisconsin where Uncle Karl, her mother's brother, and his family awaited them.

Those days in Whitewater were so happy. She pictured herself and her friends running and dancing in the meadow behind their house. She remembered the feeling of having a safe haven as she sat on Papa's lap listening to stories read from a big German storybook. She could still hear his calm, deep voice speaking in his native language.

Then Papa's employer, the Easterly Works Wheat Processing plant closed and moved to Minneapolis because Wisconsin, they said, was switching from growing the wheat they processed to growing dairy cows, and Papa found a new job in Beloit. They all moved to Beloit, and within a year, he was dead.

The night he died, Ida had gone to a Saturday evening program at church with Mama and Clara. She had wanted to stay home, but Mama had insisted. The paper wrote – she would never forget it – "Henry Doering, aged 49 years, dropped dead at his home at Beloit, from heart disease last night, while his wife was attending church." And that was it. An inauspicious obituary for such a wonderful man. His own father had died from the same at a young age. Did such diseases run through the men in a family? They had held the vigil at home in Beloit and then again at Uncle Karl's in Whitewater where her father was buried. All happiness had drained from the world the day Papa died, and it had taken a long time before it began to seep back into their lives. Ida sighed.

At the time of Papa's death, Emma had just married Floyd Fisher and set up housekeeping in Racine where Floyd worked for the United States Express Company – a mail carrier on the rails. Herman was living with the Fishers, making a name for himself clerking at Zahn Dry Goods Company.

Mama sold the house in Beloit, and they all moved to Racine to be near Emma, Frank, and Herman. Ida had spent a year in Chicago, completing the McDowell French-Cut Dressmaking Course, and when she returned to Racine, she and Mama had begun a dressmaking business on her credentials. Even Clara, who was ten, quickly learned how to hem a skirt. And they had done well in Racine.

Then last year, J. Nicholas Stoffel, who had lost his wife just about the time they moved, let a room in their house to be closer to his work at the J. I. Case facility just down the street. They had met him through the St. John's German Lutheran Church, and he had become a part of their lives. He and Mama had become close and were just like an old married couple except for separate bedrooms. Could it be that her mother would marry again before she would? Ida shook her head at the irony.

Emma had mentioned last Sunday that she was again expecting – number four – and hoping, if it was a girl, to name her Marion. If a boy, Howard. Ida liked the name Marion for a girl's name. "Don't tell Mama, yet," Emma had whispered. And now, here was Ida looking marriage straight in the face and the possibility of leaving the hearth also.

"Don't tell Mama, yet," Ida whispered to no one.

Mr. Stoffel and Mama seemed a good match. They were kind and polite to each other. Maybe…

"Ida? Ida!" Mama's voice, a bit severe, brought her back to her senses. "Was machen sie?"

"Nothing, Mama."

"Ich sehe das! Wie kommt das Kleid?"

"The dress is coming fine," she hedged. "Mama, what would you do if I got married?" So much for saying nothing.

"Ich wäre so glücklich!" The dress was all but forgotten.

"You would be happy? I'm just worried that I would leave you in the lurch."

"Lurch?' Was bedeutet das?"

"It means I would leave you without much income if I wasn't here in Racine." She rubbed her thumb and two fingers together, the universal sign for money.

"Uns wird es gut geben. Ich habe, so Gott will, Mr. Stoffel," she crossed her fingers on both hands. "Unt Clara. Wo wirst du hingehen?"

Hm, Ida thought, she, God willing, 'has' Mr. Stoffel, eh? "Woodstock. Woodstock, Illinois."

I SEE BY THE PAPER...

McKinley Club Changes Age Limit.

The Young Men's McKinley club held a business meeting last night, removing the age limit so as to allow all Republicans to join, authorized Capt. Eichelberger to organize a flambeaux club, appointed a committee of five to solicit members, chose C. F. Renich, D. T. Smiley and John Wienke to arrange for a public meeting next Wednesday evening, and transacted other important business.

Woodstock Sentinel.

"Der Mann ist?"

"Lena's fiancé's brother, John. Remember we talked of him when she was here? John Wienke."

"Ja."

"Ich bin mir nicht absolut sicher, aber…I think he might be the one," said Ida, a little smile playing on her lips.

"Ich muss ihn zurest treffen," said Louisa.

"Of course, you'll meet him first. I promise. Now I must work on this dress," Ida smiled at her mother and received a pleased smile back.

November 30, 1900
Woodstock, Illinois

Dear Ida,

I hope that your quick trip did not wear you out too much and that this letter finds you well.

I very much enjoyed our time together and hope that we will see each other again soon. As a matter of fact, I just had the opportunity to talk to Al, and he says that Lena is coming to Woodstock for New Year's Eve and staying at a friend's house. I was wondering if you might think about doing the same. I believe you met many nice people when you were here, and I'm sure I can find someone to give you lodging overnight which will be a necessity on New Year's Eve, unless we just stay up all night and I put you on the morning train back to Racine, ha. You will probably have to work on New Year's Eve day but you could take the 4:30 p.m. train which would get you here in plenty of time to celebrate with your new friends, including me. I do hope you consider me one of your new friends.

There will be a dance at the Armory on New Year's Eve and fireworks all over town at midnight. We may be small, but we throw a good New Year's party.

I know this would be a lot to arrange at short order, but if you could, I would be glad to take you a few turns around the dance floor, as long as you go easy on me.

Thank you for considering this invitation and let me know if you accept as I must quickly find lodging for you. All of Woodstock looks forward to your return, and especially John Wienke

---

I SEE BY THE PAPER...

LOCAL INTELLIGENCE.

Oysters at Conklin's.
Next horse sale, Jan. 9.
Ideal Christmas weather.
Oysters found at Huntzinger's restaurant,
Short orders and lunch at all hours a Huntzinger's.
The happiest Christmas is the first one we remember.
He was a foolish man who have his neighbor's boy a drum.
Good sharp winter weather - the days have begun to lengthen.
A storm house has been erected over the entrance to the postoffice.
It won't be long now until we begin swearing off bad habits for the next century.

Woodstock Sentinel, Dec. 27, 1900.

"Com'on, Herman. You simply must come with me!" Ida plied her brother with her most beseeching look. "I need you!

Mama won't let me go overnight alone." They were standing in the kitchen of the house on Huron Street, Ida having made Herman a late-night sandwich as he claimed he had missed supper while working. She was hoping she could persuade him with food.

"I don't know. I—"

"I know. I must find a way. I am becoming an old maid, and at twenty-six, this might be my last chance! Once we're there, you can stay with Al, and I with Lena. Or we can all stay with Al. Goodness, we aren't children. All it will cost you is the train ticket and entrance to the dance.

> **I SEE BY THE PAPER...**
>
> Art thou one of the many that has drained the golden nectar that maketh thy heart full of strength and gladness? If not, take Rocky Mountain Tea. A. M. Murphy.
>
> *Woodstock Sentinel*, Dec. 6, 1900.

I'll even pay for that! Do you have a date lined up for Silvester?"

"Maybe...," he trailed off thinking.

"Oh, never mind! I'll just turn into a dried-up old spinster taking in sewing in Racine, Wisconsin."

"So why don't you just go?"

"Mr. Stoffel does not believe in women traveling alone especially at night. Women don't belong out in the world; they must be protected by strong virile men." She grasped Herman's bicep and squeezed.

"Ouch! Stop that! Since when does Mr. Stoffel make the rules of this house?"

"See, I'm as strong as you are, stronger even. Since Mama listens to him. But who has the right to stop me from going to see my beau?" Ida wailed.

"Oh, your beau. I didn't understand the question. Will I facilitate you seeing your beau? How in the world can I say 'no' to that? Does this beau have a name?"

"John Wienke of Woodstock, Illinois, born and raised. Good German stock. Member of the German Lutheran Church in Woodstock."

"High or Low?" The question was one that was often asked by parents, but it didn't reflect a social position...not as such. High German was spoken in the southern part of Germany where the elevation was higher. It was also the older version of German. The Doerings were high German. Low German was what one might call a simplified German common to Bavaria.

"Low," Ida admitted. "But this is America, that shouldn't matter."

Herman raised his eyebrows with a grim look. "Looks like you are doomed. Romeo and Juliet; John and Ida. How will you ever understand each other?" Then he broke into a smile.

"Oh, you! We both speak English very well, thank you."

"How long have you known him?" Herman asked. He was still rubbing his arm.

"Since October. He sent me a nice invitation, even offering to arrange lodging with one of his friends. If I can't see him, I'll have a broken heart," she fluttered her eyelashes at Herman with a coy little smile.

"Ach meine Gotte! You are such a little flirt! This man doesn't have a chance." Herman laughed, shaking his head.

John ran as fast as the frozen, rutted sleigh track would allow. Dressed in his best wool suit and overcoat, he had fallen only once....so far. His galoshes flapped against his legs as he ran. He had stopped to pull them on before bolting out of his mother's house, which was lucky because twice a sleigh had trotted past forcing him into the crusty snow along the side of the road. The New Year's Eve revelers could have at least offered him a ride down to the square. It was cold out here. Their hail-fellow-well-met greetings were fine, but a ride would have been much more appreciated.

His breath was coming in great puffs of steam as he rounded the corner onto the square, alive with sleighs and couples scurrying here and there even in the cold weather. He skirted the park on the north side and then went north on

Benton Street, toward the armory, just a few blocks ahead. Light reflecting off the low hanging clouds guided the way. He slowed in order to catch his breath. He didn't want to show up huffing and puffing like an old man.

As he pulled open the door, Brubaker's orchestra was playing a waltz, and all the young people seemed to be standing along the sides of the room while most of the older couples were dancing. Was thirty years old or young, he wondered?

He hurried to the men's cloakroom and removed his coat, tucking his cap and gloves into his galoshes. He would need them for sure on the mile walk home. Emerging, he scanned the crowd – where was she?

John smiled as he looked out across the crowd. His height allowed him several inches on most of the assembly. He acknowledged a few friends from afar. Ida and her brother Herman had taken the train down from Racine to be here for the celebration and were staying at Al and Lena's new house. Al must have gotten some beds. John wondered how long they would be staying. Not that it mattered greatly. This night was what was important, but he must find her soon or her dance card would be full. He wanted to feel her in his arms. Where the heck was….?

There she was! Dancing with Bob's business partner, Albert Schneider. She looks like the belle of the ball, he thought as he made his way through the crowd, greeted Lena and Al, and was introduced to Herman. The music stopped, and Albert, always the gentleman, guided Ida back to the circle of friends. Her beautiful light blue gown, with a high collar and lace across the breast and around the wrists, swirled delightfully around her ankles. Did she have golden slippers on, he wondered?

"Well, it's about time, John," Albert teased. "You shouldn't leave your girl lollygagging around for the likes of me to take advantage of." His attention turned toward Ida, "There you are, m'lady. Safe and sound. Save for a few crushed toes, but who's counting."

Albert and Ida laughed.

John reached over and took Ida's hand. "I hope you haven't bruised those beautiful feet, Schneider, or I'll have to take you out to the woodshed," he teased back. Albert looked appropriately chagrin. Then John laughed also and said, "Al, can you find a nice Woodstock girl for my friend Herman here to dance with? He's come a long way to be stuck talking to my brother."

Without waiting for an answer, John led Ida out on the floor. As long as they kept up the waltzes, he'd be OK, but once the orchestra moved on to the Turkey Trot or the Bunny Hop or the newest one he just heard about yesterday, what was it...ah yes, the Texas Tommy, what then?

"Can you dance the Texas Tommy?" John asked.

"The WHAT?" Ida replied. He hadn't even said hello yet.

"I hope you cannot dance the Texas Tommy or the Turkey Trot. Because if you can, I'm a cooked goose," he said. His attempt at humor meant to get his nervousness under control.

"No, I'm from Wisconsin, not Texas. I can, however, dance a pretty fast polka," Ida gave him a poker face. His face had fallen, his bravado gone. And then she laughed. "Don't worry, I won't make you polka. Waltzing is just fine with me."

They waltzed; his arms full of this beautiful maiden. After a few minutes, John relaxed, and for the first time in his life, he enjoyed dancing.

As they counted down the clock to midnight, John made sure he was still at Ida's elbow. "Five...four...three...two... one! Happy New Year!" the crowd hollered. And John Wienke leaned down and placed a proper kiss on Ida Doering's lips. And then gave her a brief cheek-to-cheek hug, saying, "Happy New Year, Ida."

"Happy New Year, John," Ida replied, her lips so close to his ear that he could feel her warm breath.

Ida and John stood, hand in hand, drinking in the intoxication of the moment. This was going to be a good year, a good century! They both could feel it.

Ida Doering circa 1895.

John Wienke circa 1890.

Vas You Dar, John? - 1901

John Wienke and Ida Doering sat, huddled from the cold, north wind, on a bench on the leeward side of the depot waiting for the train that would take Ida and her brother back to Racine. The typewriter factory had given the boys January first off, and for once John was glad to have a no-pay day if it meant he could sit here and talk with Ida for a few minutes more. Herman had made himself scarce, walking down the platform, pretending to read notices and wanted posters. They sat in silence properly close, John's knee touching hers as they discussed the night before and the days to come.

John felt like he'd just been gut-punched. He didn't want to let her go. Say something, fool.

"It was pretty quiet here last night…I mean…for a New Year's Eve. We usually have a lot more fireworks and parties.

"Mm. Maybe because last year was the people's new century, and this year was the government's new century."

John laughed, "You are right. For the people, January 1, 1900, was the beginning of the Twentieth Century. The people all celebrated last year."   He took a deep breath, cleared his throat, and started to tell Ida about how much work the factory was expecting in the months to come. He wanted to be honest about this long-distance courtship.

"…six days a week and sometimes Sundays, too, depending on the orders."

"Nooo!" Ida whined. "When will we see each other? And Mama wants to meet you."

"I'll do what I can, but I don't want you to get your hopes up too high for frequent visits. But on the sunny side, I will be earning a lot of money which I am saving for my store."

"Well, it looks like I'm going to have to make a few visits down here then. First visit will be the wedding of the century."

> ## I SEE BY THE PAPER...
>
> ### OPENING OF A CENTURY.
>
> ---
>
> #### Event Celebrated without Usual Noise in This City.
>
> ---
>
> The dual event - the opening of a new year and of a new century simultaneously - did not create any unusual excitement in Woodstock. As soon as Father Time had indicated the hour of midnight, Monday night, the announcement of the new year's arrival was made by the ringing of the church bells and the blowing of the whistle at the city power house, the firing of guns and cannon crackers, but the noise was not nearly as bewildering of as long drawn out as we have known it on previous announcements of the birth of a new year.
>
> Aside from the watch meeting services at the M.E. church and the celebration of midnight mass at St. Mary's, there were many cases of individual and family watchings of the old year out and the new year in, and the usual hearty expressions of good wishes on the part of the participants.
>
> None of THE SENTINEL readers ever before witnessed the birth of a century, and it is highly improbable that any of them will again, hence it behooves all to make the most of the years of this century that may be vouchsafed to them, realizing our dependence on and our responsibility to a Higher Power, and our duties to our fellows.
>
> THE SENTINEL wishes all great joy and prosperity in this century, which, if men realize the possibilities that stretch out before them, is destined to be the greatest in the history of the world.
>
> Welcome the new century! May it treat us no worse than its predecessor has done, and may it witness a greater and grander appreciation of the fatherhood of God and the brotherhood of man.
>
> *Woodstock Sentinel,* January 3, 1901

John chuckled. Al and Lena's house was ready for the new couple to move in. Lena's things being moved before the snow. Al, Lena, Ida, and Herman had served as their own chaperones the night before. The girls in the marriage bed and the boys on pallets on the floor in the parlor. John had been invited but bowed to formality and custom by walking the few blocks home. But he had joined them for breakfast and the walk to the station.

The train whistled its approach, and Ida rose to gather her belongings, with Herman coming over to help. The men shook hands.

"Nice little town you have here, John," declared Herman.

"Thanks, it is," agreed John. "I'm glad you came to the festivities," he paused and looked at Ida, "and brought this wonderful girl with you."

"You betcha!" laughed Herman, and he gathered up the cases and climbed aboard, waiting at the top of the steps for Ida.

John turned Ida toward him and kissed her lightly on the lips, "Thank you for coming."

"You betcha!" said Ida. She held the gaze for another long moment then turned and pulled herself up onto the first step still clasping John's hand. The train began to move, and their hands slipped apart. She stayed on the step until the train was past the platform then waved her handkerchief at him, turned and went into the train.

John watched the train until it disappeared – until he could no longer hear the whistles at the crossings – until he realized that he was standing on the platform as if he had missed the train. He chuckled and said, aloud, "This is a train I do not want to miss." And he turned and headed back up Main Street to the square, whistling.

February 17, 1901
936 Huron Street
Racine, Wisconsin

Dear John,

In a week's time, you will be enjoying the wedding festivities while I will be in Racine playing nursemaid to sick people. Mr. Stoffel was the first to come down with the grippe and so is the first to feel better. He was completely down for two days and then resting for two more. He says he will return to work tomorrow, although Mama is trying to persuade him to go back on Monday. Then comes Clara home with it – did I tell you that she is clerking for a doctor's office now? She was told she must stay home a week so as not to spread it to the patients, but it would seem to me that it's the other way around…the patients have spread the germs to her – they should stay away. Ha! And lastly, Mama is feeling poorly this morning. So, I have chamber pots to empty, soup to make, and cool sponge baths to give…and I'm just waiting to begin to feel

---

I SEE BY THE PAPER...

Local Intelligence.

You should endeavor to discover your natural tendencies and apply them, unless, indeed, your natural tendencies are all evil.

When women don't know what etiquette would demand, they kiss each other.

Boys are, of course, taught to rise and give a seat to any lady who enters a room also to rise and remain standing till a woman is seated, but the rule is often in abeyance to their own mothers and sisters. You may enter it on your records as a rule without exception, that no one will ever be at ease in society who fails in the little daily amenities in the home.

Have you been vaccinated yet? Arm or-?

Beware the tax collector will soon be abroad in the land.

Woodstock Sentinel, January 31, 1901.

---

feverish myself any time. So, I am quarantined here and cannot come to the wedding!!! It's not fair! But I wouldn't want to have all of you sick also. At least this grippe isn't as hard a one as it might be. When Mr. Stoffel came home, we were all very afraid. But the doctor said with rest and plenty of pea soup, he should be fine. I do not look forward to my sick time and am doing my best to stave it off.

Mama is calling. Must go and give this to the postman who will pass in about an hour.

I remain truly yours,
Ida

Woodstock Pleasure Club
Woodstock, Illinois

February 25, 1901

Dear Ida,

I am so sorry that you will not be here for the wedding, but I do understand your nursing assignment. I do hope you do not fall ill along with everyone else. I will miss your presence as I'm sure Lena and Al will. However, I would suggest that you come on Monday evening, March 4 for an inaugural dance we Republicans are putting on at the Armory. It is sure to please. I don't know if you can get away on a Monday afternoon and Tuesday morning, but if you can, Lena has said that you may stay at their house. She and Al will be in Beloit making the after the wedding rounds of family.

If you can come, please let me know by return post so that I can make arrangements. It would be very nice to see you.

Sincerely,
John

March 1, 1901
936 Huron Street
Racine, Wisconsin

Dear John,

Thank you so much for your short invitation to the dance, but I will have to decline as the weather has been horrible here by the lake and Mama, while much improved, is still unable to keep up with the housework and cooking. We have had feet of snow instead of inches and the city is working hard at shoveling out. I'm not sure how deep the drifts are in Woodstock. Probably the drifts all melted the next day in that blessed city, but here they are even disrupting train service now and again. I'm sure you will be able to fill your dance card without me, but just don't hold those ladies too tightly or I'll be jealous. I won't even have Lena to spy for me. Ha!

We've been busy this winter with many engagements for Clara and her instruments. I've told you that she plays piano and sings beautifully, but I don't think you know that she also plays the mandolin. She has joined with two friends, and they are singing for their suppers at various gatherings, especially during the breaks in cinch card parties. The reviews have been good with more invitations each day. The girls have even had to turn down some due to conflicting dates. Today she is off to a St. David's Day celebration. I guess it is a common Welsh celebration, although I have never heard of a St. David, have you? Here in Racine, we have a St. David's Society which is sponsoring the day. Clara and her friends will sing two songs, as will a Methodist ladies' and men's quartet along with a few solos and other recitations and speeches. Clara had to learn the Welsh national song in Welch, so she can sing it with gusto at the appropriate time. She is now sure that she wants to be an entertainer. Can't you just see the theater poster "Clara Doering and Her Mandolin singing The Welch National Song"! Ha! Ah, the pipedreams of youth.

This isn't going to be a long letter like I usually write because I'm punishing you for your short letter of last week. You can do better than five lines, can't you? Your life can't be that busy, can it?. On the other hand, maybe it cans. Maybe life in wonderful Woodstock isn't all it's touted to be. What do you say to that, kind sir?

Have a fine time celebrating McKinley's win. Save a dance for me next time we see each other.

I remain your friend,
Ida

Woodstock Pleasure Club
Woodstock, Illinois

March 15, 1901

Dear Ida,

I finally have time to send a note. My brothers and I have finished our move to town. It took some doing. Ma's house was small, but twenty-five years of living were packed into every closet and cupboard. We easily found a buyer because housing is at a premium here. The fellow who bought it owns a lot of rentals and will probably do some renovations and then rent it to someone at the Oliver factory. I was amazed as I walked through one last time how my parents were able to raise eight children in five-rooms — three bedrooms, a parlor, and a kitchen. Luckily, we were spread out enough that the older boys were gone before the younger needed a bed, I guess.

We bought a house on Washington Street for Ma which is a residential street going out of town toward Hebron. The house has been updated with a good coat of paint, concrete paths, and modern conveniences. We are most happy with the change, and I think she is also. It's a bigger house with five bedrooms upstairs and one down. Each of us can have a bedroom with two left over plus a kitchen, parlor and a formal dining room. Best of all, it is fully

I SEE BY THE PAPER...

Local Intelligence.

Delightful sunshine and moderating temperature greeted the people this morning.

The Wienke place west of the cemetery has been sold to Wm. Corr who will soon take possession, and the Wienke family will become residents of this city. They are the kind of people who make good citizens.

The Wienke brothers have purchased the E. A. Stone residence and property on Washington street.

If you want your organ or sewing machine repaired, call on E. B. Conklin. Leave orders at Hooker's grocery store.

John Wienke was a visitor at Beloit last Saturday.

Woodstock Sentinel, March 7, 1901.

modernized. It has city water and a modern septic system with indoor plumbing! She is so happy!! No more chamber pots. I wonder why she is happy about that. Ha!

I missed you at the dance. I only danced two waltzes all night, and they were not fun at all. I'm sure it was more fun than being snowed in at Racine under five-foot drifts with a north wind, but mostly it was just a lot of cheering and beer drinking. I left early and was abed by midnight. I hope that does not make me a bore in your mind.

I am still hoping you will be able to come down for the minstrel show in March. Let me know so I can make arrangements.

I had thought to come visit a few weeks ago because I had a Sunday respite. But then I got bogged down in the details. If I come on Saturday after work, I will arrive after supper and will have no place to lay my head. If I wait until Sunday, I will arrive while you are away at church and will have to leave on the 4:30 p.m. train so will have very little time with you. If I came on Saturday, I could go to church with you and see you for a longer time…but would have to make my bed in a snowbank outside your house. (It is Spring here, but I assume you still have piles of snow). Such a dilemma. Please advise.

Must close as I work early tomorrow. They have been keeping us to a twelve-hour day, but I don't complain. More work, more money saved.

Yours truly,
John

Ida sat at her writing desk and read and then reread the letter. Yes, she thought, she would get to Woodstock for that show no matter what. Seeing John in a minstrel show would be so funny. She imagined his face painted black and him singing with his mouth in an O like a cigar smoker making smoke rings. She was glad he wasn't a smoker, now that she thought about it. Well, except for cigars when out with the boys. But not cigarettes, another plus.

And yes, a place for him to lay his head was a dilemma. She could ask her mother and Mr. Stoffel if John could stay here, but that was a bit difficult with the number of people who lived

I SEE BY THE PAPER...

LOCAL INTELLIGENCE.

Mud, mud, mud, everywhere.

Be sure to come out and vote next Tuesday.

The best show of the winter will be the Pleasure Club minstrels at the City Hall, Friday evening, Mar. 29.

Will April showers in March result in May flowers in April?

The advance sale of seats for the Pleasure Club minstrels was immense last night. Anxious purchasers waited from 10 o'clock in the forenoon until night in order to get first choice of seats.

The bowling alley is being conducted for men these days. Andrew Lascelle is in charge.

See the Coon Town County Fair at the Pleasure Club minstrels, Friday Evening.

If you want your organ or sewing machine repaired, call on E.B. Conklin. Leave orders at Hooker's grocery.

Every Republican will do his country a service by coming out next Tuesday and voting the Republican ticket straight.

Laugh and grow fat at the Pleasure Club minstrels.

Woodstock Sentinel, Mar. 28, 1901.

in the house now. She and Clara shared a room and Herman had the other. Maybe John could just bunk on the couch in the front room. Herman called it the best bed in the house.

Mama often said, "Lass den, der kalt ist, sich rühren die Kohlen." Let the one who is cold stir the coals. Ida was without a doubt going to stir the coals. Even if they'd known each other for only six months and seen each other but a few times, he was the one she wanted. She would ask Mama about John staying, and then she'd see if she could get those coals glowing.

In his favorite chair in the parlor of the new house, John paged through the paper starting with the last page looking for the story. He wasn't sure why he started with the last page ...maybe just low expectations. "Men never get too old to acquire experience," said a quote on that last page...isn't that the truth!

Next page had an ad that caught his eye, "Gold dust in the water makes your dishes come out perfectly clean and free from grease. It is almost a pleasure to wash dishes with Gold Dust Washing Powder."

"Ma?" he called out to Sophia in the kitchen where she was washing the evening dishes. "It says by the paper that you can get cleaner dishes if you put gold dust in the dish powder."

"Acht, no?" She appeared in the doorway wiping her hands on the dishtowel. "Was meanst du? My dishes nicht so clean fur deine Hoheit? Vhy dey try'n to get rid of golt?"

John laughed, "Did you just call me Your Highness? Me? Why yes, fair maiden, come and look at this!"

She looked over his shoulder. "Well, what bout dat? Must have too much golt in 'laska. Soon in everytink."

"Like gold underwear."

"Unt golt Korsetts."

"Gold in flour. Maybe that's the secret ingredient in Gold Bond Flour."

"Unt in Zucker. 'Zugar…a bit more sweeter mit golt'," Sophia wrote the ad for the sugar company. They laughed, and John began turning the pages. When he reached the front page, he said, "Well, what do you know! We are front-page news!" and began reading the article aloud as Sophia sunk onto the davenport.

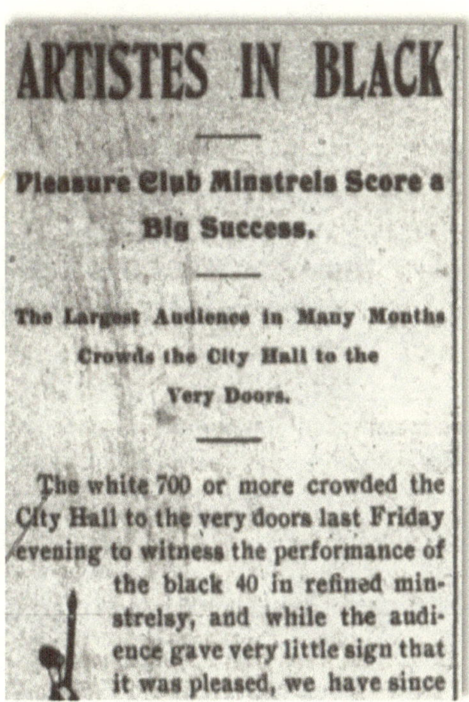

ARTISTES IN BLACK

Pleasure Club Minstrels Score a Big Success.

The Largest Audience in Many Months Crowds the City Hall to the Very Doors.

The white 700 or more crowded the City Hall to the very doors last Friday evening to witness the performance of the black 40 in refined minstrelsy, and while the audience gave very little sign that it was pleased, we have since heard no one express himself in any different manner. It is a peculiarity of Woodstock audiences that, when a local company of performers puts up a good show, they seldom express their appreciation in the way they do when an outside company appears and presents a program far inferior, very often, to the one given last Friday evening. We don't know why this is, but local talent has often noticed this defect, and the habit, if it may be called by that name, is one that ought to be overcome. But to resume our account of the program:

Interlocutor Field to the gallery gods

"Ja," said John, interrupting himself, "the audience was very quiet at first, but we pulled them in."

"Mmmm," said Sophia, picking up her tatting. He read on.

The audience, which was one of the largest ever seen in the hall, crowded the building to the very door, not a seat being vacant, the total from the sale of seats aggregating about $310.

Jas. Sullivan giving a joke

"Three hundred and ten dollars! That's three times what we made last year," said John. "Makes all the work worth it. Of course, this year's performance was much better than last. I think we are getting the hang of it."

"Mmmm," said Sophia. Her hands worked swiftly making a lace fringe for a pillowcase.

> With Director John L. Carroll and the Brubaker orchestra occupying their accustomed places in front of the footlights, the curtain went up at 8:15, revealing a very beautiful tropical scene, with potted plants, trailing vines and a profusion of colored lights. In the rear of the stage was a balcony scene that was quite realistic. As the curtain went up the chorus, or circle, broke out

"Vat dat…circle," Sophia broke in, looking up from her handiwork.

"That's just what they call the singers in a minstrel show," John explained.

"Warum?"

"Why? Well…because…they sit or stand in a semi-circle when they sing, I suppose," John replied and continued.

> chorus, or circle, broke out with the opening chorus, "Hail, Little Children, All Hail," and from the balcony came the end men, with a song appropriate and beautiful, who marched to the front of the stage, and, after a few minutes' work with the bones and tamboes, took their places.
>
> D.C.Akers making a spiel.

"Was ist dis bones and tamboes?" asked Sophia. She had left her tatting behind, as the article had caught her attention.

"Well, there is the Interlocutor who is the master of ceremonies…Der Zeremonienmeister…and the two end men who do the comedy with the…um …funnymen…the tambo and the bones. Sometimes there are more than just two, but they make jokes and make fun of the Interlocutor behind his back."

"OK," said Sophia, trying to understand.

John cleared his throat and continued...

> Then Interlocutor Geo. W. Field appeared on the balcony with a song that began, "Now tell me, little children, do you hear me calling you?" to which there was a prompt and unanimous response. He descended the stairs, and his pages, Masters Richard and Edsall McHatton, the bright and winsome sons of Mr. and Mrs. W. B. McHatton, followed with his chair, which they placed at the center of the circle, winning the applause of the audience by their skill and their neat and attractive attire.
>
> C. C. Harting growing loquacious.

Sophia interrupted, "Kleine Kinder in dis?" She shook her head. "Waren sie auch Neger?"

"No ma. None of the people were Negroes. The children were little white boys with their faces painted black, so they would look like little Negerjungen."

"Hmmm," said Sophia. She looked confused. "Not sure bout der Kinder? Not gut."

"Ja, I know. But the rest is very funny, like a play – ein Spiel. We all pretend to be Negroes and then horse around."

"Hmmm. Warum scherzten Sie nicht mit weissen Gesichtern."

"Come on, English please, Ma."

"Vy du not hoss 'round vid vhite faces?"

John looked at his little mother, now perched on the edge of the couch, "It wouldn't be as funny," he said, and went back to reading, not giving her a chance for more questions.

The interlocutor and end men were attired in full evening dress and white gloves, with sparkling "diamonds," while the make up of the circle was suits of white duck, black gloves and sashes and red neckties, the effect being very pleasing.

E. J. Field waxes funny.

Sophia was frowning. "Vhen du hoss 'round?"

John looked up, "I was in the chorus and in the third part of the play." Reading ahead, John skipped down to the third act of the show.

The program concluded with a roaring farce entitled, "The Coonville County Fair," in which the histrionic ability of several young men was shown to good advantage. The stage was set to represent the McHenry County Fair in full operation, and Secretary Arnold got in his work by having a banner suspended from the flies advertising the next annual exhibition. There was the ticket office, where many tried to gain admittance by reminding the secretary that "I voted

H. Brubaker trying to change color.

for you," the pool-seller's box, the judge's stand on the race track, the "blind pig," the side-show with its bewildering array of attractions, and many other scenes familiar to Fair attendants. As the keeper of the side show G. L. Mullen fairly brought down the house, no one who knows him realizing for a moment that he was gifted with such a "gift of gab." F. W. Kniebusch, as Madame De Gambo G. Louison, the wonderful snake charmer, was certainly a "peach"; Harry McLaughlin, as Madame De Bruski, the operatic marvel, was strictly "all right"; John Wienke, as Prime Ursus, the strong man, acted as if he could lift almost anything, even to a pocket-book; Owen Corr, as Signor Owenierous, the wonderful pedestal clog dancer, convinced everybody that he certainly knows how to handle his feet; and the Cherry Brothers, Wm. Colberg and J. B. Cronk, in their buck and wing dancing, demonstrated that they have missed their calling by confining themselves to manual labor. Four of "the finest"—G. L. Mullen, F. W.

"Vat knowst du! Mein Junge ist beruhmt…famous!" Sophia slapped her knee, interrupting John mid-sentence. "Maybe he is too gut he not dry dishes!" she baited him as she rose and returned to the kitchen.

"I'll be right there. Just leave 'em," he said, thinking about the night of the show when he had looked up during the first chorus and had seen Ida in the second row grinning at him. He was so proud and had hammed it up during the finale. They only had time for a quick hug and a peck on the cheek, and then she was off and away with Lena to get some sleep. The next morning, he brought Ida home to meet Ma, who had served a nice lunch of corned beef and cabbage. And then she was off on the 4:00 p.m. train back to Racine. He sighed. I must make more time for romance.

"I'm abed goink," said Sophia. "Dishes stand im der Waschbecker…zink."

"OK." Still lost in his reverie.

Ma paused at the parlor door. "Best be tending to das Madchen 'fore she forgets du."

"Yes, du hast recht! G'night, Ma. Sweet dreams."

She was right. He did need to tend to his girl.

I SEE BY THE PAPER…

Personal Mention.

Wm. Wienke was reappoined as engineer at the power house by the mayor. Mr. Wienke has at all times filled the requirements of that exacting position, and, with the assistance of the electrician, has kept the city's plant in an admirable condition.

Dr. Emil Windmueller went to Milwaukee last Thrusday, where he purchased a new automobile, which he brought home overland. It is of a much finer make than the one the doctor had a year or two ago, and is guaranteed to give him far greater service over all kinds of roads. This is the first gasoline automobile stationed in Woodstock.

Births.

Born, to Mr. and Mrs. Ed Wienke, on Saturday, April 27, 1901, a son, Edwin.

Woodstock Sentinel, April-May, 1901.

April 5, 1901
936 Huron Street
Racine, Wisconsin

Dear Prime U,

I am overcome by your manliness and strength. Please come rescue a damsel in distress in Racine, Wisconsin. I have been captured and am being forced to sweat out a living by sewing my fingers to the bone every day. I beg you to use your power to come to release me very soon from this tedium.

Your captivated audience,

Ida Doering

Woodstock Pleasure Club
Woodstock, Illinois

April 20, 1901

Dear Captivated Audience Member,

I am very gratified that you have acknowledged my strength and ability to rescue you from the dungeons of Racine, but I have been very busy with work and other manly endeavors.

I would be very happy to see you when the weather is warmer and maybe go for a picnic. I know some fine places around Woodstock where picnics are quite pleasant. Do you have the same near Racine? I must say that I have missed your company and adoration, but my days are so full, and I do not see an opportunity for traveling to your fair city in the next while.

I SEE BY THE PAPER...

New Arrivals.
Born, to Mr. and Mrs. Ed Wienke on Saturday, April 27, 1901, a son.

Woodstock Sentinel, May 2, 1901.

Please come see our beautiful Woodstock in the summer. You will love it. If you will, I will plan an outing with our friends (other admirers of my strength). Or we could have a nice long walk and talk without the noise of the crowd. You need not be afraid. I will protect you. My weaker brother, William, was hurt falling down the basement stairs last week. It took three of us to get him back up the stairs because of the narrowness of the exit. The doctor took a look, and he seems to be no worse the wear except for a broken leg and a good bump on the head. I'm sure he'll be right back at work as soon as he masters the crutches.

You see that I do not hold your short note against you. I have written a very long letter in response. I am sure you will learn from my good example.

I SEE BY THE PAPER...

They Come in Carriages.
We could not help but notice on Saturday last the large number of carriages that were hitched to the chain around the public park. The time was when it was the exception for a farmer to own a carriage. Now nearly all are able to come to town in carriages to do their trading, which indicates the changing conditions that have come over this portion of our population as a result of the great prosperity brought about by continued Republican administrations, and we know of no one who begrudges the farmers this comfort and thrift. We hope the time may come when they will all be able to use automobiles.

Woodstock Sentinel.

I hope you can see clear to come down and that I will see you soon.
Your devoted,
Prime U

May 31, 1901
936 Huon Street
Racine, Wisconsin

Dear John,

Oh! how I wish we were sitting on a blanket in the wilderness as we were at this time last week. Hasn't this spring's weather just been heavenly? I would love to see blue eyes...er...skies looking down at me.

I loved just sitting and talking about your plans for a grocery shop. It's amazing, but Herman was discussing the same thing with Mama and Mr. Stoffel the other night... you two must talk next time you come to Racine....and please do come to Racine when you can.

The story you told about your Madison friend CJ running away to Woodstock to get married was hilarious. Maybe you should run away to Madison and challenge HIM to find a preacher? Or maybe he just wanted Prime U as a best man.

Mama has set upon a goal to have the whole house cleaned and aired out by the Fourth of July, one room at a time. She believes that the grippe germs hide in the dust. So, since Clara is gone at least twelve hours a day between work and her singing engagements, that leaves the furniture moving to me. But then, I am a big strong girl. Not as strong as you, of course.

Shall I complain some more? I dread the heat and humidity of summer in Racine, but I doubt it will be much better in Woodstock, maybe worse. Have you thought about starting a grocery shop in Fond du Lac where the breezes are always cool? Or up the shore in Manitowoc where

I SEE BY THE PAPER...

O.T. Factory Squibs.
News Concerning the
Industrious Boys Who are
Oliver.

Last Call. Will someone let us know why we can't celebrate the 4th of July in Woodstock. Have we forgotten how, or don't we want to get the streets littered up with fire crackers?

"Beware" of anybody who says they are not going to Madison. Saturday, on the O.T. train. They are making a sport of you and you will be the only one left in Woodstock.

Woodstock Sentinel, June 20, 1901.

we would be snowed in for six months of the year? Let me know your decision so I will not anticipate melting away into nothingness forever.

I SEE BY THE PAPER...

MATRIMONIAL

Derring—Stoffel

J. Nicholas Stoffel, one of the best known residents on the north side of the river, was united in marriage last evening to Mrs. Louisa Derring. The announcement created considerable surprise as it had not been intimated that Mr. Stoffel was to take unto himself a bride. Congratulations are in order.

Racine Journal Times, June 18, 1901.

I'm not sure if it made the papers in Woodstock, but Mr. Stoffel had an awful occurrence in May when his grandson killed himself at the family home. Mr. Stoffel has been keeping a room with us here on Huron Street to be close to work, but his sons called him home when his grandson, who has lived there with him for a number of years, did not come to work. Mr. Stoffel and his daughter went to the grandson's room and there he lay with a hole in his head from a gunshot. He wasn't yet dead, so they called the doctor who told them there was no hope. It was quite a dark time. Since then Mr. Stoffel has been lodging with us full time even on weekends. I feel so sorry for him, but what can one say to make things better? He and Mama have been having long talks in German which I am sure it is helpful.

I suppose I had better go to bed; my eyes are forcing me to do so although I would rather write all night to you. I hope your dreams are filled with the selling of fresh tomatoes and sweet corn. Ha!

Truly yours,
Ida

July 10, 1901
936 Huron Street
Racine, Wisconsin

Dear John,

What a nice surprise to see you standing on our doorstep on Saturday morning. And you having the whole weekend to be idle. I was glad to see you although you might have warned me so I could have warned Mama and Mr. Stoffel, or I should say Papa Stoffel. I was relieved to see they took you in like a lost waif and didn't just dump you unceremoniously out at the curb.

I quite enjoyed the fireworks at the park…I'm not sure why they were on Saturday instead of the Fourth. Maybe this will be the modern way to keep us working all week — moving all celebrations to the weekends so men will not have an extra day off. But still, it was good that you were here to see them with us. Do you think the Racine fireworks were more beautiful than those we would have seen in Woodstock? Thank you for giving me shelter from the lake breeze under your arm.

Oh, how I wish you could come to Racine in a month's time… August 16 to be exact. We are to have a motorcar race! Everyone is so excited to see it. Two motorcars, one a Locomobile and the other a Winton, will start downtown and race out into the country and then back for 15 miles. There are posters all over town for it. My disappointment is that it will be on a Thursday, and I doubt you will be able to come. I'm hoping to sneak away to see at least the end.

It is getting late. The boys and girls are all in tonight and everybody is abed, except this nighthawk. I guess it is time I was at least beginning to think about it. Usually, it takes some time before I can make up my mind whether it is best to retire or sit up all night. It does not make very much difference tonight as tomorrow I do not have to work and can sleep late, until about half-past six. I never sleep later than that. Ha!

With regards,
Ida

I SEE BY THE PAPER…

Local Intelligence.

Next horse sale, Aug. 14.

Glorious summer weather.

A Michigan man who is lecturing on What I Know of Hell, exhibits four marriage certificates among his credentials.

Many arms are just as beautiful at the wash tub as they are hanging from the shoulders of an actress.

Music from a large graphophone now issues from the store of J.C. Choate to give enjoyment to passers-by.

Many of our people are planning to attend the Pan-American exposition the coming few weeks.

102 in the Shade.

That was the record made by the weather yesterday. A strong southwest wind, right off the oven, prevailed all day. Vegetation wilted and shriveled, and humanity sweltered and suffered. The people who could flocked to the park and stood around the mineral spring like bees around the bunghole of a molasses barrel. A little relief was brought in the afternoon by the sun becoming obscured by clouds.

Woodstock Sentinel, July 11, 1901.

Woodstock Pleasure Club
Woodstock, Illinois

August 24, 1901

My Dear Friend,

 I would have very much liked to have seen the road race. Your description of the end of the race with the winner losing all the way until the last half mile was very exciting. I can hardly wait to try a motorcar.

 Doctor Windmueller's Milwaukee car has gotten all the boys here to dreaming. The city will surely have to do something about the dirt roads if we go to horseless carriages. They kick up a lot more dust than two horses plodding along. Dr. W's auto does help him to get to house calls faster although one of the boys at the Pleasure Club said that he has had a need to be pulled out of the mud by a team of horses multiple times when it rains. Not enough HORSE power I guess, ha.

 Your little Clara is a real spitfire, isn't she? You best rein her in a little or she'll be off to climes unknown before you can say Jahn Jahnson. The concert she provided us with when I was there was pure vaudeville. Tell Herman, if she was my sister, I wouldn't let her out of my sight.

 Time to quit for now. I so look forward to your letters…more so, I daresay, than you do to mine. Please write soon and tell me what is going on in modern Racine.

 I remain as ever,
 John

I SEE BY THE PAPER…

Shipping Beer to Milwaukee.
The quality of the Woodstock, Brewing Co's. beer has gained for itself so prominent a place that Jung Independent Brewing Co., of Milwaukee, has placed an order for 5,000 barrels. The first two cars went forward Tuesday, to be used for their export and bottle trade exclusively, which speaks volumes for the purity of the beer brewed by the Woodstock Brewing Co. Shipping beer to Milwaukee is indeed carrying coal to New Castle.

Woodstock Sentinel

"Ma? Emil?" John called out as he came quickly through the door.

"Here," his mother's voice replied from the parlor. Emil and Sophia sat together on the sofa holding hands. "We were praying for the President," his mother said.

John pulled up a chair and sat down, "I will pray with you." They held hands and bowed their heads for two or three minutes, each silently saying pleading words to spare the life of McKinley, and then they released each other from the grasp.

John looked at his little brother. "Are you OK," he asked.

Emil nodded.

Emil's company in Beloit had offered the boys time off to go to the Pan-American Exposition in Buffalo. Emil had, of course, jumped at the chance to travel east and had gone off to Buffalo with several others. He had listened to the President's speech on September 5 and had thoroughly enjoyed it. The exposition was fantastic, and he and his buddies were having a great time. Then on September 6, the news spread that common people could shake the President's hand in the Temple of Music.

"I heard the rumor," said Emil, reliving the experience, "and I headed right over there and squirmed up near the front of the line – sometimes it helps to be skinny. A lot of people waiting to see him. They had it set up like a cattle chute…one person at a time walked in. But inside a lot of people were crowded around the dais. There was this nice string orchestra music playing, and I went down the chute and was able to walk right up to him standing on the steps. He shook my hand, and I gave him greetings from Woodstock and Beloit. He said he loved the West and wished me the 'best of luck.' I wasn't even out of the Temple when I heard the two shots. I turned and tried to run back toward the steps, but the guards stopped me. All I could see was a man being wrestled to the ground and a crowd on the steps. I couldn't believe it."

"Dat mus haf bin awful," Sophia said, looking at John.

"Then we heard that he wasn't 'badly hurt,' but I don't believe it. People who get shot are badly hurt. So, then I just came home," he said, with tears in his eyes.

The Wienke boys had not served in the military. The Spanish American War in McKinley's first term had been successful, netting the United States Puerto Rico, Guam, the

Philippines, and Hawaii, but none of the boys had been called to serve and none of them had ever seen anyone shot dead right before their eyes. The event was more upsetting than Emil had ever imagined, and even more so, since the beloved President of the United States was involved. John reached over and patted his brother's knee.

"Who vill den President be?" asked Sophia.

"Teddy Roosevelt," said John. "Do you remember him?"

"Ja, the Rough Riders, right?" said Emil.

John nodded. "America is in good hands with him until McKinley comes back."

They sat in silence for a few moments until Emil said that he wanted to go to bed. Sophia followed soon after, and John sat, wondering what the world was coming to. If an anarchist could just walk up to the President and shoot him with all those guards around, was anyone safe? He wished he could talk to Ida. Ida…and in that moment, he knew that he had to keep her safe. He would ask her to marry him — as soon as he was making good money and could build a house. Providing a home was the least he could do for a wife like Ida.

I SEE BY THE PAPER…

Death's Victory.
President McKinley's Gallant Struggle for Life is Unsuccessful.

Milburn House, Buffalo, N. Y., Sept. 14. — President McKinley died at 2:15 a.m. He had been unconscious since 7:30 p.m. His last conscious hour on earth was spent with the wife to whom he devoted a lifetime of care. He died unattended by a minister of the Gospel, but his last words were a humble submission to the will of God in whom he believed. He was reconciled to the cruel fate to which an assassin's bullet had condemned him, and faced death in the same spirit of calmness and poise which has marked his long and honorable career. His last conscious words, reduced to writing by Dr. Mann, who stood at his bedside when they were uttered, were as follows: Good-by, all; good-by. It is God's way. His will be done.

Woodstock Sentinel, September 19, 1901.

"Hi, Ma! Look what I won for you." Bob came through the door with a broad mischievous smile, carrying a bundle which he gave Sophia to unwrap.

Sophia had just sat down at the yellow checkered oilskin covered table with a cup of black coffee and an egg and corned beef sandwich made from leftovers of last night's supper.

She hefted it. Heavy. She unwrapped the prize and examined it. "Vell," said Sophia. "Dat ist sometink." It was made of a plaster called chalkware and had been painted in red and white. The shape was catlike with painted-on black eyes and whiskers. "You von it? Doing vhat?"

"Pitching a baseball," said Bob while rummaging in the larder for bread and butter. He sat down and started preparing a sandwich from the leftovers. "I had to knock over some ugly hairy dolls with a baseball. I won ten cigars and then traded five of them for this prize."

"I've not heard of dis. Vhere?"

"At the Elkhorn Fair up in Wisconsin. I went with friends to watch the surrey races, and then we saw the rest of the fair. We were walking by, and this hawker yells, 'Come on over and win yourself a prize!' You get three balls for five cents and each time you win you get a prize and if you win more than once, you can trade those prizes in for bigger prizes. It's a new and very modern approach to gambling on your own

I SEE BY THE PAPER...

WE HAD A GREAT FAIR.
Records in All Departments Were Smashed.

It was a great Fair that we had in this city last week. To the officers of 1901 belongs the distinction of bring to a successful conclusion the greatest Fair in the history of society, the total receipts of which will approximate $9,000. There was no disorder on the grounds. There was an entire absence of fake schemes and gambling devices to trap the unwary, and the program was of a high order and successfully carried out.

News of the Fairs.

A. J. Austin and Robt. Wienke attended the Fair at Milwaukee last week.

Robt. Wienke, F. G. Arnold, Ben. Stupfel and A. J. Austin went to the Elkhorn Fair yesterday.

Special trains to the Elkhorn Fair leave Woodstock on Wednesday, Thursday and Friday of this week at 8:07 a. m., Ridgefield at 7:55, Hartland at 8:15 and Harvard at 8:30, connecting with the St. Paul train in Clinton Junction at 9:10 and reaching Elkhorn at 10 o'clock. Returning, the trains leave Elkhorn at 6:45. A low fair has been made for the round trip, and it will prove a fine opportunity for residents of this locality to attend the greatest county Fair in the Northwest.

Woodstock Sentinel, September 19, 1901.

skill. It was the top prize, and I knew who to give it to! My Ma!" Bob took a big bite of his sandwich and smiled as he chewed.

"How much times must you play to get dis doll?"

"Oh, I don't know, I played thirty or so. I didn't win every time, but I won enough to keep moving up and when I got enough small prizes, I traded for this…um…doll."

"Hm…intrestink." She looked at the cat doll, "Tank you." Sophia set it down on the table. She rarely got gifts, and this thing was not at all beautiful, but it was kind of cute, she supposed. She would have to find a place to display it that was a bit out of the way.

"And da racink?" she asked. She picked up her sandwich, examined it, and went in for a large bite.

"Oh, they were great! I won more than I lost so came away the better man."

"Gut fer you. And vas plan have you for today?"

"White Stockings game! Catching the noon train. You know what I heard?" Bob's voice had dropped several decibels like he was telling stories out of school.

"Vas?" Sophia managed around a substantial bite.

I SEE BY THE PAPER...

BOARD OF SUPERVISORS.
Proceedings of the Annual September Meeting, 1901.

The honorable board of supervisors of McHenry county, Illinois, met in annual session at the court house in Woodstock, Ill., on Tuesday, Sept. 10, 1901 at 10 o'clock a.m.

Mr. Chairman and Gentlemen of the Board of Supervisors: Your committee on caims would beg leave to report that they have examined all claims presented to them, and recommend the payment of the following, and that the clerk be directed to issue orders on the county treasurer to the claimants for the several amounts allowed, as follows, to-wit:

24 iron beds, per contract . . . 118.00
Meals for jurors, May term 6.30
F J Schroeder, flag repair 2.00
Albert Wienke,
   putting rope on flag pole 7.50
MW Lake, bailiff 1 day, Jan 2.50

LOCAL INTELLIGENCE.

The coal haulers have been very busy the past week, putting coal in the bins of those who are getting ready for cooler weather that is coming ere many weeks.

Emil Wienke returned on Monday to his duties at Beloit, after a visit to the Pan-American exposition.

The school house is being painted under a contract with Albert Wienke.

Woodstock Sentinel, September 19, 1901.

He leaned closer. "I heard that the White Stockings might change their name to the Cubs. Can you believe it? Baby bears."

"Vhy?"

"I heard it was because this year they are rebuilding the team and most of the players are rookies – you know, new players – like our Moriarity from the Olivers. They are like bear cubs, I guess. But I tell you what, they will without doubt grow into da Bears, I'm sure." Bob took a bite of his sandwich and chewed.

"Vell, gut luck to dem! Take a samvich with you for trip," she suggested.

"I think I will!" Bob replied with a broad handsome smile.

> **I SEE BY THE PAPER...**
>
> City Marshal and Mrs. John Bolger, Mr. and Mrs. Theo. Davis and son, rs. John R. Kellogg, Mrs. E E. Mead, Mr. and Mrs. John McGee, Mrs. C. M. Harting, George and William Conn, L. J. Young, Ray Kimberly, John Wienke, George Tower, Elbert and Delbert Ryan, J. C. Dillion, Charles Freeman, Charles Williams, William McDowell, Clarence Short, Scott Morton, Scott Sinclair and C. W. Davis were among the number who accompanied the Oliver Typewriter band to Elgin last Saturday and enjoyed the street Fair.
>
> *Woodstock Sentinel*, October 3, 1901.

John walked briskly down the boardwalk away from the new McHenry County State Bank. His investment in this institution would open doors that otherwise would only crack a bit...even if he could find the perfect way to beg…for a mortgage on a house. But now, since he was a founding stockholder, he could expect a good interest rate. A house was a high priority now. Save up the down payment, get his own business, get the money, build the house, ask Ida to marry him, move her here. His future was set. As he walked around the square, he tipped his hat or greeted everyone he met. He was building his reputation, which would bode well if he opened a grocery shop here or ran for office.

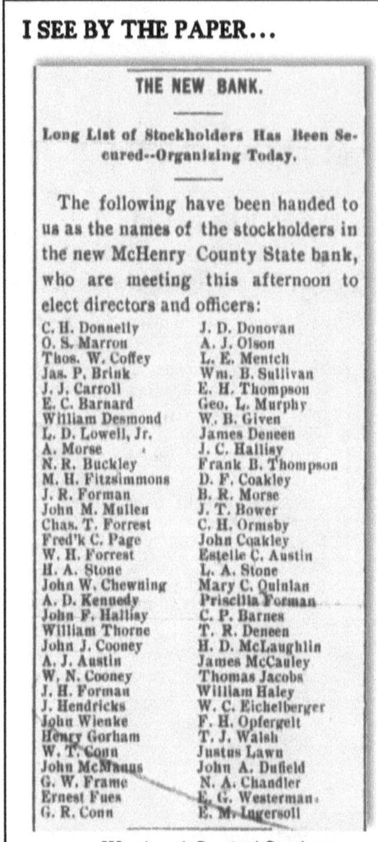

I SEE BY THE PAPER...

THE NEW BANK.

Long List of Stockholders Has Been Secured--Organizing Today.

The following have been handed to us as the names of the stockholders in the new McHenry County State bank, who are meeting this afternoon to elect directors and officers:

C. H. Donnelly	J. D. Donovan
O. S. Marron	A. J. Olson
Thos. W. Coffey	L. E. Mentch
Jas. P. Brink	Wm. B. Sullivan
J. J. Carroll	E. H. Thompson
E. C. Barnard	Geo. L. Murphy
William Desmond	W. B. Given
L. D. Lowell, Jr.	James Deneen
A. Morse	J. C. Hallisy
N. R. Buckley	Frank B. Thompson
M. H. Fitzsimmons	D. F. Coakley
J. R. Forman	B. R. Morse
John M. Mullen	J. T. Bower
Chas. T. Forrest	C. H. Ormsby
Fred'k C. Page	John Coakley
W. H. Forrest	Estelle C. Austin
H. A. Stone	L. A. Stone
John W. Chewning	Mary C. Quinlan
A. D. Kennedy	Priscilla Forman
John F. Hallisy	C. P. Barnes
William Thorne	T. R. Deneen
John J. Cooney	H. D. McLaughlin
A. J. Austin	James McCauley
W. N. Cooney	Thomas Jacobs
J. H. Forman	William Haley
J. Hendricks	W. C. Eichelberger
John Wienke	F. H. Opfergelt
Henry Gorham	T. J. Walsh
W. T. Conn	Justus Lawn
John McManus	John A. Dufield
G. W. Frame	N. A. Chandler
Ernest Fues	E. G. Westerman.
G. R. Conn	E. M. Ingersoll

Woodstock Sentinel, October 3, 1901.

There were a number of grocery and mercantile shops in Woodstock already, so competition would be strong, but he had connections in Chicago with the wholesalers, and he was a good negotiator, so he was sure he could beat their prices and make a success of it. Today, he had taken the first step.

"Judge Donnelly, good afternoon," John said, stopping near a man who was gazing out at the plot of land in the middle of the square. The trees, planted some years ago, were reaching a good size now, and it looked like a park. Boarded paths crisscrossed the grassy plot.

"Why hello, John." The judge removed a cigar from his mouth to speak and pointed with it at the park. "Don't you think this park could use some sprucing up? I'm going to talk to the mayor and get the trees trimmed while the leaves are down. We can get someone to pull the weeds and get grass growing under the trees better for next summer. And maybe the city can cobblestone the paths through from one side to the other and keep them shoveled during the winter, so we don't have to go the long way around."

"I was just thinking how nice it was to see a natural park in the middle of the square," John demurred.

"Well, yes, but we can do better. Do you think that they allow the parks to get so overgrown in Chicago or New York? I don't think so. We can do better," and with that, the judge put the cigar back between his lips, sucked in, and blew out a huge billow of smoke. "Good to see you, John," he said, reaching out.

John took the proffered hand and firmly shook it. "Same here, judge. I'll be watching for the changes," he said, smiling. As the judge walked back toward the courthouse, John once again felt the urge to run for office. Mayor would be nice or even alderman. Then he could provide ideas to improve the town. He shook his head wondering if this part of his dream would ever come true.

> **I SEE BY THE PAPER…**
>
> **Personal Mention.**
>
> Fred G. Arnold and Robert Wienke left on Monday evening for a trip to Memphis, to take in the great races.
>
> Mr. and Mrs. Albert Wienke spent Sunday with relatives and friends at Clinton Junction, Wis.
>
> Dr. W.V. Hopf, the dentist, will keep is office open every evening in the week, except Sunday, from 6 to 9 o'clock, for the benefit of those who cannot call during the day.
>
> **Local Intelligence.**
>
> The public library will be closed on Sunday afternoons until further notice by order of the board of directors, who feel that six days of labor for the librarian should be enough.
>
> The weather of the last week has been very Indian summer like, and has been greatly appreciated by all.
>
> *Woodstock Sentinel, October* 24, 1901.

Woodstock Pleasure Club
Woodstock, Illinois

November 1, 1901

Dear Friend,

Talk about snow. It is snowing very hard here just now. It is not unlike the storm you told me about in your last letter. If it keeps up, we will have a foot of snow by morning. Does that sound like a big one?

I was planning to come up to see you about two weeks ago yesterday, but we had to work Saturday afternoon and three nights besides. If they keep that up, I do not know when I will be able to come, for I do not get a chance to make up my lost time which I have to do when I am off. If Oliver closes on Saturday afternoons, I could come every Saturday, but I'm sure you would not want to see me every Saturday, and I understand.

I will be up there two weeks from today and spend Sunday with you. If I leave here on the 12:30 p.m. train, I can get up there sometime around four o'clock on Saturday if I can have the couch. I know that you wouldn't want me to come every Sunday and wear out my welcome with Mr. and Mrs. Stoffel. So, I will stretch out my comings and goings and keep them guessing.

I would like a photograph of you husking corn. I would be glad to have one of you even not husking. Lena has such a picture in her parlor. If you have any more, I would be pleased to have one. I will send you one of mine in exchange if you will do so.

If I were your sister, I would not play for you at all. When I come up, I guess I better tell her what you said about her music. You ought to hear Lena play. She has a piano now so when you come down again you can play for us.

I had a good time in Madison last weekend. Went up on Saturday to Sunday night. I enjoyed the game and am planning to go again on the ninth for the last home game against Iowa State. The Badgers have a good chance at the conference championship this year.

> *Well, I better close. Hoping to hear from you again,*
> *I remain yours as ever,*
> *John*

I SEE BY THE PAPER...

'Phone Your Items.

Woodstock people who have phones in their homes will confer the favor on THE SENTINEL, by sending in short news items. If you have visitors or are going away, call us up and tell us about it. It doesn't cost a cent.

Woodstock Sentinel, November 7, 1901.

I SEE BY THE PAPER...

Local Intelligence

The usual capers were cut up by the young people last Thursday evening (Hallowe'en), horse-blocks being over turned and other minor offenses committed, but we have heard of no serious damage. Youngsters will be youngsters.

Woodstock Sentinel, November 7, 1901.

November 8, 1901
936 Huron Street
Racine, Wisconsin

Dear John,

Why do you say you know I don't want to see you every Sunday? Of course, you are right, but how did you know it? I would have been glad to see you last Sunday because I was so lonely. Went to church in the morning with my "Mudder" and "Fodder." In the afternoon they both slept, the Mr. on the lounge and Mama went to bed for the rest of the day as she was sick with a cold; everybody else had gone out and I spent my time in blissful solitude. In the evening it was the same. Mr. Stoffel went to church and the others were all away, Mama sleeping and myself keeping watch. Watching so no one would carry away all our money.

Don't flatter yourself and think I should have been glad to see you drop in and share my solitude. That would have been too bad since I love to be all alone, because it is my opinion that I'm in good company when I'm alone. How is that for conceit? It almost equals yours, but not quite.

> ## I SEE BY THE PAPER...
>
> **Personal Mention.**
>
> E.C. Jewett, Geo. W. Field, Albert Wienke, John Wienke, L.T. Hoy, C.T. Donovan, Geo. L. Murphy, Fred Joorfetz, W.P. Hoy, George W. Lemmers, Geo. B. Richards, B.C. Young, D.C. Akers, Harry Cross, John Whitworth, L.E. Copeland and William Colberg were among the number from here who witnessed the great Wisconsin-Minnesota football game at Madison last Saturday.
>
> *Woodstock Sentinel,* November 21, 1901.

Do you mean you have every Sunday afternoon off now? Dear me, what do you do with so much time to dispose of? You ought to be ashamed to spend all that time in idleness. What in the world will become of such a lazy fellow?

I expect the next time you write you'll say you can't come next week. That's alright. Put it off another four weeks, then it won't make any difference.

Would you like to know what Lena wrote? You won't find out for I'll not tell you. Had a letter from Emma the same day Lena's came; I will tell you what she said when I see you. If I see you.

Have I talked mean enough to you tonight? I'm very sorry, honestly, I am. It shall never happen again, not until the next time.

If you cannot come next Sunday then plan on the Sunday before Christmas, won't you? I promise I won't tease you so badly as I have in this letter. It so long since we've seen each other, and I miss you.

> *Until then I remain lonely,*
> *Ida*

I SEE BY THE PAPER...

LOCAL INTELLIGENCE.

A lot of new ads in this issue; read them.

We have not had time to mention it, but say, wasn't it cold last week? Coal bins were relieved of a lot of their burdens.

There were several cases of malignant diphtheria in the Bull Valley community, which are being quarantined and properly treated by the physicians of this city.

The Eminent Ladies will give a charity ball, New Year's night, in Murphy's hall. Music by Brubaker's orchestra. Supper at Dirrenberger's, extra.

We wish all of our readers a most happy new year, may the sun of happiness and prosperity shine upon you during 1902 with even greater effulgence than during 1901.

PAINTERS AND DECORATORS

The principal painters and decorators of this city are Albert Wienke, who keeps a large force of men at work and who has done most of the finest work in the city for several years, Henry Burdick, E.W. Ercaubrack and A.P. Baker.

Woodstock Sentinel, December 16, 1901.

"Oh, for pity sakes," Ida cried. "I don't think he's coming again."

It was Saturday evening. The family had just finished supper which had started at the normal five o'clock. She had hoped with John's train coming at four o'clock, he would arrive in time to eat with them, but that was not the case. And now as she and Clara washed up in the warm kitchen, it was already 6:30 p.m. and no word and no one. Ida threw a pot into the dishwater. She was hurt and mad and frustrated.

"I'm sorry, Ida," Clara said. "Maybe it's time to do a bit of a push."

"He says he doesn't have the money to take the train and walking would take too long."

Clara snorted. "Well, at least, he's funny. Can't say that any of my beaus right now are funny."

"I don't want funny!" Ida wailed. "I want married."

"He seems to like you quite a lot. Does Lena see him around with other girls?"

"No," Ida admitted, downcast.

"Well then, you'll just have to be patient. What did Mama say the other day, 'Alles zu seiner Zeit'? All in good time."

"I don't want good time! I want now! By the time, he gets around to even asking me, I'll be all shriveled up and barren."

"You are funny. You look ten years younger than you are. Babies take a toll on women. I don't think I'll have any. I want to stay young forever!" Clara threw her long hair back over her shoulder in defiance.

"Thank you for the compliment, but I DO want to have babies…lots of them…boys and girls. I'm just going to have to be more forward or let him know that it makes me angry when he says he's coming and then doesn't or…oh…I don't know. I need to do something!"

"Why don't you write Lena about it. Maybe she'll have some ideas. She landed a Wienke. Lena always has good ideas. Or let's ask Mama if we can go to Woodstock next weekend or in two weeks if Lena says we can stay with her. Then he'd have to see you and maybe you could tell if he is serious or not. Maybe he's just shy."

"Shy, shmy. He wasn't so shy when he kissed me at last year's New Year's Eve Party. He wasn't so shy when he showed up at the door on July Fourth. It's like hot and cold water. He's here and then I don't hear from him for weeks,

I SEE BY THE PAPER…

LOCAL INTELLIGENCE.

Were you among the number from here who witnessed the great Wisconsin-Iowa football game at Madison last Saturday?

Personal.

Will the lady who fell in a swoon last Thursday, in front of the post office, call at our store? She suffers from biliousness. Dr. Caldwell's Syrup Pepsin will surely cure her.

It avails little to the unfortunate to be brave.

Sure of Approval.

A girl may not be able to write poetry or paint sunsets, but if she can bake a biscuit that is somewhat softer than flint and can crochet a section of weather-boarding on the gable end of a pair of pantaloons, she may be pretty sure of the approval of some good man.

Enjoyable Smoker.

On Saturday evening, Dec. 7, the Woodstock Pleasure club will give another of their enjoyable smokers at their club rooms in the Hoy block, and every member of the club is requested to be present.

Woodstock Sentinel, Dec. 5, 1901.

months even, and then he's here. Anyway, Mama won't say 'yes' to going to Woodstock unless Herman goes with us, but he's so wrapped up with his own plans! And I'm sure Lena is tired of hearing me whine."

"Herman might go."

It makes me so mad I could spit tacks! He has all the time and money in the world for his friends and football games and smoking at the Pleasure Palace. But he can't even write me a letter every week. Once a month is what I get, the leftovers," her voice broke. God, she hated it when she got so mad that she cried. And what good did crying do anyway?

Clara came over and gave Ida a hug. "Maybe he isn't the one."

"He has to be, Clara," she withdrew from the embrace. "I've wasted so much precious time already on him, over a year. Maybe it is time to cut my losses, but I do like him very much and when we are together, we seem perfect for each other."

"You could…," Clara's voice trailed off.

"Could what!" Ida demanded.

"You could move to Woodstock."

"Oh, don't be a fool. I'm not going to degrade myself chasing after him like that. If he wants me, he knows where to find me."

"Oh, I'm the fool, huh? Well, I'll have you know that I have a date for Silvester, do you?"

"No," admitted Ida dejectedly. "I had hoped…." Now it was she who trailed off.

"Just put him out of your mind. Cheer up! It's almost Christmas. What are you making all of us this year?"

"Scarves," said Ida. "You get the lavender one."

I SEE BY THE PAPER…

Current Gossip.

Mrs. Elizabeth Cady Stanton celebrated her eighty-sixth birthday on Nov. 12 at her home in New York city. She is still in excellent health and spirits and retains all her zeal for her favorite reform, woman's suffrage.

Racine Journal Times, Nov. 19, 1901.

December 25, 1901
936 Huron Street
Racine, Wisconsin

Merry Christmas John,

The very cold weather has precluded any attempt that Clara and I might have made to come to Woodstock. I am very frustrated that we see so little of each other, but it is too cold to stand on the train platform in the wind awaiting the train and then riding in its unheated seats for hours…and Clara is just feeling better from a cold…and well, Mama won't allow it. She says we will come down with consumption or worse. I don't know what is worse than consumption, but there you are. We will just have to see what happens in the new year.

If you would like you can go to the ball alone and hope that the ladies of Woodstock have pity on your bachelor self. Or go visit Bob's saloon, maybe he'll let you drink for free, so you don't have to spend a precious penny. Or you can just stay home and read the paper or possibly a miracle will happen, and you'll write to me. If it is too cold for us to "go gallivanting," as Mama puts it (she can barely speak English, but she knows gallivanting), it is too cold for you to do the same. Or is the Pleasure Palace having an event? Anyway, don't freeze your toes off.

Clara is calling us to dinner. We are having roast duck with apple and sausage dressing, potato dumplings, red cabbage, and fruitcake for dinner. Aren't you jealous? I did the baking and Mama did the cooking. There…Clara is again calling. Must run.

All of us on Huron Street hope all of you in Woodstock had a very Merry Christmas and have a fine new year!

Your friend,
Ida

Not a word! Not a single word from him! Neither a Merry Christmas nor a Happy New Year. Nothing! Ida sat down in a total huff at her writing desk. She was fuming. That's it!! I don't care if I ever see him again. What a fool I've been wasting over a year on a man who can't make a commitment. Even when we are together, he's so polite – too polite. I must hold his hand and initiate every kiss. I don't know what the quandary is, but I AM FINISHED. I will write and call the whole thing off. I should have done it months ago. I refuse to just sit here and wait and wait! She took pen in hand, looked at the blank page before her, and began…

> *December 31, 1901*
> *936 Huron Street*
> *Racine, Wisconsin*

Dear John,

I think it only fair that I send the news that I have found another beau due to your inconsiderate neglect of our friendship. It is a boy here in Racine. It is easier for him to call and attend various functions without the long distance between us. I have much appreciated your attention and thought there might be a hope for a mutual understanding, but I do not see that happening, nor has our mutual admiration progressed to a point that—

"Ida!" Mama called up the stairs. "Jemand ist an der Tür für Sie."

Someone at the door? Ida realized that as she started writing she also began crying. "Oh Mama," Ida called back wiping the tears with a hanky, "I'm not fit for company. Tell them I'll see them tomorrow at church. Ich werde sie in der Kirche sehen." Ida turned back to her desk.

"Ida!" Mama called. "Sie möchten diesen Anrufer annehmen."

I will want to take this caller? Oh, good heavens! She did not want anyone to see her right now! She took a great breath and blew it out in frustration. "Wer ist es?" she called back in a calmer voice. She listened. Silence…then…

"It's me, Ida," a baritone voice called up the stairs.

Her heart skipped a beat. Her breath caught. She put down her pen, looked at the letter she had started, picked up the piece of stationery, and crumpled it into a ball.

John!

Ida ran to the top of the stairs and looked down at him. "Vas you dare, Charlie?" she said, using the Racine colloquial greeting to cover her nervous excitement.

John laughed. "I'm John, not Charlie, remember me?"

Ida was not smiling. "Almost not at all. I guess you don't know how to be polite and let a family know when you are coming for a visit?" She came a few steps down and stood with arms akimbo, towering over him.

John chuckled, but Mama and Clara swiftly withdrew to the kitchen. John took a step up and leaned on the newel post, "Aw, Ida. Don't be mad at me." He looked at her like a bashful little boy. Her heart thawed just a bit.

"Why in the world would you think I was angry with you? Did you do something naughty?"

John thought about what he should say. Should he admit guilt, or would that just make her even angrier? On the other hand, maybe she just needed some concession from him. "I'm sorry I didn't let you know I was coming. I just couldn't resist."

Oh, well played, she thought. She stepped down a few more steps. "I've missed you and your letters. I had almost given up on you. Seemed like you lost interest."

John took a step up to the landing, "Lost interest? I'll never lose interest. I've just been busy and haven't had a chance to come up. I've been—"

"Working hard? I know. But to what end? To make yourself rich and lonely, Mr. Scrooge? Maybe that is who you are, not Charlie. Is that the future you want?"

John took another step, "Of course not, but—"

"No buts. Do you want to keep this friendship, or do you want to be filthy rich and alone?"

"Of course, I want to keep this friendship, but I would like to be able to provide for my family before I make one," he said, a little heat in his voice.

Ida considered this. They weren't betrothed. He sounded like they were. "I'm not family yet," she said.

John took another step, "I know that, but I was sure that—"

"That what? That I'll just sit here and wait until you decided to give me the time of day?"

"No…I thought…I was sure that," he paused, thinking. "That we had made permanent plans."

"Permanent plans! You are lucky, mister, that I don't slam the door in your face!" Ida said.

John took another step. He was within arm's reach now. His voice was soft and calm, "Aw, come on, Ida. You know how fond I am of you. Don't be angry. Give me a chance to make it up to you."

Ida looked at his earnest face and the hand he was holding out to her. She looked down at her feet. She could feel the tears welling up. She did not want to cry but was not sure that she could stop the emotional waterfall inside her. She reached out and took the proffered hand, her other hand went to her face. She took a step down. They were only one step apart now. His arms encircled her and lifted her off the step and into him. Then she was crying, wetting his wool-covered breast.

He held her and let her cry for a few minutes, mumbling to the top of her head. "I'm so sorry. I hate to see you sad. I do care for you."

After a bit, Ida got her tears in check and pushed back. John pulled out a clean handkerchief. She wiped her eyes and dapped at her nose. Then she smiled, "I'm glad to see you."

John laughed out loud and turned to descend the stairs with his arm still around her, and they came down the stairs together.

As if cued in from stage left, Mama and Clara came scurrying in from the kitchen. Each took a turn for a hug and a kiss on the cheek, and Clara took John's coat and hat, which had found rest on the back of the davenport. Mr. Stoffel appeared out of nowhere and gave John a hearty handshake and a clap on the back and welcomed him to sit down. John wasn't sure that he had ever in his life been greeted with such enthusiasm. But it was Ida who stayed utmost in his thoughts throughout the greetings. They could not keep their eyes from each other. Ida took a seat on the couch a respectable distance from her beau. She watched him talking easily with her family and took a deep breath, letting it out slowly. John gave her a look of concern. She returned a quick smile. They would talk later. Now was family time.

They sat together on the sofa, holding hands. Just having him here was a wonder, and he had said he could stay until tomorrow evening because the typewriter factory was closed on January 1. She still wasn't sure where they stood long term, but she was sure that he wanted to be here with her as the year turned over. She was encouraged by his presence. Mama and Papa Stoffel had made their way to bed, and Clara and Herman had taken their leave to go celebrate the new year out on the town. So, here they were…alone…together…a first. He smelled of wet wool, perspiration, and a little cigar smoke…AND he had just brought her hand to his lips for a kiss.

"You know Mr. Wienke, that I had almost given up on you. Six months without a visit and only a few brief notes. I was sure you had met another."

"Well, Miss Doering, it isn't that I haven't thought about you or thought about sitting here with you on this very comfortable sofa holding your hand. It has not been easy for me either."

Ida pulled back, dropping his hand and looking him straight in the face in mock astonishment, "I should say NOT with all the traveling to and from Madison and various other locations to curry the favor of your future customers, I assume, while I was left sitting here wondering about your intentions."

John blushed. He had told her of all his comings and goings in his letters but never expected that she would feel that he didn't have her foremost in his thoughts. His brow furrowed in concern. "Well…I…was just trying… I'm sorry…I…I can see now that I should have made one of those trips to Racine. I do apologize."

She left him there to hang for a bit, just so the lesson would make an impression. "OK," she said, lips in a little pout. "Just don't let it happen again or I'll find a fine union factory man here in Racine to marry. I could do that you know. There are plenty of anarchists to go around."

John looked somewhat stunned. Did she know anarchists? Did she have a new beau here in Racine? "I thought…," he started.

Ida put him out of his misery. "Oh, John. At present, I only have eyes for you. I'm just expecting a bit more…," she searched for the word, "a bit more attentiveness from someone I admire so much and who, I think, admires me."

He reclaimed her hand. "I am so sorry I caused you to question my desire to continue this courtship," he said, making direct eye contact, as one must do when coming to an agreement of great consequence. Ida didn't break the gaze but kept it straight and true like she was attempting to read his honesty.

"I will do better at showing you my attentiveness," he said. Was this what she wanted him to say? What had he been thinking? Did he think that he was such a fantastic catch that she would still be waiting for him when HE was ready? He looked at her earnest, beautiful face. "I do greatly admire you, Miss Doering, and I would like nothing better than to show my admiration with a kiss."

Oh, for heaven's sake, stop talking about it and just do it, thought Ida. She smiled, "Well, Mr. Wienke, what are you waiting for? It's time we get serious about this pairing or give this courtship up, wouldn't you say?"

"I WOULD say." And he gathered her into his arms, and the embers were glowing again.

And that's how Herman, and then Clara, found them when returning from their New Year's Eve celebrations. Fast asleep in each other's arms, fully clothed, mind you, but very content, nonetheless.

Ida Doering and John Wienke,
circa 1890, before they knew
each other.

Ida Doering and John Wienke, circa
1900, around the time they met.

Clara Doering
circa 1900.

Herman Doering
circa 1900.

Henrich and Louisa Döring
on their wedding day in
Breslau, Germany in 1868.

Henry and Louisa
Doering of Whitewater,
Wisconsin circa 1890.

Two Cities - 1902

> Yule's come and yule's gone,
> And we hae feasted weel;
> Sae Jock mann to his flail again,
> And Jenny to her wheel.

Sophia Wienke sat in her comfortable chair in the generous parlor. She had pulled her hair back into a bun at the nape of her neck as she did every morning. She wore a drab-brown, ankle-length house dress and sturdy shoes of black leather but no jewelry or other adornments, as this was not the way of the German Lutheran ladies. Her hands moved swiftly as she tatted a doily that she would add to her gift bag. Sophia liked giving handmade gifts.

She had spent the night before, New Year's Eve, and this morning alone with all her boys were off on their own business, and she was a bit at a loss for things to do. Emil had been with her overnight, coming home in the wee hours and slipping out just before dawn. He gave her a quick kiss on the cheek, before catching the early train back to Beloit. She could, she supposed, cook that lamb shank out in the icebox, but who would eat it? She had eaten a bowl of oatmeal, kuchen, and coffee for breakfast and was getting hungry at a bit past noon.

She was happy enough in this new house, she supposed. The rooms were sizable, and she could easily fit everyone

> **I SEE BY THE PAPER...**
>
> ### Personal Mention.
>
> Robert Wienke visited with friends at McHenry, New Year's night.
>
> Chas. Wienke, of Beloit, is in the city for a few days visiting with relatives and friends.
>
> Emil Wienke was home from Beloit for the holidays.
>
> *Woodstock Sentinel,* January 2, 1902.

around the dining room table even with the grandchildren. She sighed. Here she had gotten the large house with five bedrooms just in time to be alone. She needed only three rooms – a kitchen, a parlor, and a bedroom. Oh yes, and a bathroom…she loved the indoor bathroom! Four rooms then.

She got up and made her way to the kitchen. She must shake this feeling from herself. This was a lovely house, and she had such wonderful sons to buy it for her. As she stood at the sink looking out at the railroad track which ran close behind the house. A train was approaching from the north. The whistle a lonely sound to her ear. She took a New Year's Day inventory. Eight boys. Five married to good women. Nine grandchildren and another on the way. Of the three unmarried sons, John would soon be married she was sure. Bob might never marry, although he was quite a catch. Handsome and fun. And little Emil, a real worker, dedicated and athletic. He would meet a girl from Beloit soon.

Sophie turned from the window and looked around the kitchen with its many cupboards, heavy wooden table, running water and new cookstove. Yes, she had fine sons. Out of the blue, it came to her, and she knew what she would do. She would make a German New Year's cake for each family, well, at least the ones in Woodstock, and one for this house. A generous New Year's gift, she thought. And then she'd invite her sons over to pick them up, and she'd get to see them. It was a wonderful idea.

She went to the cupboard and found the fillings for the three layers. Poppy seeds for the first layer for good luck in the new year. Almonds for the second layer for good health in the new year. And for the top layer, cinnamon apples, canned last fall, to add sweetness to the new year. She laid out the ingredients along with the milk, eggs and clabbered cream from her new icebox, and set to work.

She worked the dough and set aside four portions in the icebox to chill while she prepared the fillings for the layers quadrupling the amounts to provide for four cakes. She put poppy seed, butter, sugar, raisins, milk, honey, and nearly a cup of rum for flavor into a pot and let the mixture slowly come to a boil and then removed it to rest. She shelled and chopped the almonds and mixed them with the sugar, milk, cinnamon and crushed cloves together in a bowl, the spicy fragrance tickling her nose. Then she opened the first mason jar of apples, using her apron to grip the cap, and poured the contents into a second bowl. They looked fresh and delicious. It was everything she could do to not eat them right there. Two jars for four cakes.

Retrieving and cutting the first dough ball into four pieces, Sophia rolled out each into a thin layer. Using the ten-inch springform cake pan like a cookie-cutter, she cut out four circles of dough. She greased and floured the pan and then placed the first circle of dough at the bottom. She added the poppy-seed mixture and covered it with another thin layer of dough. Pouring the nut mixture in to form the middle layer, she added more dough followed by a single layer of apples. She used the last quarter of the dough to cover the whole cake. She then broke an egg into a bowl and beat it thoroughly, but not enough to foam. She poked the top layer with a knife and brushed the egg over the entire cake letting the golden liquid soak down through the holes to the layers below.

She replenished the water in the pan that would accompany the cake into the oven and placed the pan next to the firebox to absorb some of the heat from the hot spot, a practice which kept the whole oven at a more constant temperature. Then she placed the cake in the hot oven and closed the door. She had not baked very much with this stove, so she would watch this cake closely and adjust the fire and time based on this experience. It should, she thought, take about three-quarters of an hour or maybe an hour. She turned the hourglass, so she would not lose track of time.

With a satisfied smile on her face, she started the process again for the second cake. The only steps left for the first cake after it came out were to let it cool, release the spring so the sides of the pan could easily be removed, slide the cake onto a plate, and then sprinkle powdered sugar in a thick layer to cover the top. Ideally, the cakes should sit in a cool place overnight before removing them from the pan, but since she had but two pans, two cakes would have to jell overnight without the pan. But where. She thought about putting them out on the enclosed porch off the kitchen, but it was too cold. They would freeze rather than jell. She decided that the icebox would be a good temperature, keeping them cold until morning. She would have to make room for four cakes, not an easy task.

> **I SEE BY THE PAPER...**
>
> **PERSONAL MENTION**
> **A Four Days' Vacation**
> The employees of the Oliver typewriter factory are enjoying a four days' vacation, the factory having shut down on Tuesday evening until next Monday, in order to allow time for annual inventory. The employees of the factory appreciate the rest, for they have been given a taste of the strenuous life in real earnest the past few months.
>
> *Woodstock Sentinel,* January 2, 1902.

She was glad she had thought about this gift. She would call the boys tonight to pick them up in the morning on the infernal telephone. How surprised Minnie, Anna and Lena would be to have a wonderful New Year's cake for dinner tomorrow evening. And how surprised John and Bobby would be upon their return home. If they returned today, the cake might not last overnight.

Her stomach growled. In her enthusiasm for the cakes, she had forgotten to eat. She went to the icebox and gathered sandwich fixings. She'd have time to eat a little while the cake baked. It was a wonderful New Year's Day.

January 10, 1902
936 Huron Street
Racine, Wisconsin

Dearest John,

How I miss you and wish you were here in Racine rather than there in Illinois. I can barely stand going to work, traveling through the drifts and ice only to sweat in the laundry for hour upon hour and then get a chill walking home. If you were here by my side, I would be warmer, and you would be colder I'm sure.

I'll have you know that Mama and Papa Stoffel and even Clara had nothing but good to say about you after you left on New Year's Day. It was John this and John that and wasn't it nice of John until I told them to desist. That I like you just fine now and they shouldn't worry. I must agree that you were most generous with your good nature during our short time together. I know I appreciated it and I guess they did too.

Did you catch your death on the cold train on the way home? We certainly have had a cold spell since you were here. Some nights the stoves must be stoked halfway through the night so that there will be coals in the morning. It's snowing again now so we can expect drifts in the morning and boots full of water by the time we get anywhere. Oh, wait! Tomorrow is Saturday! I can just stay home and sew. What a lucky ducky I am!

I suppose you will not be able to be lazy tomorrow. I can hardly believe what that factory expects from you boys. Days, nights, Saturdays. You better not be working yourself to death. I will be very upset with you and will punish you by not writing for a full month. Ha.

I must start thinking about heading to bed even with a day off tomorrow. I will have to get up and feed the boys before they go off to work and then I'm sure Mama will have chores for me before I can settle down to sew. Such is the life of the handmaiden. I will be thinking about you slaving away at your station.

When will I see you again Mr. Blue Eyes?

Soon I hope,
Ida

I SEE BY THE PAPER...

An Addition Being Made to the Oliver Typewriter Factory.

The predicted addition to the Oliver typewriter factory is well under way. This addition, which is being made on the north end of the factory building, is 40x60 feet, and we understand that it will be two stories high and built to conform the character of the main building. More room has been badly needed for a long time, and the officers of the company being progressive men, they are determined not to be cramped for room in turning out the best and most popular typewriter on the market. The factory force is again working three nights a week, and the force down stairs works every night, and even then it is a difficult task to keep up with the demand for the machines.

Woodstock Sentinel, January 16, 1902.

"What are you doing here?" Ida exclaimed as she pulled open the front door on Huron Street in Racine.

"Is that any way to greet a person you admire?" said a smiling John standing big as life on the stoop on a Monday afternoon.

Ida pulled him in from the cold and threw her arms around him. He acknowledged her admiration by holding her tight and kissing her cheek.

"Here give me your wet coat and hat. What are you doing here?"

"Well, the union boys pushed a little too hard at good old Oliver and so they closed the shop for three days so we could all consider our sins against the company and the management and Woodstock itself. I decided that, if you'll have me, I could consider from Racine as well as Woodstock."

"What do you mean 'pushed too hard'?"

"Three-quarters of the shop or more decided to start a local trades union to negotiate better hours with management. Management, however, was having none of it and has closed down the shop rather than let it unionize."

> ### I SEE BY THE PAPER...
>
> #### O.T. Shut down.
> From Monday noon until Thursday morning of last week the works of the Oliver Typewriter Co. in this city were shut down. This move on the part of the management of the factory was made, because a large number of employees had organized a local trades union. The management of the factory, while not opposed to organized labor as a principle or to union men working in the factory as individuals, did object to the local union, composed mostly of unskilled workmen, attempting to unionize the factory.
>
> Soon after the shutdown notices were posted stating that work would be resumed on Thursday morning and all former employees could return as individuals but not as members of the local union.
>
> On Thursday morning the factory was reopened. All of the former employees who had not affiliated themselves with the newly organized local union were on hand and took up their former positions. A large percentage of those who had joined the union, surrendered their membership and returned to work. The others, about sixty in number, stood pat and remained out, and are still out.
>
> *Woodstock Sentinel,* February 1902.

They had settled themselves at the kitchen table where Ida could keep track of supper while they talked. Mama had gone up to dress and the other workers would soon be home and hungry.

"May I ask which side you took?

"Well, it was a hard decision. Oliver has been very good for Woodstock. We have almost no one unemployed and the housing and other markets are booming because the workers have money to spend. On the other hand, I would love to see you more often. Did I tell you we won't be called back until Thursday?"

"Indeed!" Ida's heart took a little jump. Three days!

"On Thursday, when they reopen everyone has to either drop their union membership or they are fired. Those of us who didn't sign on with the union will be welcomed back with no extra requirements."

"So, you didn't join." Ida got up to stir something on the stove. Her back was to John, and he didn't know how to take the comment.

"Would you have wanted me to," he hedged.

"Sixty or more hours a week seems a lot for a man…and for his family. I don't know. I would just want you to be home more than that if we were married."

"But just think what sixty-some hours a week will buy. A grand house, a business, a fine horse and coach-"

"True, but at what cost to your family or your fiancé?"

It was a blatant hint, but it seemed to go right over John's head or maybe he would have noticed had Mama Doering not come bustling in and reacted with joy at seeing John sitting at the kitchen table. They weren't quite on the same page, John

---

I SEE BY THE PAPER…

Woodstock Supports Oliver Management

About town the sentiment of the people of this city has in a large degree been opposed to the local union not because they are opposed to union labor but because of the laudable desire to actively support the Oliver Typewriter, Co. and the management of their factory in accordance with their best judgment. The citizens of Woodstock are justly proud of their factory and they are extremely jealous of any movement which they fear may interfere with its successful operation.

THE SENTINEL has observed that a large number of its exchanges, have contained garbled reports of the happenings here regarding the factory and of the conditions surrounding. We regret that this is true and that our friends of the press in neighboring cities did not better inform themselves before they published long-winded articles under big scareheads.

Woodstock Sentinel, February 13, 1902.

reflected the next day as he enjoyed a day off in Racine,…but almost.

I SEE BY THE PAPER…

Racine Situation Alarming.

Racine, Wisc. — State health officers were called here today and made an examination of three cases of smallpox. Dr. Wingate, secretary of the State board at once ordered that the houses where the sick persons were confined by quarantined and that

"Smallpox" signs be posted. Local health officers were criticized by the State officer for allowing persons to enter or leave the houses as it was found that the cases were severe.

Chicago Tribune, February 16, 1902.

February 16, 1902
Woodstock, Illinois

Dearest Ida,

I just put down the Tribune after reading about the smallpox outbreak in Racine. Please tell me that you and your family are being
careful and staying away from the public squares that bring this sickness upon the unwary receiver. I want to come and snatch you from that vile city this instant, but I know that I cannot. If you want to escape to healthier environs, please but come! Or maybe I should come there rather than you bring the pox here with you…please write and tell me that you are healthy, and I will be so pleased.

I am working many hours and have a plan now for a house. Al has a lot on Lincoln Avenue and I have one out a bit just off McHenry Avenue that I invested in a few years ago, and I am going to talk to him about trading with me because I would want to be close to the square if I…or we…were to open a shop. We shall see what he says. Al and Lena seem happy. She is going to have a baby, which you probably know. Ma is overjoyed, of course. Not that she doesn't have other grandchildren, but as she always says, the more the better.

Please write and tell me you and yours have not come down with any deadly diseases.

I remain truly yours,
John

February 21, 1902
936 Huron Street
Racine, Wisconsin

Dear John,

A quick reply to ease your mind. The paper has reported smallpox in another part of town where rooming houses are the rule rather than the exception and then only two actual cases. Most of the cases are varioloid which is a mild case of smallpox that someone gets after they have been vaccinated. We have not had a single case of the pox or varioloid that I know of here close to downtown and the lake. We are all as safe as we can be as we go about our usual business. I am careful about meeting people at the laundry when I work. I do not offer my hand and try to watch for blemishes which give away infected individuals. Besides, a few sniffles here or there we have all been healthy this winter. And now we can look forward to spring in the near future.

I do hope that we may see each other soon. I so enjoyed our last meeting and would entertain any plan to meet again.

You seem to have very negative feelings about Racine, calling it a "vile town." I will have you know that we have all the modern conveniences in Racine without the crowding of Milwaukee. Our streets and streetlights are very modern along with our very good rail system both to Milwaukee and to Chicago to say nothing of points westward. We have the very finest stores and a grand hotel with high society luncheons. We have not just one theater, but two, where the best plays come to town, I daresay, long before they come to the Opera House in Woodstock. We also have access to all that the lake brings by boat and steamer. Our fresh fruit and meat are practically still on the vine and hoof. The opportunities for employment are vast. If someone wants to work, they can find work. The laundry is thriving. and we have not seen any downturn in the sewing business due to Mama's fine handiwork.

On the other side, I will concede that we have more Democrats and anarchists in Racine which is sometimes troublesome as they make up most of the union members who are demanding additional benefits, marching in the streets, and so forth. But this just makes life more exciting, don't you agree? I know you do.

> **I SEE BY THE PAPER…**
>
> ### COUNTRY GOING MAD.
>
> Dr. R. B. Hoyt, of Detroit, is authority for the statement that by the year 2162 the world will be populated by madmen. He bases his bellef on the statement that during the past fifty years insanity and fanaticism has increased 300 per cent, and that the same pace continued for 100 years will absorb all the common sense and sanity there is left.
>
> The doctor appears to be a pessimist of pronounced type. He is perfectly café in making his prediction, because he will not, be present to verity his claim. While the statement is extremely radical, it contains more than a grain of truth, so far as fanaticism is concerned and it not unfrequently develops that danger to the welfare of humanity lies close to the surface; requiring but a breath to fan a flame that is threatening.
>
> The various political fads that are constantly coming to the surface, under the alluring guise of reform, are paralleled in the religious world by creeds that are loose and equally dangerous. The age is restless and unstable. There are more people chasing phantoms and riding hobbies than ever before. This is doubtless the danger to which the doctor alluded. What the world needs, especially this land of rapid progress, is stability.
>
> *Janesville Daily Gazette*, Feb. 19, 1902.

As for Wisconsin, it is very progressive. Why a proposition that a man could divorce his wife if she is insane for three years was just voted down in Madison. So, you would not be able to get rid of me so easily if we lived in Racine. Do you have such a law in Illinois?

All in all, I doubt that there is a more up-to-date or exciting city anywhere in the United States than Racine, Wisconsin. So much more cosmopolitan than the small village of Woodstock.

That said…I am sure we are as safe here as anywhere these days, as you will surely agree.

Must run! A seamstress's work is never sewed up. Ha.

Truly yours,
Ida

"Hello, Al…and Lena! And Evie! Come, come in out of that wind," said John, as he held the door wide and inviting.

"Hi John," said Lena. "Evie meet your Uncle John." And with that, she placed the baby in his arms while she removed her coat and hat.

"Um…hi there Evie. I think she smiled at me."

"Gas," said Al.

"Albert!" said Lena. She playfully slapped Al's arm and then turned her attention back to John. "She might have smiled at you. You *are*, after all, her favorite uncle."

Lena took the baby and unwrapped her from the blanket. She is so tiny, thought John. Are they all so tiny? Lena handed her back now clothed in the one-piece flannel slip dress common to babies of both sexes. She felt so small in his big hands. Her eyes were open, but now her face crumpled, and she began to cry.

"John, you are holding her at arm's length like she is going to break, cuddle her in. She's just a little cold from taking off the blanket." John pulled her in and tucked her in his right arm as he would a football, and she quieted.

"Vat's dat I hear!" called out Sophia as she hurried in from the kitchen. "Aw, da littl' one."

John, without hesitation, transferred Evie to his mother's arms who began to bounce and cluck like a mother hen. John smiled. That lady knew how to comfort a child.

Al and John retreated to the parlor leaving the women with the baby.

"How are you, brother," Al asked. "How's your love life?"

"Never better. Sorry about the caucus vote. Maybe next time."

I SEE BY THE PAPER…

Dorr Caucus Results.

Hendricks — 307;
Wienke — 191;
Hendricks majority — 116.

Popular Vote.

Madison, Wis., Feb. 13. — A joint resolution was introduced in the assembly today requesting congress to forthwith issue a call for a constitutional convention to pass on amendment relating to the election of United States senators by popular vote.

Personal Mention.

Mrs. Sophia Wienke and Robert Wienke went to Dundee, Monday, for a short visit with friends.

Born to Mr. and Mrs. Albert Wienke in this city, on Tuesday Mar. 4, 1902, a daughter, Evelyn Theolinda. The respected parents have the congrat- of their many friends.

To Increase Output.

The Oliver Typewriter Co. are gradually increasing the ouput of their factory in this city. Superintendent Whitworth was in Chicago a few days ago and purchased about $10,000 worth of new machinery, to be placed in the works here, and they expect soon to be manufacturing seventy-five type-writers per day.

LOCAL INTELLIGENCE.

The office of Dr. E. Windmueller has been greatly beautified by the skill of Albert Wienke in the paperhanging and painting line. Doc is never happy unless things are looking pretty sleek around him.

Woodstock Sentinel, March 20, 1902.

I SEE BY THE PAPER...

The Annual Tramp Crop.

The keeper of the tramp house, Charles Roth, states that the number of knights of the road who are sheltered at his resort is not decreasing. This army of those who have fallen behind in life's struggle for supremacy begin to put in their appearance at nightfall and before 9 p. m. the register often shows fifteen signatures. While there is nothing luxurious about the local quarters, it is a paradise in comparison to other towns along the line, Kenosha especially, where there is nothing by a dingy, cold room. The boys who hit this town find comfortable quarters with good anthracite coal at ten dollars a ton to toast their shins. The claim to represent men from all lines of industry, mechanics now and then a professional man. The other evening a patron claiming his home in the east registered for the night. He claimed to be an M. D., but the crowded condition of the profession coupled together with a strenuous life made it necessary for him to drop out, and while his present existence was not a matter of choice, it was nevertheless compulsory, for the time being at least. Still he hoped to see better days.

Racine Journal Times, April 1902.

"I should have put more effort into campaigning, but with the baby and all the painting jobs, I just didn't have time. Yes, maybe next time."

"Your work is getting pretty well known around town, so you'll have a better chance next time."

"You know, you should run, John. You are the one who is on a first-name basis with the politico. Me, I'm just John Wienke's brother, the painter."

John chuckled, "Maybe. I've been thinking about it. I have a lot on my plate right now trying to get ready to ask for Ida's hand an—"

"What? Excellent!" Al interrupted. "Did you hear—" he began to call out to Lena.

"No, wait," John shushed him. "I don't want Lena to know yet because she'll break the surprise before I do."

"No, she won't."

"Yes, she will, or she might without meaning to. Let's just keep it between you and me. I'll let you know when you can tell her. I've still got a long row to hoe. I've been trying to figure out how we can get married before we have a house. I just don't have enough saved to get a mortgage yet. My money is tied up in real estate and in the bank and here." He gestured to the house. "I guess I could sell a lot for a down payment. Or I could buy an old house and fix it up or—"

"Whoa, slow down," said Al. "Sounds like you have a lot on your mind besides politics."

"Ja, I guess I do," John admitted.

"Lena and I got married before we bought a house," Al reminded him. "As a matter of fact, we are still living in the rental and are only starting now to look for something permanent."

"But that was because of timing, not money."

"True, but also wanting Lena to have a say in the new house. So, one thing at a time. If you feel you want or need to ask Ida, do it. Then work it out between the two of you when you'll marry and when you'll buy a house, and when you'll open a business. It's much more fun to make plans with a helpmate, I assure you."

John sighed. The task just seemed overwhelming.

"John, don't let your fiscally conservative ways stand in your path to happiness. There is a lot more to life than having money. You are going to need Ida to help in all the ways a wife can as you go forward. Don't push it off until she has given up on you. Neither of you

---

I SEE BY THE PAPER...

600 Converts in Four Weeks.
Rev. William A. Sunday, known as the baseball evangelist, has closed a series of meetings at Fairmont, Ind., securing in all 600 converts in four weeks. A large tabernacle was erected for use of the evangelist, and at least 1,200 people heard him every afternoon and evening. The evangelist is not paid a regular salary for his work but is given the collections taken up on the last day. Mr. Sunday received $1,600 for his work at Fairmont.

Woodstock Sentinel, April 1902.

I SEE BY THE PAPER...

Racine Fears Mob Rule as a Result of Labor War.

Racine, Wis., April 11 - Attacks on the jail and the J. I. Case plow works by a mob are feared as a result of the shooting of a union molder by a non-union employe this afternoon. Both places are guarded by special deputies and the police.

The shooting was the outcome of the lockout by the Case company of its union molders, and union men of all trades are aroused over the affair. Should the wounded man die it is promised that the jail doors will be battered in and the prisoner lynched.

Chicago Tribune, April 12, 1902.

> ## I SEE BY THE PAPER...
>
> ### MORE HOUSES NEEDED.
> #### Demand Is Great for Residences for Factory Employees and Others.
>
> There never was a time in the history of Woodstock when there was such a crying demand for more houses for renters. The employees of the factory are living in whatever places they can find, in the hope of soon finding better quarters, every hotel and restaurant in the city is crowded to its fullest capacity with table boarders, and men who have families refusing to come here to work for the reason that they cannot find places in which to house them.
>
> The men of Woodstock who have money are jeopardizing the great prosperity we now enjoy by not putting up houses needed for the families who want to locate here, drawn here by the certainty of profitable employment in the Oliver typewriter factory, which is now about 3,000 machines behind in its orders. The output of the factory is now fifty machines a day, and the time will so be here when the demand will be for sixty and finally 100 machines a day. This will take men to manufacture them, and the men will not come unless they can get houses in which to live, and if the time comes when the factory grows faster than the city, then will come the chance of losing the splendid growth we have made the past year, and that would be a disaster the consequences of which cannot be estimated.
>
> What is wanted is the erection of a number of comfortable cottages that can be rented for from $8 to $12 per month, where a laboring man can live comfortably and within his income, and we must have a lot of these this summer if we hope to keep up our degree of growth and keep in our midst the institution that is responsible for this growth.
>
> *Woodstock Sentinel*, April 17, 1902.

is getting younger, and I assume you want children. If so, you better get cracking."

"I want children. I never thought about that being an issue."

"OK, go, have these discussions, and if everything seems good, ask her. If she says 'no,' you can stop worrying."

"What?" John looked up in alarm. "Says no?"

Al laughed, "I'm just kidding, but you don't know until you pop the question! Oh, here they come, my darlings."

Sophia came in with Evie in her arms followed by Lena with a tray of lemonade and kuchen fresh from the oven. The smell of it had permeated the air and now the sight of it sent all their mouths to desire.

"Get it while it's hot," Lena said, as she began cutting the cake and sliding healthy portions onto the dessert plates.

April 15, 1902
Woodstock, Illinois

Dearest Ida,

I hope this finds you well and safe inside the confines of your home, away from the anarchists and union thugs. The Tribune says that Racine is just short of mob rule. If you and your family need to escape, we can find respite in Woodstock for all of you.

You are of the opinion that Racine is superior to Woodstock? My what a sheltered life you have led in the big city. One major way that Woodstock is better is that we don't have armed marauders traveling the streets at night. We do sometimes have young boys with firecrackers who set them off under windows and then run away. We also have the best crime fighters for a town our size and the county courthouse and jail where hoodlums, if we have any, pay their dues. Woodstock has not had an outbreak of the grippe this winter as you have in Racine, nor have the pox taken any lives or even been reported. We have had a few cases of consumption, but no more than any other municipality. Maybe less.

Everything in Woodstock is in walking distance of everything else eliminating the need for streetcars and taxis. If you walked eighteen or nineteen blocks in Woodstock, you would have walked across the whole town. We do have, as does Racine, trains that run through town and bring danger in their crossing of the public thoroughfare. But we do not have streetcars killing people or unions revolting and shooting guns at people. We do have people who celebrate by shooting off guns in the air, as is common, but we have not had a single murder. Everything in Woodstock is fairly new, thanks to the destruction of the old by fire. As the wooden structures burnt down, we replaced them with brick and stone, so we are somewhat fireproof. Well, at least downtown around the square is. Each year we see new buildings being put up and wonderful new commercial spaces being let to entrepreneurs, like me, I hope.

I SEE BY THE PAPER...

Personal Mention.

Mr. and Mrs. Charles Wienke of Beloit, Wis., visited with relatives and friends here, Sunday and Monday.

Woodstock Sentinel, April 3, 1902.

Everyone in Woodstock, basically, knows everyone else. How many of your neighbors and fellow citizens do you know? Only a handful. I know your friends are precious to you, but it seems to me that they are few and most often from church. I cannot count the number of my friends and acquaintances. Some are from church, but many I have met in the day-to-day life of the citizenry.

I know that I am totally besotted with my town and if you lived here, I'm sure that you would be also. I am coming up next weekend. I hope you will agree to see me.

As ever,
John

I SEE BY THE PAPER…

LOCAL INTELLIGENCE.
The interior of the German Lutheran church is being repainted and repapered by Albert Wienke and his helpers, and it will look beautiful when the job is finished, for Mr. Wienke is an expert in his field.

Woodstock Sentinel, April 17, 1902.

Ida smiled up at John who had just come through the door. The broad grin on his face said he was glad to see her. He took Ida in his arms and kissed her. Now that was a greeting any girl would swoon over.

"Oh, I have missed you," John sighed.

"And I, you. Your defense of Woodstock's values was very…um…moving."

He laughed and swung her around. "It's all true!!" He kissed her again.

"Ahem!" Mr. Stoffel cleared his throat. They separated, and John hastily crossed the room to shake hands with him as Ida's mother hurried into the room wiping her hands on her apron. John realized that there was a wonderful aroma in the house of baking bread or strudel. His mouth began to water. He hugged Mama, kissing her on each cheek.

"Something sure smells good," John said. "Es riecht gut."

"Wir haben etwas Besonderes fur Sie gemacht," she replied.

"Something special for you," Ida translated smiling. "Schneckennudln."

Now John's mouth was already watering from the smell and the memory of warm Schnecken, the rich pastry with raisins and hazelnuts and a modicum of rum. This pastry was only prepared on very special occasions.

"What is the occasion?" asked John.

"Your being here," said Ida, as she slipped her small hand into his.

Later after dinner of bratwurst and cabbage, and of course, die Schneckennudln, he said, "I feel like a celebrity. That was an absolutely wonderful meal and fantastic company." They had adjourned to the parlor after Mama and Clara had insisted that they would wash up, and Mr. Stoffel retired upstairs. They sat close on the couch facing inward a touch so they could see each other's smile.

"See I told you, Mama," Ida called out. "Er ist ein gutter Esser." And then to John, "I told her that you are—"

"A good eater," John interrupted.

"You understood?" Ida said.

"Ein bisschen. Although your accent is difficult at times."

"My accent? We don't have an accent."

"In German, you do. Wait until you are struggling with Ma's German; you'll hear it. Myself, I understand better than I speak. We are having a bit of a struggle at our church right now because the first generation and even some of the second generation want to keep everything in German. Alle auf Deutsch! But a good number of us want at least one service in English so that we can understand the sermon. My brothers and I have talked about adding a service, but the church Väter are not in favor. And as you know, church Mütter can't vote, even in German."

I SEE BY THE PAPER...

THE INDUSTRIAL HOME.

The association known as the Chicago Industrial Home for Children, whose buildings are located in Woodstock recently held its annual meeting. The report of the treasurer showed a small balance on hand, after all current expenses were met.

The manager, W. E. Bardell, reported that seventy children had been taken in and provided for, forty have been placed in comfortable Christian homes and there are now in the institution twenty-three boys and four girls, three of whom are infants under 2 years of age.

Under the economical and efficient management of W. E. Bardell and his wife, the matron of the institution, the home has been greatly improved and the board of directors feel highly pleased.

The children who are old enough attend the public school of Woodstock. It requires a great deal to feed, clothe and keep warm so many children.

Contributions of food, clothing, coal and cash always will be accepted and thankfully received.

Woodstock Sentinel.

I SEE BY THE PAPER...

Spell Iowa Out.

The post office department has issued a bulletin asking that the name of the state of Iowa should never be abbreviated in addressing letters, as it has so often led to mistakes in the distribution of mail. It is explained the abbreviated, Ia., might be mistaken for Indiana while the abbreviation, Io., might be mistaken for Idaho, these abbreviations being used in those states as they are in Iowa. No one ever gained anything by the use of abbreviations. The suggestions are well worth heeding and practicing. - Harvard Herald.

Personal Mention.

Clayton Harting, Harry Cross, John Carroll, Frank Martin and Robert Wienke drove to Pistaqua Bay, Sunday.

Woodstock Sentinel, May 1, 1902.

"Yes, but do the women want to be church mothers who can vote?"

"I'm not sure, but I would think that women would want some part in the running of the church, wouldn't they?"

"Maybe," she drew the word out, considering. "I suppose that women should have a voice, but we don't even have a voice in political elections. How is it right that we have a vote in the church?"

"It is right because…," he hesitated, thinking, "because it is right!" John asserted. "You are no less God's child than I am. You have every right to have a vote in what happens in our church."

"OK. I do agree, but I doubt you'll convince the Fathers of that," said Ida.

"Don't just agree. Say that you will take part in making sure our church will accept our daughters as total equals with our sons."

"Our church?" Ida asked, smiling coyly.

"Yes, our church," John said. He reached into his breast pocket and took out a small box. He opened it and showed it to her.

"This is how the boys do it today," he said. He slid off the couch onto one knee and said, "Ida Doering, will you marry me?"

She smiled down at him. Her eyes filled with tears. Finally, it was her turn!

"Yes, John Wienke, I will marry you!"

He slipped the ring on her finger, and she kissed him in a way that left him breathless.

"Hello, hello, is anyone there?" John's frustration was beginning to grow even as his purse shrunk. "Hello?"

He had decided to call Ida to see how everyone was, but for some reason, the call had gotten stuck. He clicked the hook switch a couple of times and the hello-girl came on the line. "Number, please?" she said.

"I was calling Racine and the call got stuck."

"I'm sorry. Number?"

John gave the number and the girl said, "Racine, Wisconsin, you say?"

"Yes."

"One moment, please."

The receiver proceeded with clicks and clacks and static and then he could hear the phone ringing at the other end and a small voice said, "Hello?"

"Clara, is that you? It's John Wienke."

He heard a small gasp followed by a loud bump. He pictured the receiver bouncing off the wall after being dropped

> **I SEE BY THE PAPER…**
>
> **Good Advice About Telephoning.**
> Marshall Field & Co. of Chicago have on each of their telephones a printed card reading as follows:
>
> The manner in which a person uses a telephone indicates his character to a great extent and makes either a good or bad impression. And this impression is reflected directly upon the establishment from which such message comes. It is a pleasure to do business with a house which performs every detail in a clean-cut, satisfactory manner; but it leaves a sting to be answered abruptly or discourteously over the telephone. It is a folly to lose one's temper because one does not get immediate connection. This is rarely ever the fault of the telephone operators who are nearly always courteous and prompt. When one is called the telephone he should respond quickly, and the person calling should not be left holding the wire too long, something decidedly irritating, and often unnecessary. Let us, throughout the whole house, strive to excel in satisfactory telephoning.
>
> The forgoing is considered of sufficient importance by the Chicago Telephone Company to be printed in large type on the back cover of its latest directory.
>
> *Chicago Tribune*, 1902.

and now swaying at the end of the cord. He heard, "Ida, Ida, Ida" being called out far away. "It's John."

Then another voice, "What do you mean it's John. Did something happen? A letter?" He heard quick footfalls and then close-by, "No, Ida. On the telephone."

"What? Oh dear! How do I do this?"

The first voice said, "Listen with this and talk in here."

Ida's shout of "HELLO! JOHN?" about broke his eardrum.

"You don't need to shout, Ida. Hello, it's John Wienke." He heard some scrabbling around.

"SAY THAT AGAIN JOHN…I can't hear him."

"Oh, for heaven's sakes, hold it this way." Now John was laughing.

"I hear him laughing," said Ida. And that set Clara off, and soon they had spent twenty or thirty seconds of precious time laughing together.

"Good afternoon, Ida, how are you?" said John, trying hard to recover his composure.

"Good afternoon, John, I am fine. How are you?"

"Ida," whispered Clara, "Just talk like normal, like he's standing right here."

Ida elbowed her away, "Ouch!" cried Clara, and John began laughing again.

"He's laughing again," said Ida.

Clara grabbed the receiver, "Hi John. Clara here. Sorry, this is Ida's first talk on the telephone, and she's a bit flustered."

"I guessed. Put her back on. Thanks, Clara."

"Ida."

"Yes, John."

"I miss you," he said. His voice was still alive with laughter.

"Clara! Claarrraa! Clara, where are you?" Ida dashed along the dock looking from face to face. Where was she? Other people were being brought off the boat, but she couldn't find her sister. What if she had been swept overboard, and they didn't realize it? Did they know for sure that everyone was still on board? And then she heard her sister's voice through a megaphone no less. Ida came to an abrupt halt and slowly turned looking up at the disabled launch.

"OK, that's good! That's the last of them, boys. Let's give a round of appreciation for the crew and captain of this ship for keeping us safe even in the dire straits of the middle of Lake Michigan. We have not succumbed but are safe and sound on God's green earth again." The crowd hooted approval, and several men let loose with whistles appreciating not just the affirmation but also the pretty girl broadcasting it.

Oh boy, thought Ida, she's not merely safe but she's running the show, as usual.

"Clara!" Ida waved up to the deck and caught Clara's eye and Clara sent back an enthusiastic wave like this was the greatest adventure on earth. Ida beckoned and mouthed 'come down.' Reluctantly, Clara gave up the megaphone and made her way to the gangplank. Then she rushed down into Ida's embrace.

"Are you OK?" Ida asked pushing Clara back so she could look at her.

> **I SEE BY THE PAPER...**
>
> **Twenty-Five Women for Hours in Peril on Lake.**
>
> With a strong west wind blowing, a steam launch, in charge of S. Larson and Bert Russel, and having on board a party of twenty-five women, was blown out on the lake today and only rescued after hours of work. The engine of the launch was disabled and the craft rapidly drifted three miles out into Lake Michigan. The Racine life saving crew went out and after two hours hard work landed the party safely.
>
> **Cyclone Kills One.**
>
> One man was killed and several persons injured, houses and trees blown down, and stock killed in a strip ten miles long and half a mile wide by a cyclone which swept the country from the town of Raymond to the village of Washer. Crops were ruined and great damage was done.
>
> Reports on the district state that there were many barns and houses blown away, and that it is hard to estimate the exact number. Telephone lines are down through the country.
>
> *Chicago Tribune*, June 1902.

"Oh yes, fantastic! It was great fun. A lot of the girls were scared, but not me. I figured I could swim back to shore if I needed to."

"Do you know how to swim?" asked Ida.

"Oh sure. Learned at the beach. It's just floating and paddling," Clara assured her as they turned back toward main street and home.

"But the wind would have been blowing you away from shore. And the water is very cold."

"Hmph…I hadn't thought of that, but no matter, the brave men of our life-saving squad came and rescued us. Weren't they handsome? I was their special mascot because I didn't faint or run to my cabin or act like a scared little girl. They put me in charge of all the fainters, and I got to nurse them back to health before we docked."

"You are such a strange girl, Clara Doering," said Ida.

"Why am I strange? I knew the men would come to rescue the damsels in distress. They always come to rescue the damsels in distress," she flicked her hair in the general direction of the docks.

"When we heard that a boat was in distress, you should have heard Mama. We were sure it was yours, just knew it! Mama straightaway went to bed and pulled the covers over her head, and I headed down here to wait. I hope you are impressed with how much we care about you."

"Oh, thank you, kind sister, for your concern, but I am fine. Never better."

"Well, let's get on home before Mama dies of dread." And they began to walk toward Huron Street.

"Maybe I should be a reporter. Reporters get sucked into this kind of thing all the time. I loved it," she twirled around and skipped up the block ahead of Ida.

"Watch out for the mud in the street," Ida called after her. "It rained tod—"

Clara took a mighty leap into the street at the end of

I SEE BY THE PAPER...

Anachists Ordered Out.

Pittsburg, Pa. — Because President Roosevelt is to spend the fourth of July in Pittsburg all known anarchists have been ordered to leave the city this week and to stay away for the week. Detectives have just finished the rounds of their haunts and told them if they did not obey the order they would be arrested as suspicious persons and locked up for the week. The detectives also visited the coal mining towns where there are groups of anarchists and notified them that if they came to Pittsburg any day this week they would be arrested. Allegheny anarchists have received similar warnings.

Racine Journal Times, June 1902.

the boardwalk and went ankle-deep into the mud.

And so falls the queen from her steed, thought Ida, as she worked her way carefully across the street with her skirts held high, while Clara, unscathed by her dangerous hours at sea, stomped and jumped and most likely ruined her shoes, her petticoat and her dress crossing just one street.

As they came back together on the other side of the street, Ida was shaking her head.

"Now Clara, tell me truthfully…did you sabotage that boat?"

Clara's face took on a mischievous grin, "I'll never tell."

June 5, 1902
936 Huron Street
Racine, Wisconsin

Dearest John,

Oh, how frightening the past few days have been. First of all, there was a storm that narrowly missed carrying me away across the lake. It was headed right for Racine, and we watched the sky grow quickly darker and darker until it was black as midnight. Of course, we didn't even know how bad it was until we read about it the next day.

That day, that same day mind you, Clara and her friends decide to go out on the lake, and the storm overwhelmed the motoring ability of the launch, and they were blown out to the middle of the lake where they couldn't even signal for help because they couldn't see the shore. Eventually, someone on shore noticed that they had not come back and sent out the life rescue boys who pulled them back in and there was Clara, unhurt, up on

---

I SEE BY THE PAPER…

Local Intelligence.

It is not necessary to go away from town on the fourth for a good time. The ball team will play the Chicago Maroons and the band will give a concert during the game and at the park in the evening.

There is absolutely nothing impossible these days. A southern mob lynched a white man a few days ago.

The white sox and the cubs both seem to be on the downward grade at a fearful rate.

Friday's Parade.

The committee on amusements of the 4th of July celebration has arranged the procession to beheaded by the Oliver Typewriter band, followed by the Woodstock Guards, the fire company and the calithumpians, and the prade will move promptly at 10:30 o'clock. The committee is anxious that more volunteer to participate in this parade, and especially in the calithumpian end of it.

Woodstock Sentinel, July 3, 1902.

*the top deck with a megaphone bossing everyone around. Now she wants
to be a newspaper reporter so that she can have such adventures daily.*

*AND we all got smallpox vaccinations which hurt like the
dickens and festered all up like they were royally infected. The scabs soon
dried up and just fell off. I guess we are now safe from the disease you will
be glad to know.*

*That's all the mundane news from here. When will I see you
again, Mr. Blue Eyes?*

Yours always,
Ida

Lena threw down the paper. "Why is it always the woman's
fault?" she wondered aloud. She took a deep breath and picked
up the paper to read. The headline that had made her angry
was "Tried Thrice for Insanity was this Lady." She picked up
the paper again.

> After three trials by a jury in the county court
> covering a period of nearly a year, Mrs. Julia Jaap,
> wife of Arthur Jaap of Harvard, was declared
> insane Tuesday afternoon. The first trial occurred
> Nov. 4, 1902 and resulted in a verdict of not insane
> from the jury. The second trial occurred Friday,
> July 3, of this year and the jury was unable to
> agree. That there was a close question as to the
> woman's sanity is shown by the three different
> trials.

Three trials? What kind of man would put his wife through
that, she wondered? What had she done to make this man want
her "put away" as Lena had heard it phrased?

> Mrs. Jaap appears to be sane on every question
> except one, a peculiarity found in the majority of
> insane cases. Her hallucination takes an unusual
> turn, however. She believes her husband is in love
> with other women and that his attentions are so
> pronounced she is even neglected. With this
> hallucination in her mind, she becomes so
> irrational at times she has to be restrained.

Aren't we all irrational at times? Surely, we are, and as for a man having lovers, that also happens often. With as much as Al was gone, who knew? He was always back at some point during the night. She could just see herself in the position of this woman, making claims with no proof, just a feeling. Women use feelings quite a lot to decide dilemmas. But no one in this fine city would believe unfaithfulness of their favorite son if she did question Al's loyalties.

She had taken of late to smelling his shirts to see if she could find any perfume residue, but all they smelled like was cigar smoke which covered up any other odor. There was nothing to do but trust that he was being loyal, but why should he be. She had been acting like a shrew. She never went with him to the lake, and she knew that girls were always available there. She ceased her reverie and turned back to the paper.

> Judge Gillmore has not yet issued the order that will send the woman to the Elgin hospital for treatment. The jury was so late in reaching a verdict Tuesday evening, the court decided to send the woman to her home in care of Sheriff Lake, who resides at Harvard. Later, if the woman's mental aberration continues to be displayed, she will be taken to the hospital at once. This action is taken by the court because of the fact that Mrs. Jaap has a little baby of only a few weeks old in her arms, and he feels it would unwise to separate them at the present only under the most extreme circumstances. It is believed that the woman is not so mentally weak, but what she realized now is her condition and that she will make an effort to restrain herself.

What in the world! In the midst of this ordeal, the woman was pregnant! "Yes, crazy pregnant woman! Restrain thyself!!" Lena said, too loud.

There was a very good chance that her loving husband had found comfort during her pregnancy in the arms of another woman. They would put her in Elgin for being sensitive while with child? Mein Gott! This is disgusting! She ripped the page from the paper and tore it into small pieces. Then she realized what she had done. Al would want to read the paper in the morning. She frantically put the pieces on the table and tried to arrange them into the page again. There…no…here…no…okay…start at the top and…she sank into a chair and put her head on her arms and began sobbing. Woman, restrain yourself! She mentally slapped herself to try to regain composure, but she couldn't. The tears continued in great gales of despair.

Bit by bit, she became aware of the fact that she was not alone in her crying. Another voice was also wailing. A baby…that woman's baby was crying hard. She looked up. Where was it? She followed the sound into the parlor and found the baby in a cradle. Shhhh…quiet baby. She rocked the cradle, but the sound continued.

"OH PLEASE STOP!" Lena screamed putting her hands over her ears, sitting down hard on the floor beside the cradle. "STOP CRYING!" But the cries from the child continued. Where was this child's mother!? Oh yes, she was in Elgin.

Poor child. Lena reached in and lifted the child and her blanket into her arms and began rocking. The child quieted and began pushing its face into her chest. Lena pushed the little face away, but then felt her milk let down staining through her bodice. What was going on? She looked down at the child. This wasn't a strange baby of an insane woman; it was Evie. The

> **I SEE BY THE PAPER…**
>
> ### Seventy Followers of Dowie Arrived Yesterday in Racine.
>
> One of Zion's Seventies, or in other words, seventy followers of Alexander Dowie of Zion City, arrived in this city yesterday morning and assembled on the green plat just east of the Chicago & Northwestern depot. They were loaded down with literature touching upon the teachings of Dowie.
>
> During the day there was preaching and the town was flooded with tracts. In the afternoon Rev. O. Jacobsen of the Trinity M.E. church happened to pass along State street. One of the Dowieites acosted him and offered a circular and invited him to the meeting. Rev. Jacobsen politely refused the invitation and discussed the nature of Dowie's teachings with the man. The discussion was animated and a crowd of several hundered gathered and applauded the Racine minister, who completely floored the follower of Dowie.
>
> *Racine Journal Times*, August 18, 1902.

baby's eyes were dark, her face red, her hands angerly punched the air as she looked up – her eyes accusing. My baby. She held Evie tightly, sobbing into the blanket. Evie squeaked, unable to get enough air to cry out. Oh no, I'm killing her. She tried to loosen her grip. It seemed impossible. The squeezing had stopped the crying. But a loosening was accomplished, and Evie began to nuzzle again.

Lena stood, took her to the rocking chair and undid her bodice, unconcerned with propriety. She tucked the material into her right armpit and brought the baby's mouth up to her nipple. Evie began to suckle even before she made contact. Lena tried to relax so the milk would flow easily and leaned her head back against the chair before closing her eyes. Tears continued to run down her cheeks. She hummed a familiar tune, and then, looking down at her baby, she began to softly sing. Evie's eyes opened in surprise – had she never sung to her child? "Schlaf, Kindlein, schlaf," she sang. "Der Vater bewacht die Schafe; De Mutter schüttelt die Bäumchen, Dann fällt ein kleiner Traum herunter; Schlaf, Kinlein, schlaf!"

Sleep, baby, sleep; Thy father guards the sheep; Thy mother shakes the little trees; There falls down one little dream; Sleep, baby, sleep! How often had she heard her mother sing those words? The tune calmed her and calmed Evie, too, who eagerly took to nursing.

How Lena missed her mother! She must go home soon and see her mother. Very soon. She sang the stanza again and then the bits and pieces she remembered of other stanzas. And as she sang, the world fell back into place.

I SEE BY THE PAPER...

Local Intelligence.

And still it rains.

Next horse sale, Oct. 8

A husband in hand is worth two that are beyond control.

The heavy wind of the last few days has worked havoc on the standing corn, and the farmer who has his cut is indeed a lucky fellow.

Personal Mention.

Frank Wienke went to Dundee last Saturday to visit friends for a day or two.

Mr. and Mrs. William Wienke and family returned Sturday evening from a visit of his brother in Beloit, Wis.

Woodstock Sentinel, September 1902.

September 25, 1902
936 Huron Street
Racine, Wisconsin

Dearest John,

I hope this finds you fit as a fiddle. We are fine here also. No diseases to speak of. The unbelievably good weather of this Fall has fallen to the wet cold rains of the coming winter. The leaves are still beautiful, maybe even more beautiful wet, but the heavy rain is removing them from the trees so one must look smartly before they are gone.

Shall I see you in the near future? I did appreciate, I think, the telephone call. I liked it much more than the last time when we laughed through it. I would like to see you tomorrow or the next day, but I know that it is impossible with the work they have you doing at the factory. You said that they were going to be hiring more people so that your long hours would cease. Is that happening? I hate to think how little I will see you once we are married, and I will be in a town where I only know one other person. I suppose I will quickly make friends through church.

Speaking of church, Clara has stopped going to the Lutheran church. Mama is having a fit, but Clara says she needs to explore other religions then she'll be back. She has gone to the Universalist church with a friend the last few weeks. She says it is so relaxing to hear the service in English, although she misses the formality of the Lutheran service. This church doesn't believe in hell, can you believe it? I said, what keeps people from doing dastardly deeds? She couldn't answer. Like most of her endeavors, I'm sure this will be short-lived. I sympathize with wanting to speak English in church, but I'm not sure about completely changing one's religion for it. She says that the Universalists don't require a change of religion — that it is Christian but just more forgiving. It gives the responsibility to the believers. What do you think?

I must move on to my next project now. The sewing has been slow this fall so I've been working more at the laundry and the YMCA. Trying to put aside a nest egg like my betrothed is doing. Write and tell me when I shall see you.

Sincerely yours,
Ida

Woodstock Pleasure Club
Woodstock, Illinois

October 1, 1902

My Dearest Ida,

I wish we were together this evening to just sit and watch the rain. It was a very warm day, but the rain tonight bodes for a cooling down to autumn temperatures. I'm sorry I have not gotten up to your tempting city for well over a month or has it been two. I am a very bad beau, but we will see each other soon, I promise. The factory hired fifty new people in the last month, so our hours are going back to normal this week. So, soon, my girl.

You write of Clara's change of faith. Here we have faith all around us and all good choices except maybe the Catholics and their strange ways. My brother Emil has been drawn into the revivals since his high school days both here and in Beloit. I've gone a few times but find it more emotional than substantive. Our papers are filled with news of the churches and each week a sermon is published in the paper from a pastor far afield from Woodstock, mostly based on the Bible stories or the clerical season. It is in fact hard to escape from the message of the good news, even if one would want to.

We did have a Universalist church here in Woodstock, but it was shuttered last year. It was very much in line with the Congregationalists and their bottom-up leadership style. Myself, I believe in a strong minister who guides the church for the parishioners, not the other way around. I would not want our children to become Universalists. That said, I do believe in freedom of religion as guaranteed to us as citizens. It's difficult to know which should take precedence.

> **I SEE BY THE PAPER...**
>
> **Personals.**
> Miss Clara Doering entertained the L'Cameas at cinch.
>
> *Racine Journal Times*, October 8, 1902.

> **I SEE BY THE PAPER...**
>
> **Fine Woman for Loud Praying.**
> Arrested on the charge of disorderly conduct, found guilty, and sentenced to pay a fine of $3 and costs, Emma Leopold of the Metropolitan holiness church of Chicago was advised to return to Chicago, the $50 bond being furnished by F. J. Hanche, who recently joined the church. The woman admitted that the police told her to stop screaming, but she said she could not, as the inspiration had entered her soul.
>
> *Racine Journal Times*, 1902.

I think I've used up my words for now and I shall get this in the mail to you tomorrow. I hope your evening has been as delightfully rainy as mine. I send you my undying devotion.

Sincerely yours,
John

John bounded up the steps to 936 Huron Street in Racine. Before he could throw up a hand to knock on the door, it flew open, and Ida jumped into his arms. Their kiss lasted a little too long for standing out on the stoop.

"There you are," John said. His voice was husky, as he smoothed back her hair which had started to unravel from its bun. "There you are," he repeated.

> **I SEE BY THE PAPER...**
>
> > **Stretching Things.**
> > What is the sense of some evangelists in stretching things so? It has gone so far that women have been charged with being immoral who have danced or played cards, and the men charged with committing wrongs they never even thought of.
>
> *Racine Journal Times.*

"Yes, here I am," she said.

He felt a wonderful urgency in his britches and felt her hands guiding him into the house before closing the door. He had taken a day off to come to visit her. They didn't get many days off at the factory, but he had found that the supervisors were understanding about such things as doctor's visits or other family emergencies. They could often be taken, without pay. So, he had claimed one just so he could see Ida.

"I've never seen your hair down," he said. He reached up and began to unpin her bun. She was beautiful and…but wait, what was he doing? He stopped. "I'm sorry…I… I…I'm sorry."

Ida laughed. "It's OK. It's a mess, I need to re-pin it anyway." She reached up and pulled the rest of the pins out and allowed her hair to fall around her shoulders. Then she put her arms around his neck and allowed him to pull her close for another kiss. Her hand caressed the back of his neck. As the kiss stretched longer, the urge to allow his hands to roam a bit down her back to her waist was overwhelming, and then down…he broke off the kiss. He pulled away. "I am so sorry. I don't know what's gotten into me."

"A little bit of the devil, I'd say," Ida purred. "You know, John, I truly don't mind at all." She drew him over to the sofa, and they sat much too close. She kissed him again with great enthusiasm.

John was trying not to give in to the impulse to touch her everywhere. He pulled back. "Where is everyone?"

"Gone," said Ida. She kissed him and then said with her lips still against his.

"Gone to work." Kiss.

"Gone to ladies' aid." Kiss.

"Gone for at least two hours." Kiss.

"We are all alone." The next kiss became deep and long, and he realized that he was nearing a place where he would not want to turn back.

"Ida, I'm not sure this is a good idea," John said. This time he did not try to pull away.

"What isn't a good idea?" said Ida. Her body was draped across his, touching places that it shouldn't.

"How about we go walk around downtown, and… and…I'll buy you a new hat," he suggested, made breathless by her proximity.

Ida looked him up and down and smiled. "OK." She pushed away from him.

John's mind raced. Oh no, what had he done? Was she giving up so easily? She reached down and took his hand and

> **I SEE BY THE PAPER…**
>
> **Women Should Sleep More.**
>
> A physician who is a specialist in nervous disease say that women should sleep at least nine hours at night and one in the daytime, says a New England Farmer. A woman will plead that she hasn't the time to lie down for a few minutes in the daytime, and she will infringe upon the hours of night, which should be given to sound, healthy, needed sleep, in order to finish some piece of work which could as well be completed on the marrow. She will rush and hurry all day long, and then when the household is hushed in slumber at night she will sit to read the daily paper thinking she will not have to pay for the time she is stealing from the health-giving sleep that comes before midnight.
>
> *Woodstock Sentinel*, November 6, 1902.

pulled him to his feet. Yes, this was better, he reasoned. They'd go for a walk and....

Ida led him to the stairs. She kissed him again, and he brought his hands to her hips. She turned in his grasp and proceeded up the stairs holding his hands steady on her hips.

They reached the upper hallway, and she drew him into her room and closed the door. After two years of yearning, they could not wait one minute longer. She turned away from him, reaching back to uncouple the button loops. He reached to help. His fingers were tentative and clumsy, but he disengaged each one. Her dress fell to the floor, and she stepped out of it. Turning around, she removed his jacket, sliding her hands over his muscular shoulders and down his arms. Then she put her hands on either side of the row of buttons running down his shirt and ripped the lapels apart. Buttons popped and flew. John stood wide-eyed and open-mouthed at what she had done.

"I'll fix those later," she said. Her hand caressed his chest during another prolonged kiss.

She pulled down his suspenders, undid the three-button fly and pushed his wool suit pants down around his ankles. Noticing the bulge under his white cotton underwear, she casually brushed against it while turning. As she pulled her slip up over her head, John attempted to rid himself of the underdrawers by pulling them and his pants off without removing his boots. In frustration, he pulled the boots off with the pants and underwear all in a tangle. She pulled down her bloomers and removed them over her shoes. She never made it to the buttons of her shoes. As she turned, they came together feeling flesh on flesh, both eager to consummate this relationship.

Ida stepped backward toward the bed, never letting go of John and pulled him down on top of her. Her hands guiding him into her as she wrapped her legs around his torso. It took very little time to find that they were compatible.

Afterward, after the sighs of delight had faded away, they lay spent in each other's arms, and Ida whispered, "You know what this means, right?"

John nodded. "I'm in love with you."

Ida snickered. "Well yes. I hope that is true, because I love you. But this means that we must get married very soon. It's good to find that we are well suited to each other before we are married, but we also don't want to have a baby too close to the wedding date."

John sat straight up. "You are going to have a baby? Whose baby?"

Ida looked at him. "You are so sweet. There is only you, my dearest. I might be having a baby because of what we just did, but we won't know for a month or two. When do you want vows? I will talk to Mama and Papa Stoffel and see if they have any other ideas, but how about the beginning of next month? That will give me just enough time to make a dress and to invite people. That will be enough time to get things in Woodstock set up, right?"

"November? I was thinking more like a year from November."

> **I SEE BY THE PAPER...**
>
> **From Louisville Courier-Journal:**
> There is an evangelist going about from church to church in northern Illinois announcing his terms as $40 a week and fifty conversions guaranteed or money refunded. He seems to be doing business, and yet if he were, say a Mormon, the very people with whom he is doing business now would probably do it with tar and feathers.
>
> *Racine Journal Times.*

"Funny boy. No, we must do it soon, because IF I am pregnant, you do not want me walking around nine months pregnant next summer with no husband, right?"

"Well, no, of course not." The satisfaction he had felt moments before had turned into full-fledged panic. "But I'm not ready. We don't have a house, and I don't have a profession and… and …I'm NOT ready!"

"Well, I'm ready. And it's time, John. Girls don't like such long courtships. It's time. I would call the pastor right now, but we are too rosy-cheeked at present, and he'd surely catch on."

She put her hand on his inner thigh and felt it tense. "Let's just say that we are not going to do this again until we are married. Is that enough incentive?"

How could I have given in so easily? John's mind raced. I'm not ready? He couldn't get married AND start a business.

"I'm not ready yet?" he said.

"But, sweet man, when WILL you be ready. We are already along into our prime. We want a family, right? If we wait a year or two or three, I may not be able to bear because of my age. We must strike while the iron is hot." She smiled broadly and patted the comforter right over his crotch. He reflexively reached to cover it with both hands, too late. He felt the desire well up. He cleared his throat.

"Of course, I want children," he managed. "I've seen many women who bear when they are…um…older. There is no hurry. I am also glad to know we are well suited, but…." He paused and looked at her. Gott in Himmel, this woman was exactly what he needed.

"John, do you want me?" she asked, looking him straight in the eye. "Do you want to marry me?"

"Yes, Ida, I do." He smiled, holding her eyes for courage.

"Then, November it is! First week, if possible," she said.

She stood and the click of her high-topped shoes on the hardwood floor as she began gathering up their clothes echoed in the room.

> ### I SEE BY THE PAPER…
>
> #### Local Interest.
> The Oliver Typewriter Co. announces that the month of October was a record-breaker for them in the typewriter business, and, that November starts out as though to eclipse its predecessor.
>
> #### Personal Mention.
> John Wienke left for LaCrosse, Kansas, Sunday morning. It is rumored that he will do a little courting. We hope it is the right kind.
>
> *Woodstock Sentinel*, November 6, 1902.

"I'll be there," said John. He was amazed at the very look of her, standing there confidently unclothed in her boots. She was a force to be reckoned with.

I SEE BY THE PAPER...

Doering — Wienke Matrimonial.

Miss Ida Doering was united in marriage yesterday afternoon at the home of her parents, Mr. and Mrs. J. H. Stoffel, 936 Huron street, to John W. Wienke, of Woodstock, Ill. At three o'clock the guests began to assemble and at 4 o'clock under the strains of a mandolin orchestra, the bridal couple proceeded to the east parlor where they were met by the Rev. Burger, pastor of the German Lutheran Church, who in a few words united them as man and wife.

The bride was attired in white chiffon, trimmed with point lace and carried a bouquet of white chrysanthemums. She was attended by her sister, Miss Clara Doering, who was also attired in white. The groom was attended by his brother, Robert Wienke. The beautiful home of Mr. and Mrs. Stoffel was decorated with white and green flowers and formed a neat appearance. Immediately after the ceremony a supper was served and the newly married couple departed on an afternoon train for an extended wedding trip to the northern part of the state. The dining room was decorated with autumn leaves, carnations and roses. The bride is a popular young lady of the north side, having resided in this city all her life, and the groom is a hustling business man of Woodstock, Ill. The guests from out of town were Frank, Robert, Charles and Fred Wienke, of Woodstock, Mrs. C. Wienke, also of Woodstock, Mrs. William Kuff, of Portage and Miss Emma Ardilt of Whitewater.

Racine Journal Times, November 6, 1902.

I SEE BY THE PAPER...

Wienke — Doering Nuptials.

John Wienke, one of the popular, typewriter force, surprised many his many friends in the factory and about home the past week by taking unto himself a wife. Mr. Wienke started by way of Chicago for Racine, Wis., the fore part of the past week and informed his associates that he would not be here to cast his vote as he had important legal business to attend to. His friends all unsuspicious believed this to be the case and were considerably surprised several days later on hearing the nature of the business, which was legal alright but of a different character than they were led to believe.

The bride, formerly Miss Ida H. Doering, was a popular young society lady of Racine, Wis., in which city the ceremony was performed, Nov. 5, 1902, at the home of Mr. and Mrs. Stoffel, of No. 936 Huron street the Lutheran pastor officiating. Mr. and Mrs. Wienke will no doubt make this city their home and will be given a hearty welcome by the many friends of the groom, who extend congratulations and wish them much happiness and joy.

Woodstock Sentinel, November 13, 1902.

John and Ida lay cuddled in each other's arms on their last morning at the grand Hotel Doering located in Marshfield, Wisconsin. Of course, they had selected the hotel for its name, but it turned out to be modern and delightful with a dining hall and maid service. It was like heaven, no work, and much play.

Marshfield was a quaint little town with gambling halls and mud streets. It was surrounded by forests and rolling hills. They had taken several carriages out into the surrounding environs. The weather had been excellent. Cool and crisp, but no snow, as yet. The people were hospitable Scandinavians for the most part, but they had also encountered native Indians. The Indians looked much less frightening than Ida had thought they might, dressed as they were in the everyday clothes of the white men, but predictably with a straw hat and an eagle feather or two. All in all, it had been a relaxing and exciting honeymoon, but today they would catch the train back.

Ida's fingers played along her husband's chin, feeling the stubble of whiskers. "Have you ever thought about growing a beard?"

John considered a moment. "I will if you want me to, but I always thought I'd look mighty strange in a beard. Bare-footed head and flowing beard don't see to go together."

"Mmm. I don't know. Maybe we can find a fake beard and try it on…see how it looks before you take the plunge."

He laughed. "Sure. It would be nice not to have to shave. Frank grows a beard for winter sometimes."

"Does he? How does he look?"

"Good, but he says it itches once the weather gets warm."

"Are you sure we must go back today?" Ida changed the subject.

"I'm afraid so. Duty calls. They won't hold my job forever."

"I'm glad we shipped all my goods to Woodstock before the wedding so we can go right to your mother's."

"Yes, you are a smart cookie, that's for sure. You think of all the things I don't. We make a good pair."

"Yes, we do," said Ida. She hoped it was true. "Take me home to Woodstock, John."

And he did.

I SEE BY THE PAPER…

Factories Close.

Three factories in the Fox river manufacturing district in northern Illinois have shut down because their employes, numbering nearly 1,500 refused to promise, in individual agreements, not to strike. These factories furnish rods and sheet metal to a number of manufacturers, and we are likely to see a ripple effect.

News from Factory.

John Wienke was layed off last Wednesday on account of the lack of stock.

Woodstock Sentinel, December 18, 1902.

"But, John. How could this happen? What did you do? People don't just get fired over nothing." Ida was beside herself. Married but a month and already – tragedy.

"Ida, I didn't do anything. It has to do with getting the materials that they need when they need them. The suppliers are struggling with unions and have shut their doors, so they aren't getting in the raw materials to make typewriters. It's good for business to be flexible. And I didn't get fired. I got laid off."

"Did the other workers get laid off? How long will you be 'laid off'?"

"I was the first to go since, I'm inspecting finished machines, but there will be more. And they didn't say how long – a few days or maybe a few weeks. Could be as much as a month or two, depending on the strikes."

"Well, I am sorry, but it doesn't make sense to me. You are a supervisor why would they lay you off and not someone who had been there a shorter time? Or give you a different job? Something is fishy. You go back in there and tell them that this isn't right, and if you are being fired for something, what is it?"

"Ida." John rubbed his face, trying to think of a way to explain. "I wasn't fired. I was laid off. I am an inspector, and without stock, there is nothing to inspect."

"Why can't you question them? You bring me down here to live in your mother's house," tears sprung to her eyes, "and now you are idle. What am I to think? Did you miss too much work for the wedding and honeymoon? Did you do something wrong that caused a shortfall of stock? What? You can tell me."

John looked down like a guilty little boy unable to meet her blazing tear-filled eyes. They were sitting at his mother's kitchen table. Sophia had excused herself to her bedroom early on in this conversation. He didn't know what to say. As far as he knew, he had done nothing wrong at work, but he agreed that the layoff was strange, especially when the factory had claimed they wanted to increase production. But he was sure there were good reasons.

"I don't know, but they will most likely call me back soon and until then—"

"Until then we will live on bread and water!" said Ida.

"No, of course not. Ma will feed us, and I'll look for a temporary job."

"No, I'm not going to live off your mother! I will go back and live off my own mother and hope that I can get my job back at the laundry or I'll sew."

"Couldn't you sew here?"

"I don't know anyone here. How would I get customers?"

"I could—"

"You could what? You don't even have a position! You could end up at the poor farm."

"Come on, think about this. Think about what your parents will think of me if you go running home."

She looked at him, incredulous. "The only thing I can think about is if you have been lying to me about a steady job. I'm not thinking about your reputation at present," said Ida. Her eyes were cold.

"I will not for one moment consider losing you because of this." He rose and took her up in his arms. "You are the love of my life." He paused, holding her tight. She was

---

I SEE BY THE PAPER...

Personal Mention.

Mrs. John Wienke is visiting her parents, Mr. and Mrs. M. Stoffel at Racine, Wis.

Many Deserted Wives.

Many cases of wife desertion are reported from various sections of the city. All told there are possibly forty women here, some with large families, who cannot tell where their husbands are, they having disap-peared as long ago as one year and at least six months.

Most of the women are on the poor list, being forced to apply for help. District Attorney Gittins is obligation to listen to many sad and pitiful tales by deserted women. A great many of them have made good and economical helpmates, but for some reason, unexplainable, their husbands suddenly disappeared.

In a great many cases letters have been received from these truant men, stating that they will never return and in others that perhaps they will come home after the winter is over. Efforts have been made to apprehend a number of the heartless fellows, but without success, for when a city from which letters were received was searched the men could not be located.

The expense to the city of Racine in caring for the unfortunate women and children is quite heavy and it does seem as if some measures could be adopted to bring a number of these heartless husbands to justice.

Woodstock Sentinel, December 25, 1902.

stiff in his embrace. He considered the options, and then ventured, "Okay, why don't you go home for a few days, for the holidays, and I'll work on arrangements. Our own place and a job. I don't want you to worry about anything. It will be alright I promise."

She relaxed a bit – but then pushed away. "I have to go pack. I want to be on the 10:00 a.m. train tomorrow."

"Tomorrow? But—"

"No, buts. You get your house in order, John Wienke, and then we'll see where we are." With that, she turned and headed up the stairs to their bedroom.

John stared after her. What was going on? Was she leaving him? What was wrong with her? After pushing him into marriage before he had time to establish himself, now she was leaving? So much for Al's idea of a helpmate. Maybe she'd calm down by morning. Maybe she was just homesick for her mother. Maybe… John sunk down into a chair and put his head in his hands. OK, fly to your mother, little Ida. I'll be waiting right here when you return.

John sat, eyes distant, nursing a drink and his ego at the Pleasure Club. The place wasn't jumping on this last day of the year. A few men came and went, working with the weights, jump ropes or punching bag. They greeted him but then retreated without question. He would stay here as long as they would let him.

He had secured a job at the same grocery shop he had worked at as a kid, as the delivery, stocking, and clean-up person. It would be steady work until something else came up, or he could sell several of his lots to make ends meet if it came to it. Still, he was unwavering in his decision to marry Ida; it was by far the best choice he'd made in the last year no matter this difficult situation. He put his head in his hands and took a deep cleansing breath.

"Hey, brother! What are you doing here?" Bob's voice rang out in the vacant hall. "Shouldn't you be home with your wife and mother?"

Ach meine Gott! John thought. Bob. This is all he needed to complete the fall from grace.

"Ida is in Wisconsin, and I am here drowning my sorrows," said John. He had always believed that honesty was the best policy.

"I came in for calisthenics."

"Go ahead. You won't bother me."

Bob sat down. "What's going on?" he asked.

John looked up, "Oh Bob, don't worry yourself. Go, get strong." He took a sip of his drink, touted as a healing elixir.

"What are you drinking?"

"Sarsaparilla."

"Hm. Wanna go get a real drink?"

John considered. A waste of money, but then hadn't he broken other rules on the books this year. "OK," he said, "Lead on."

Bob led him down the stairs and out the door. A little beer wouldn't hurt him and might help him through the night – particularly *this* night – New Year's Eve.

As they headed toward Wienke and Schneider's, John asked, "How are you? Got a real job, yet?"

"I'm still thinking about the factory."

John sniffed, "Well, I can't help you there anymore."

"What? Why not?"

"Got laid off. Got married and got laid off."

"You're kidding," Bob considered this, "Why?"

"Lack of inventory."

"Anyone else laid off?"

"You and Ida ask the same question! No, no one else was laid off or at least none that I know of."

Bob let the silence stretch a bit. "So, what now?"

"Back to being the boy at the grocery shop," John admitted.

Bob's voice was upbeat. "You better let me buy tonight."

"Gladly," John said. Maybe having a saloon-keeper brother at a time like this was a good thing. No judgment. "Thanks, brother.".

"Not a problem. Thanks for going out with me. I needed some company tonight, too."

At midnight they sang "Auld Lang Syne" with the others and toasted the new year. Bob stayed to help close the bar, and John
walked home alone with his thoughts about Ida, Bob and the passing years. This new year had better bring luck, he thought. He looked up at the night sky and experienced utter loneliness as he had never felt before. It was as if even God had turned his back.

His despair overwhelmed him, and he fell to his knees on the hard boardwalk, his hands clasped together, his head bowed, and he prayed. "Father, do not forsake me. Please, I beg you…forgive my indiscretion with Ida. I love her so…as I love and praise you and your son. What we did was wrong. By your grace, please bring my wife back to me that we can be true to our vows. If you bless our union with a child, we will bring him up right in the church. I cannot promise that I will never again stray from your path, but I will try my best to provide a loving Christian home for my family." He paused. "Thy will be done. In Jesus name, Amen."
John looked back up at the Milky Way as it spread across the winter sky. He felt better. He would sleep better knowing everything was now in God's hands. At least, he hoped he would.

The Wienke brothers at John and Ida's
Wedding.
(L to R): William, Frank, Al, John, and
best man Bob.

J. Nicholas and Louisa Stoffel
Circa 1902.

Learning to Play Ball - 1903

Bob hustled up the boardwalk and rounded the square toward the grocery shop, his feet carrying him swiftly. He crossed Main Street, leaping across puddles still there from the freak rain on New Year's Day. He jumped up onto the walk and whooped, causing people to back away in distrust, but he just smiled his infectious smile and got one in return.

> **I SEE BY THE PAPER…**
>
> **Personal Mention.**
> Joe Connors and Robert Wienke were initiated into the mysteries of the order of Elks at Elgin the past week. It is said that they didn't do much to Joe.
>
> *Woodstock Sentinel*, January 1, 1903.

He burst into the shop, "Oh my God, John. John! Oh my God!"

John hurried out of the back room where he had been cleaning up onion skins from a new shipment. The onions were beautiful, baseball-sized, firm and ready to eat. He could just about taste a thick slice on a juicy ground beef patty sandwich, his favorite.

> **I SEE BY THE PAPER…**
>
> **Happenings.**
> Mrs. John Wienke of Wood-stock, Ill. is spending several days with her sister, Miss Clara Doering of Huron street.
>
> *Racine Journal Times*, January 2, 1903.

"Shhhhh. Language," he cajoled as he grabbed the boy's arm and ushered him to the back. Mr. Austin looked up from his newspaper. Luckily, there were no patrons in the store.

"Oh, sorry," Bob whispered, but then burst out, "I heard at the Elks meeting that the leagues are going to have a WORLD SERIES!!! Can you believe it! The Chicago National leaguers against some no-name American League team. A real shoot out! What a day it will be! Can't you just see the crowd! It's the best news in…well…forever!!"

"Wow. That's great, Bob." John dropped his arm. "But how can you be so sure it will be the Orphans and not the Cardinals or the Beaneaters?"

"I just know! And don't call them the Orphans or the Remnants or the Microbes or even the Colts. They are Selee's Cubs now, and the best team in the world. You'll see."

Johns demeanor sobered. He took up his broom and looked down at the job still to be done, his voice flat, "Well best of luck to them. I hope you get to go."

Bob's enthusiasm seemed to drain. "She's not back yet."

"Nope."

"Have you talked to her?"

"Nope."

"Does she know you have a job."

"Nope."

"Stop being such a stubborn Deutscher! Call her."

> ### I SEE BY THE PAPER…
>
> #### Blizzards for January.
>
> According to Rev. Irl R. Hicks January begins in the midst of unsettled weather with rain and snow striking many localities. A sharp, short change to cold, northwesterly winds and rising barometers will follow closely these reactionary storms.
>
> The second storm period will be central on the 6th. As this change moves eastward falling barometer will attend with growing cloudiness, causing general rains with winter lightning and thunder, ending in sleet and snow. Snow blockades and blizzards over the northern and western sections need not cause surprise.
>
> Four other regular storm periods are scheduled for the month, attended by sharp, cold weather, snow and blizzards. They are central on the 12th, 15th, 23rd and 29th. As a rule one to three bright, pleasant days are enjoyed before the actual storm periods, and readers are cautioned to plan during these days for the stormy ones which are sure to follow.
>
> Put yourself in sympathy with nature, provide fuel and provisions at your command. January is one of the most severe months of the year, so heed these timely admonitions.
>
> *Woodstock Sentinel*, January 8, 1903.

"Call her? I can't make my case over one of those damned contraptions."

"John. Language." They looked at each other and began to laugh. The laughter continued a bit too long and was a bit too hysterical, but in the end, they just patted each other's shoulder and started over.

"Maybe it's time for a trip to Racine?"

"I didn't leave…I'm not going up there begging. I suppose I could write to her."

"Great idea."

The front bell dinged. John looked up and started for the front then stopped when Bob said, "Mr. Austin's there. He can handle it. OK, if you write, what would you say?"

John turned back to Bob considering for a full minute. "Well, I'm not sure…I think I'd say something like…Ida, I love you, and I want you to come back to Woodstock. I know we hit a rough patch right out of the gate, but I love you, and all I want to do is make a good life for you and our family. And you can trust me when I say I will do it, because—"

"I know you will," a female voice interrupted.

John froze looking at Bob's smiling face. Bob nodded over his brother's shoulder and moved around him, attempted to tip his hat to Ida, but he realized at the last minute that he had on a knit stocking cap and instead changed it into a salute of sorts and continued out to examine the groceries on the main floor.

John turned and dropped the broom to the floor with a smack. Ida. She rushed across the room and into his arms.

"I'm back, and I'll never leave you again," she said. Tears wet his grocer's apron.

"Oh, Ida!" He closed his eyes and held her close. *Thank you, God!*

January 17, 1903
365 Lincoln Avenue
Woodstock, Illinois

Dearest Mama,

    I hope this finds you healthy and glad for your sound house in this cold and snowy winter. This last storm had everything, rain, thunder, sleet and then piles of snow. We were nearly at a standstill for a full day. It was nice. John even had a chance to go to one of the infamous Woodstock evenings a few nights ago but chose to be at home with me. Such a loving husband.

I think I can tell you now that, yes, I am with child. My red-headed aunt failed to appear again this month and we are so excited. I do hope it's a boy so we can get that whole thing about junior out of the way. But we best start thinking about girl names also. What do you think of Frances? John's middle name is Francis so it would seem appropriate if the baby isn't a junior.

We are still under Mother Wienke's roof, of course, and will be for some time I suspect, although in his excitement of seeing me, John did begin talking about building "me" a home with a large kitchen. John is getting called back to the typewriter factory as of February 2, as he says now that he expected to be. I doubt he did. He thinks his brothers made it happen by talking to the powers that be. And Bob has applied for work at the factory, also. That would make four of the brothers all building typewriters. They'll soon be taking over the whole company, I suspect. John is none too happy working there. I think he was happier pushing a broom at the grocery shop this past month. He genuinely loves grocery work.

When I was home, Herman and I were talking about his desire to open a mercantile. Interesting how my two favorite men both are drawn to the same things. I must write to him about John's plans. Do you think he'd consider coming to Woodstock?

Well, I better run this over to the train. I miss all of you. Please greet Papa Stoffel for me and give my love to Clara and Herman. Tell them I'll write soon.

Love,
Ida

"Mama," Clara called out distractedly as she glanced through the mail. "Lots of mail today. A letter from Emma. Also, one here from Ida."

"Lies mir die von Ida," said her mother. She came into the parlor from the kitchen wiping her hands on her apron.

Clara handed over Ida's envelope. "Why are you so wrought up, so aufgeregt?"

Mama tore open the letter and tried to read it. "Ach, es ist auf Englisch!"

"Here, give it to me," Clara said. And she began to translate Ida's letter into understandable German.

"Acht, you Deusch ist no gut," Mama commented, her English strained, but also understandable.

Clara forged on and upon reaching the second paragraph she squealed with glee. "Ein Kind!! She's going to have a baby!"

"Lessen!" Mama commanded.

"I AM reading! She says, 'Ich denken, ich kann jetzt sagen, yes, ich bin mit Kind.'" Clara danced around the room as she read on and a big smile broke out on Mama's face. She muttered under her breath, "Danke, gnädiger Herr." Thank you, gracious Lord!

Clara finished off the letter and handed it to her mother, smiling. "I'm going upstairs and write to her, right now. She wants to name a girl Frances? How horrible. I'm going to push for Daisy; isn't that a nice name? Like in the comic strip. A little girl named Daisy Mae that I can dress up and take to the Hotel Racine! Oh Mama, das ist wunderbar!!" She took two steps at a time as she raced to her writing desk.

Mama sat down on the couch, letters in hand. She would read Emma's in a moment. It would be in German. She folded her hands and said a short prayer asking God to bless her middle daughter and her husband and their life together. She had been surprised when Ida showed up in Racine barely a month after the marriage and stayed so long without contact with John. Ida had said that she was thinking. Mama had told her to remember that even the best plans don't always work out the exact way that one sees them from afar. One must be flexible. Ida had also told Mama that she had missed a period.

"Vielleicht ist John nicht ganz bereit eine Familie zu haben," she had said to Ida.

"He's not ready to have a family? He's thirty-three years old…how long should I wait, until he's forty, fifty, how about sixty when we are too old to have children," Ida had countered.

"Ja, aber jetzt könnte es ein Kind zum Nachdenken geben."

"I know. There may be a child to think about," her eyes welled with tears. "I'm not going to tell him about that until I know for sure. That should not be the solution to our disagreement. Das sollte nicht die Lösung sein."

Mama had hugged her daughter and let her cry, then had given her the space to think. When she had said on New Year's Day that she was going back to Woodstock the next day, Louisa had been glad but worried. And now this first letter verified their reconciliation. Gott ist Gut, she thought.

"Ver goest du?" Sophia asked as Ida made her way, as quietly as she could, down the stairs toward the front door.

Ida paused, "I'm going to my friend Lena's house for lunch and catching up."

Sophia came around the corner and looked at her. "Bist du warm genug angezogen?"

"Yes, Mother Wienke, I am dressed quite warmly. I'll be fine. It's a bright sunny day."

"OK. Haft gut time," Sophia gave in with reluctance. Ida was pregnant and shouldn't be out walking on the ice and snow. What if she fell? But Sophia didn't have any authority to keep her housed up. If one of the boys had been around, she would have insisted Ida be taken by buggy, but no boys today. "Achtung, vatch stepping," she called out as Ida made her way down to the plank sidewalk.

> **Fat Lady.**
> Don't sleep too much; exercise; don't eat fats and sweets. To reduce flesh rapidly take Rocky Mountain Tea. Acts directly on the fatty tissues.

"I will," Ida called back. Imagine, she wants me to just sit in that house and do nothing for the next five months. Maybe if I was further along, it might be smart, but I'm fine right now, barely showing. She was quite toasty and confident with the hat, muffler, and boots she had splurged on last winter at Gimbel's in downtown Milwaukee. She had never been better.

It was a bit of a journey from Sophia's house to Lena's but not much more than a mile. Ida walked up Washington and turned onto Dane Street and then turned left onto Hoy Street and on down to West Jackson. There were places where the boardwalks were blocked with snow, and she had to move out into the muddy street, but all in all, it was a very satisfying walk.

"You WALKED?" Lena gasped, when she saw Ida's face at the door.

"I'm fine. I walked everywhere in Racine. The only time I hopped a streetcar was when I would go up to Milwaukee."

"Racine had streetcars to Milwaukee?"

"Yes, we do." Ida laughed. "That's how I got these fashionable boots. Bought them last spring at Gimbel's."

"Oh, I would love to go shopping at Gimbel's. Here give me your coat. Come, sit down. Evie is asleep, so we will have at least a few minutes of adult conversation. How are things at Sophia's?"

"Fine, except she treats me like a carton of eggs," Ida grumbled.

"I can't imagine myself living with her. Maybe she is overly protective because she never had girls, and now she has one."

I SEE BY THE PAPER...

Personal Mention.

Born to Mr. and Mrs. Frank Wienke, Wednesday, Feb. 4, 1903, a son, Clayton.

G. W. Webster had a runaway last Tuesday. His team became frightened at the factory whistle and ran three or four blocks before they could be stopped. In endeavoring to stop the team Mr. Webster was slightly injured but will be able to take up his milk route soon.

Local Intelligence.

Mr. Sueji Miyamori has written that he will reserve Saturday evening, Feb. 14, for the people of Woodstock and will, without fail, give us his lecture on Japan and the Japanese, at the Baptist church.

Report of Woodstock Public library for week ending Feb. 1, 1903: Number of visitors, 479; number of books loaned, 247.

Mrs. C. M. Curtis, Librarian.

Woodstock Sentinel, February 5, 1903.

"Could be, but I sometimes feel like a prisoner in that house, but it should get better as the weather improves."

"Well, I have to agree with her that walking outside in this weather is very, very…um…obstacle-filled. I'm glad you were able to manage it without falling. You didn't, did you?" Ida shook her head. "Good! Don't want to jar anything loose too early. Al will be home for lunch around 1:00 p.m. He can take you back, so you don't have to take chances in both directions."

"Oh, for heaven's sake, you'd think that a woman had never had a baby in this city before."

Lena laughed. "I'm not as worried about you as I am about your precious cargo. Would you like lemonade? And I made some little sandwiches like I used to make before Evie joined us."

"Oh, she is such a good baby; look at her sleeping so that Mama and Aunt Ida can talk."

> **I SEE BY THE PAPER…**
>
> **AN OPEN LETTER**
> **To the Woodstock Friends of**
> **the Chicago Industrial Home.**
>
> Supporting friends of the homeless and orphans and those who would like to hear what we are doing at the orphan home, we take the pleasure of writing to you.
>
> In the last week we have taken in six little helpless ones, one a babe of four weeks. Three of these were taken from our own county. This makes nineteen children we have taken and cared for from our own county in the last year and a half. Of this number we have placed six in good Christian homes.
>
> We would be much pleased if more of our friends could make it convenient to call any day (except Sunday) and see our happy family and go through our home. We endeavor to give the children good, well-cooked food, and good, comfortable, clean clothing also to keep the home in sanitary condition.
>
> Whatsoever He (Jesus)
> Saith unto you, do it.
> Yours to care for the helpless,
> MRS. MINNIE BARDELL
> The Matron.
>
> *Woodstock Sentinel.*

"She is a good baby, but I don't want to talk about children. I want to talk about shoes at Gimbel's and your family and John and well…anything…except for children."

"Well, let's see. Herman got married," Ida started.

"He DID!" Lena said, too loudly. They both held their breaths, but the crying didn't start.

"Yes." Ida's tone was hushed. "He married Bessie Leahy; I don't think you know her. They got married in the parsonage of the Congregational Pastor. Looks like we've lost another

Lutheran to his wife's religion. She didn't have a gown but wore a traveling dress. They came in together, said, 'I do,' accepted a toast from the best man, and hopped the train to Chicago. You know they will be gone for a month touring down South in the warm weather."

"How nice," said Lena. As Ida spoke, Lena put the plate of sandwiches on the table. She added small china tea plates, a teapot, and cups and saucers in a beautiful yellow rose pattern to the table.

"Oh, these are lovely," said Ida. "You know what the paper said about Bessie? Mama sent me the clipping. I brought it along to read to you." She reached into the bosom of her dress and pulled out a small piece of newsprint, unfolded it, and read, "The bride is an estimable young lady with an interesting personality." Both women burst out laughing and then hushed each other.

> **I SEE BY THE PAPER...**
>
> **Personal Mention.**
>
> Connors & Stone are fixing up their saloon on Main Street in an elaborate manner. They are putting in a steel ceiling and papering and painting the side walls and giving their place of business a general overhauling and intend, when completed, to have one of the finest rooms in the county. Albert Wienke is doing the work, which, in itself, is a guarantee that it will be properly done.
>
> *Woodstock Sentinel*, March 5, 1903.

"An interesting personality? I wonder what that means?"

"The paper said that Herman was 'well known among the businessmen and is connected to the Zahn Dry Goods company.'"

"Well, that is faint praise also. Maybe it's just the paper. They make up something when they don't know the bride and groom. Here in Woodstock, the praise is always filled with hyperbole, the best, the greatest, the prettiest, the most well-known. Everything in Woodstock is the most prosperous and up-to-date!"

"You mean it isn't? My fine and beloved husband has told me wonderful stories about this grand city. Am I not to believe them?"

"If you must. Don't listen to me. I've been here only a year, and I'm so glad to have a good friend in Woodstock at last. The people are all nice and polite, but best friends are hard to find if you didn't grow up in the area."

"Hm. Interesting. Have you and Al been going to church?"

"We have a few times, but he is less than enthusiastic about going. He and Bob like to…um… 'travel' on Sundays," she put quotes around the word.

"What does that mean? Travel?'" asked Ida, copying the gesture.

"Go places, see things, enjoy events. Like going up to Lake Geneva for the day."

"Don't you go with him?"

"At first, I did a few times, but then I got pregnant, and it was unseemly, and then I had a baby, and so now I'm stuck here," Lena's eyes filled with tears.

"But he still goes?"

"Not as often, I guess, but yes," Lena said. She dabbed at her eyes. "Oh, listen to me! Let's not talk about disappointments, but rather…," she thought a moment, "Let's talk about Gimbels! When were you last there?"

The two lapsed into a comfortable conversation about styles and the city of Milwaukee, but Ida was left with an uneasy feeling. She was sure that John would not be going off with the boys constantly, but who knew for sure. She felt so sorry that Lena was less than happy and vowed to be the best friend she could possibly be in this alien land.

March 20, 1903
365 Lincoln Avenue
Woodstock, Illinois

Dear Herman and Bessie:

I just wanted to drop you a note and say how nice Mama thought your wedding was. I'm sure you are back from your honeymoon and settling into your house by now. Everything is fine here and we are all healthy if not wealthy — ha. Time marches on. I am anxious for spring to come so I can get out and walk as I was used to in Racine. Woodstock still has wooden walkways although the issue of improving them is under continual discussion at the city council meetings. John brings back detailed accounts of those for my edification. I'm learning the players slowly, and John certainly has a desire to join them.

Herman, I was thinking about our conversation last December about your desire to open a store but finding that it was a very difficult thing to do in Racine where so many are already established. The thought has been flitting around in my head since then that you and John might be able to join forces to start something here in Woodstock that would be more successful than in Racine. This is a very nice little town that prides itself on being up-to-date and cultured. John has had the idea of opening a grocery shop or bakery since I met him and is working toward that by making good investments and saving his wages. That is a big reason we are living with his mother, to save the rent money we might otherwise "throw to the wind."

Would you consider talking to John about this possibility? He is a hard worker and very dedicated to making a life for us here in this growing town. You could lean on each other. It would be a very nice place for you and Bessie to raise a family. Anyway, I hope you will think well of us and our predicament. Talk to him…please?

Bessie, Mama said your traveling ensemble was beautiful.

Your favorite sister,

Ida

John, always the grocer, scanned the paper. "EAT TONS OF PRUNES" screamed the headline, so he read on…

A Frenchman planted a prune tree out in California in 1870. It was the only prune tree in the state. All the prunes used in the United States at the time came from France. But now as a result of the prune tree that M. Pellar planted California every year ships enormous quantities of prunes not only to France but to all European countries, says the *Chicago Tribune*.

John was amazed. We are exporting prunes to Europe. That's a feather in the American hat, and they would be most likely cheaper than the imported ones, too.

> The growth of the prune industry in California all came from Pellar's single tree. It was found that the prune, which is a species of purple plum, throve on the Pacific coast, and that the hot dry weather of the country brought out its saccharine qualities. The first orchard was planted in the Santa Clara valley, just south of San Francisco, a region which is now the prune center of the state. It was only ten acres in extent and began to yield in 1875. In four years, the trees produced $14,000 worth of fruit.
> The size of the prune crop in California is so enormous that the most cynical boarder in any boarding house in Chicago would be surprised. In 1901 the state produced 150,000,000 pounds of prunes, and the total crop of the year just passed exceeded that of the preceding year by several thousand tons. If put into ten-ton freight cars, the California prune-

"John, where are you?" Ida called out. It was Sunday afternoon, a time for family, but John had disappeared.

"I'm down here…in the basement."

Ida poked her head around the corner at the top of the stairs. "What are you doing?" she asked.

"Nothing. Just relaxing and catching up on my reading."

"Can't you relax up here in company? William and Lizzie just stopped by." John's oldest brother was the city engineer. He had been in the ranks of the civil servants since he was in his twenties. William was as steady as they came.

"OK. I'll be up in a minute," John called, going back to his article….

> …freight cars, the California prune crop of 1902 would fill a train reaching from Chicago to Buffalo.
> The American prune has found its way into the European market for the same reason that it is sweeter and pleasanter to the taste than the fruit raised there. The California prune, for

> instance, is dried wholly out of doors, for the long period of absolutely rainless weather, which prevails in California from July 1 to October 1, permits the drying trays to remain out of doors day and night. The French and other kinds of European prunes are dried in kilns for fear of exposure to rains, and the artificial heat fails to bring out all the rich sugar products of the pulp.
>
> San Jose, the county seat of Santa Clara county, is the chief prune center of California, and in its mountain-encircled valley, there are 3,567,140 bearing prune trees. There are, besides, great orchards of apricot, cherry, peach and olive trees, so that in this one county there are about 5,000,000 fruit trees. Fruit raising is carried on there on such a grand scale that some orchards of prunes 30 acres are required in the busy season simply as a drying field for the fruit trays.

John folded the newspaper. Imagine that…he pictured drying racks covering most of the area of Woodstock. Well, now he knew how—

"John, WHAT are you DOING down there?" Ida had advanced several steps down the basement stairs, and she sounded irritated.

John got up, "I was reading about the prunes grown in California, the best prunes in the world." He came up the steps and kissed her on the cheek.

"Prunes? Are you not feeling well? Do you have constipation?"

"No, I'm fine, but now I know that we will have California prunes at the grocery shop."

"Oh. Well. That's fine, but—"

"Yes, I know…William and Lizzie. Are the boys with them?" He took her hand, and they went up the stairs to the kitchen and into the parlor to entertain.

I SEE BY THE PAPER…

Personal Mention.

Mrs. Theo. Lake, a sister of Mrs. Albert Wienke of this city, died at her home in Beloit, Wis., Tuesday, March 24, 1903, after an illness of only one week. She left a baby one week old, besides her family to mourn her loss.

Woodstock Sentinel, March 16, 1903.

"Lena?" Ida found her friend at Austin's grocery shop fondling a bag of coffee beans, lost in thought.

"I can't quite decide if I should buy this or not. What do you think? Is this the best coffee I can buy or is there better? Do you think Al will like it?"

Ida looked around, "Where is Evie, Lena?"

"Evie? Oh, with Ma Wienke. I'm filling the coffers with coffee." She continued to stare at the coffee bag but smiled at her own joke.

"Well, we all need to do that now and again. I was so sorry to hear about Lillie's death. Did you go to Beloit for the funeral?"

"No, Al had important work to accomplish and didn't want me traveling with the baby alone."

"Oh no. I'm so sorry. It is so sad."

"Yes. Impossible."

Ida paused wondering where to go in the conversation. "How is the new house coming? Do you need help getting moved?"

"House? I don't know…sometimes…sometimes I think I should be in Beloit, and let the next woman have the house," she blurted out, tears springing to her eyes.

Without hesitation, Ida put an arm around her and guided her toward the storeroom. She caught Mr. Austin's eye and indicated the back room with a nod in that direction, and he nodded back. Nice understanding man.

"Here, pull up a barrel. I'll take 'Pickles' and you take 'Olives'," Ida sat Lena down on the barrel.

Lena cried into her handkerchief. Ida patted her arm and said, "Tell me what's happening."

Lena laughed without warning. "I feel such a fool. Al is about ready to throw me over for a more sunshiny model if he hasn't already."

"Oh, I doubt that."

"It's just…it's just…all I do is take care of his baby when there is a baby in Wisconsin that has no mother to care for her," she sobbed.

Ida let her cry a bit and then tried again. "Do you know what's happening with Theo and Berty?"

"As far as I know, they are still in Helenville, over by Jefferson, miles away. But," she looked Ida straight in the face and gripped her arms, "Who is feeding that child? She is but a few weeks old. Theo can't nurse her. She will die just like my sister." More tears.

"What does Al say?"

"Oh, he says I'm crazy. Doctor thinks I'm crazy. Probably Ma Wienke thinks I'm crazy."

"I don't think you're crazy. But—"

"Everyone always follows 'I don't think you're crazy' with 'but.'"

> **I SEE BY THE PAPER…**
>
> **News from the Factory.**
>
> Frank Martin left last Thursday for Florida where he has gone to regain his health. He was accompanied as far as Chicago by Joe Connors and Robert Wienke, who saw him safely started on his long journey.
>
> The Oliver factory now has a well-organized fire department, with Fire Marshall Frank Wienke in command.
>
> *Woodstock Sentinel*, April 9, 1903.

Ida waited for a beat and, in the calmest voice she could muster, said, "I don't think you're crazy. What needs to be done to protect the child?"

Lena paused and considered the question, "She needs to come live with us. I'm nursing Evie who doesn't take all she can now that she's on solid food. I have more than enough to feed Berty also."

"OK, how will Theo feel about this?"

"I don't know."

"How will Al feel about this?"

"He won't care as long as it doesn't stop him from doing what he wants to do."

"Ok, the first step then is to see if we can find out how Theo would feel about allowing the aunts to furnish care for this baby. If he says, 'yes,' we are all set, but if he says 'no,' then we have to bring in the reserves to persuade him."

"Why would he say, 'no'?"

"I don't know. Let's just check before we act. Let's go see if we can figure out that telephone and call him. Do you have a number?"

"No," Lena said.

"Then let's call your folks and see if they have it."

Smiling her thanks to Mr. Austin, she led Lena out of the shop and up Jackson to her home. She dreaded trying to get the phone to go through to Beloit, but if it would help her friend, she was willing to try. At the house, Lena showed Ida the phone.

"Do you know how to make a long-distance call?" asked Lena.

"I've only done it twice on the other end of the line, but I'm sure the hello-girl will help us." She picked up the receiver. "Do you know your parent's number?"

"Yes, 4382."

Ida double-clicked the receiver switch as John did.

"Hello, number please," said the hello-girl.

Ida swallowed hard, "Hello. This is Mrs. John Wienke. Mrs. Albert Wienke would like to talk to her mother in Beloit, Wisconsin."

"Fine. Number, please," said the pleasant voice.

"Oh yes, it's 4382 in Beloit, Wisconsin."

"One moment, please." Silence, then a buzzing which seemed endless.

"I don't think it's working," said Ida.

Then, "Hello?" said a tiny voice in the receiver. She handed the earpiece to Lena, nodding.

"Mama?"

"Ida," John whispered as he slid into bed, "are you asleep."

Ida sighed, what would she be at midnight? Without opening her eyes, she mumbled sleepily, "You jest getting home? Long meetin'."

"Yes, but guess who you are sleeping with," he cooed as he spooned up behind her.

"Tebby Roothevelt?" she said, tongue thick.

"No."

"King Edward?" It sounded more like "Ethwood."

"No."

"Governor Lahf.. La..Follette?" she finally managed.

"No, that's three guesses. All you get! You are sleeping with the newest member of the Dorr Township Committee!"

"Wondaful," Ida said, almost back asleep. "I…rather you were Tebby."

"Roosevelt? Why?"

"I'd be in da White Houth," and she began to snore lightly.

Ida sipped her coffee. Easter had been very strange here in Woodstock. Was it just the German Lutheran Church or had all the churches approached Easter with the sadness of Good Friday rather than the joy of the resurrection! She had come away from the church service without the satisfaction she normally felt – God was in his heaven and all was right in the world. She perused the front page of *The Woodstock Sentinel.* "EASTER DAY IN WOODSTOCK" read the headline. She read on…

Festival and Carol and Triumph Songs and Joyful Words in all the Churches.

More space would be required than can be allotted by even Sentinel-like liberality, if one were to faithfully report the many services held in this young city, expressing nobly the glad Easter day just past. One is reluctantly content with partially indicating the joyous, spiritual feasts which were prepared by the faithful in the various churches.

The shades of Lent were chased away when the morn of resurrection dawned in the east and the world awoke to a new life.

Well, she thought, this reporter has a way with words. Ida slid her eyes down the column. The Catholics claim to fame was being the earliest worshipers. The Baptist's service was described as "delightful and quite original." The Methodists were lauded for their offertory being "in furtherance of the system of 'benevolences' adhered to by the Methodist church at large, for the education of the colored race in the south." The Congregational church service sounded interesting with the choir and organ "re-enforced by violins, flute, and saxophone," – a saxophone in church? The paper claimed that the Presbyterian's "beloved pastor wore a smile broad enough to cover and comfort every sorrow of his great flock." How wonderful! She found the entry for the German Lutheran service:

> The German Lutheran church, Rev. Johannes Bertram, pastor, was a solemn temple of praise. Then 116 communicants advanced to the altar rail and received the symbols of bread and wine and with the more grateful hearts because a company of boys and girls joined them in taking their first communion. The chorales were: Auf Auf meim Hers mit Freuden, and Freuet euch ihr Christen alle.

Auf Auf meim Hers mit Freuden? "On, On My Heels with Joy?" she said, translating aloud. This reporter may have a way with words, but he surely had challenges with German. The "meim Hers" should be "mein Herz" *On, On my Heart with Joy.* She smiled. I suppose I wouldn't mind having joyful heels.

But the article was right about the service. Here it had been Easter, the most joyous day of the Christian year, and the paper described the service as *solemn.* These joyful songs were sung like dirges. Of course, the German language enhanced their dirge-ness, if that was a word. Maybe they did need a more progressive Lutheran church in town as John had talked about so often.

Easter in Woodstock had been solemn overall compared to her experience in Racine. Ida was used to blowing eggs and hiding them for Emma's children to find, from the Osterhase – Easter Bunny. Mama would order chocolate eggs and bunnies from Germany, and everyone, including the adults, had to wait until after church AND dinner to eat them along with the German chocolate cake in the shape of a lamb with coconut wool. Sometimes the eggs and bunnies had a surprise inside – nuts or jam for the children and a bit of alcohol for the adults.

She remembered that when they were all young, Mama would spend the months from New Year's Day to Easter in preparation for a celebration of new life. Why in Racine, Easter was celebrated for at least five days! Grundonnerstag, Maundy Thursday supper, had to include something green. The eggs in green Frankfurter sauce had always been one of Ida's favorites. And then fish on Karfreitag – fish and only fish, since Good Friday was a day of mourning – no singing, no laughing, no church bells ringing, just one meal of fish. Saturday was spent decorating the house and the yard with bright spring colors and flowers, painting eggs blown over the previous months, and stringing them together like a garland to decorate the Osterbaum – Easter tree. But best of all was Easter Sunday! It was joyful, the sermon was often funny, and there was a lot of laughing, eating, and candy.

What had happened in John's beloved Woodstock to make the Lutherans so solemn and serious. A time to pummel the sinners rather than rallying the saved. Next year, when she had her own house and a child to help blow and paint eggs, she vowed that she would change that mood around Easter and keep the German traditions alive. Yes, she would!

> **I SEE BY THE PAPER...**
>
> **Personal Mention.**
> Albert Wienke was in Chicago last Tuesday looking after business in connection with his large painting trade.
>
> *Woodstock Sentinel,* May 21, 1903.

She folded the paper and stood, looking around for something to do. This would be the time when her mother would begin spring cleaning, throwing the devil out with the dust. Did she dare to start cleaning her mothers-in-law's house? Mother Wienke had not said anything about spring cleaning. She wandered around the room she and John shared. She could at least clean this room well and then see what happened. She pulled up the throw rugs and placed them in the hall to be taken out and beaten – she would ask John to do that – and went down to the kitchen to retrieve a broom and dustpan.

"Vat's wronk. Vat are you doink?" Sophia's voice came from behind her as she leaned down for the dustpan.

"Nothing, Mother. I was just going to clean our room…you know, Easter is time for spring cleaning," she tried to sound jovial and turned to smile at Sophia.

"Ist es dreckig?"

"No, it's not dirty," she replied in what was, she hoped, a diplomatic tone, "But I haven't done any real cleaning up there since we moved in. It's the right time of year to spring clean, right after Easter."

"But du solltest nicht arbeiten. No gut for Kind."

"Why shouldn't I be working? It isn't going to affect the baby. I feel fine and just thought I'd do something productive. We have two women in this house. We should split the work up more so I'm being helpful."

"Du tink my haus ist nicht sauber – not clean?"

I SEE BY THE PAPER…

Floods and Wind Work Havoc in Middle West.

Wisconsin and Michigan report cyclones, floods, and hail storms. Many landslides and washouts have resulted from the high water, and railroad traffic, in Wisconsin especially is practically at a standstill. A huge tidal wave yesterday swept up the lake striking Racine with terrific force. Vessels lying in the harbor were lifted to the level of the docks. St. Joseph, Mich., and many points in Wisconsin report similar experiences.

The devastation in the middle West by wind and flood continues. Within the week past nearly 100 persons have been killed and many hundreds injured and millions of dollars' worth of property has been destroyed. Scarcely a town between Ohio and the Rocky mountains has been free from the fury of the storm, and numerous villages have been completely wiped out by tornadoes.

Chicago Inter-Ocean, May 28, 1903.

"Oh no, I just want to clean our room, beat the rugs and look for wool mice – Wollmause – under the bed, wash the linens and so forth. It is the least I can do for my husband and for you. But if you need help with other things around the house, please tell me. I've been very lazy and would like some chores to do."

"Vant to vork? Das ist gut auf Kind?"

"I don't think it will hurt the baby at all. If I had my own home, I'd have to clean. I won't lift anything heavy, and if I get tired, I will rest. I bet you didn't stop working when you were pregnant with the boys, did you."

> ## I SEE BY THE PAPER...
>
> **Deaths of Many Babies Blamed upon Mothers.**
>
> Many babies die every year because their mothers, for selfish reasons, refuse to nurse them, and are, therefore, guilty of the crime of child murder. This is one of the statements made by Dr. C.A. Lindsley, secretary of the Connecticut board of health and professor emeritus in Yale medical college.
>
> Dr. Lindsley asserts that more than 600 babies died last July, August, and September from cholera infantum, and that most of them were bottle-fed babies, or in other ways the victims of improper feeding.
>
> Dr. Lindsley believes that the mother who can nurse her baby but who, for selfish reasons, refuses to do so, is often guilty of crime. The natural nourishment of the human offspring during the first year of its life is found only at its mother's breast. No substitution for this can ever be made without risk of the disturbance of its digestion. While this is always true, it is more emphatically so during hot weather. A nursing baby, the mother being healthy, is immune to summer complaint if no other food is given it that that provided by nature.
>
> *Chicago Daily Tribune,* June 15, 1903.

"Nein. Bei Enkelkindern ist das anders."

Ida laughed, "Ja. It is different when it's your grandchildren, I suppose. I will be careful, I promise."

"Wie du willst! Do as you willst! I vill not stop du," and Sophia disappeared back into the parlor.

As Sophia sat back down to her embroidery, she shook her head. What a strong-willed woman Ida was. I hope John is ready for this. She will surely keep him in line.

Ida stood for a moment, her hands shaking a little, not quite knowing what to do. She took a deep breath and decided to soldier on. Picking up the dustpan, she retreated up the stairs into their room and closed the door. This wasn't her house, but this was her room, and she could clean it if she wanted!

She smacked down the dustpan and broom and then melted on to the bed sobbing. How long, John, how long?

June 1, 1903
Racine, Wisconsin

Dear Ida and John,

What a week we have had. Did you get hit by "the storm of the century" as they are calling it here? We had a storm seiche — do you know what that is? I was walking home for lunch in the rain; the worst of the storm had gone by, it seemed, so it was just sprinkling a bit, but suddenly people were yelling and screaming and running back up the hill from the lake as if a lake monster had been sighted or worse. I, of course, ran toward the lake hoping to get a story that the paper would like — I think I told you I'm going to be a reporter, but I need a good story to get them to notice me. It was amazing, but not something easily written about. The schooners and tugs and other boats in the harbor just started to lift up, higher and higher they went until they were floating above the docks, and of course, crashing their hulls into them. I never saw anything like that, and I daresay neither had most of the people in Racine. They were running and yelling "Tidal Wave!!" Since I didn't know how high this floating would go, I didn't go right down to the edge of the water, but I got close — maybe 50 yards away. A huge wave rushed forward bringing the boats with them. And then as quickly as it had started, the water began to recede. Some boats came down hard on the posts of the docks and got holes poked in them. A few came down on land, and at least one person was swept out into the lake. The larger schooners and tugs just demolished what they came down on. It was somewhat interesting to watch. But how does one write about something like that?

Then a police officer came over and told me I had to move back up the street to where others were standing. That was too bad because as soon as I turned my back, one of the schooners rolled on its side, and I missed it! I told the police officer that it was his fault I had missed the best part of the event. I was extra mad because up until then there had not been anything to write about, and I missed the only newsworthy part.

Of course, he thought my anger was funny and laughed at me! I turned around without so much as a howdy-do and walked home. I'm sure his name was Officer Common Bob Spoilsport.

We are fine here. I am working hard to save up some money so I can make future plans. I told Mama that as soon as I have $500, I'm moving to Chicago. I have about $86 already, so still a ways to go. Mama said she won't hold her breath. No one believes in me.

I know she thinks I'll just get married like all the other girls and fade away. I keep meeting nice men, but no one I'd want for the long term. They are so blah, with blah names and blah Racine ways. But don't worry, I'll keep looking.

The girls and I have been singing a bit, but for only a pittance…a donation that I am obliged to split three ways or donate to the church. Sad to have a talent and not be able to make money from it.

Have you thought any more about names for the baby? Did you like my suggestions? I especially think Daisy is a winner. I wish my name was Daisy instead of Clara. Maybe if you don't use it for the baby, I'll just start introducing myself as Daisy and

---

I SEE BY THE PAPER…

Harding—Steinke.

The host of friends of C. C. Harding will be pleased to learn of his marriage to Miss Linda Steinke of Beloit, Wis., Wednesday afternoon, June 10, 1903, at the home of Albert Wienke of this city, Rev. Bertram officiating. The ceremony was per-formed in the presence of but the immediate relatives of the contracting parties.

The bridegroom to this happy union has been a resident of Woodstock seven years. He is the skillful and efficient pattern-marker of the Oliver Typewriter factory. Everyone knows Clayt and know him to be large-hearted and generous and is an exceedingly popular young man and numbers his friends by the score. He is one of the oldest of the Oliver operatives, always attentive to business and has ever proven himself to be a valuable man to the Oliver management.

The bride is a comparative stranger in our city. She is the sister of Mrs. Albert Wienke, and is a young lady of fine disposition, of pleasant address and is well qualified to make their domestic life pleasant and agreeable.

Immediately after the ceremony the happy couple were driven to Nunda, where they took the 5:30 train for Chicago, thence to Freeport, Rockford and Beloit, expecting to be gone about one week, after which time they will be at home to their many friends at the residence of Mr. and Mrs. Albert Wienke.

Woodstock Sentinel, June 11, 1903.

see what happens. If I counted correctly from your wedding, the baby will come the beginning of August, aina? I will put in for time off when it happens. This is going to be one time when Mama is going to want to go by train to Woodstock.

I hope this finds you all well and happy. Let me know if you have any leads on a reporter's job. I'd even move to Woodstock for that.

Love,

Daisy

"John! Haven't seen you in a coon's age," Frank settled himself at the wooden lunch table next to his older brother.

"Well, they give even you a lunch break now? What's the world coming to," John said. He punched Frank's shoulder.

"Wahdid Ma pack you? Oh wait, I mean, wahdid Ida pack you?" Frank stole a glance in the paper sack in front of John.

"Yes, yes," John agreed, "they even argued about who will pack my lunch. Ida is trying to be patient, but Ma is a stubborn old deutsche dame. It's her house and don't you forget it! And the fatter Ida gets, the more she complains. She says she feels fine and doesn't need watching over, but then she carries rugs out to the line and beats them silly, exhausting herself."

Frank laughed. "Looks like you got two stubborn deutsche dames! Too many women under one roof. So, when are you breaking ground?"

John smiled, "Already have. Got your builder, Frank Keshard on that lot over east of McHenry Road." John looked a little conspiratorial. "But I also want to…," he paused, leaned closer, and lowered his voice, "get out of this place and into my own business. Two prongs one fork. Maybe it would be smarter to sell the new house for a profit that I can use to start the business. On the other hand, we might need a place before then after the baby is born. Can't you just see those two women having to go to King Solomon to decide who is more adequate to care for the child?"

Frank laughed again. "When is the anticipated arrival?"

"August, Ida says. And the surprise house is a distance from the business district. I have those two lots up in Wicker's addition, but they are also far from the square. Being close to the shopping district would mean being in walking distance to everything including my own shop if I end up opening one. I've been reading up on what goods I should carry and have decided on a grocery shop with all the best."

"Hm," Frank commented, mouth full of the Braunschweiger sandwich. He swallowed. "The best wurst in town, eh?"

John laughed. "That's not half bad…not half good either."

"So, can't you borrow some money from your bank? Aren't you vice president or something? I suppose they would be more willing to lend for a business than a house, right?"

John snorted and almost choked, "Vice President? Not hardly. Just a shareholder. And of course, the business will need more money to establish and build than the house will. So, I keep working, and Ida gets fatter as the weeks go by, and Ma just holds on tighter and tighter-"

"To her very last mama's boy," Frank teased.

John punched his shoulder again, harder this time. "Stop! She still has Bob to worry about. I'm sure he'll move back in as soon as Ida and I are gone. And your new place is up just off Washington, so you'll be close. She'll have plenty to do."

"And what do you know about the crowd at Al's house?" Frank inquired.

"Ach, it will be short-lived. Clayt and Linda will take over the rental when Al and Lena move into the house on Lincoln Avenue. Ah, there will be many grandchildren for Ma to tend eventually. How about sharing your little chitlins a bit more…take the load off Ida?"

"Ma does want the babies to hold. I'll see what I can do," said Frank. He crumpled up his lunch bag and sent it flying into the trash barrel. "Talk to Al, he owns lots all over town. He's working on a deal with Hoy to sell one near the square for three thousand."

I SEE BY THE PAPER...

Awful Horrors in Russia.

Dispatches from Odessa, Kishineff, and St. Petersburg say that another massacre of the Jews is expected between May 18 and 24, old style, which would be about June 1 of the English calendar. There has begun an almost general exodus for the Jews. Wealthy Hebrews are disposing of their property for whatever they can get. Many have abandoned homes and businesses rather than remaining and face the terrible slaughter which is anticipated. Many have already taken their departure. There is a Jewish population of 37,000 in Kieff, and all are affected. The agitation in Kieff is so great that the Jews are in dread of an immediate massacre.

A ministerial circular forbidding the Jews to defend themselves has been issues. It is expected that this step will stimulate Jewish emigration to America.

Chicago Inter Ocean.

"Three THOUSAND dollars?" John was beyond surprised.

"Ja," Frank confirmed. "I should have been a painter!" He smiled and got up, "Well, gotta run. Fire meeting... putting on a drill later in the week. Be ready!"

"So long, it's been good to know ya," John sang him away. Three thousand dollars! For a single lot? John sighed. He'd never have the money for a lot close to the square. But before that, he had a house to finish so that his son didn't come into the world homeless.

Ida's eyes flew open in horror. Wasn't it bad enough that she was as big as a house? Wasn't it bad enough that she felt like the fat lady in a circus? But now she had wet the bed. She reached for John. Not there. She rolled out of bed and observed the damage to the linens. What time was it? Light is streaming in, so it must...oh my, what was...the pain. Oh no, the baby was coming.

She pulled a housecoat around her shoulders and went to the top of the stairs, "John? Mother Wienke? The baby is coming."

John rushed into the foyer with the paper still in his hand. He looked up at her, concern written all over his face. "But...but...," he glanced at the date on the paper, "—but, it's only July second. You can't have the baby today." But the truth was, she could have the baby that day and did.

John sat holding his fussy little girl as an exhausted Ida came out of a nap. "Ugh," she complained. "Mothers don't tell daughters how much bearing will hurt. Here let me see if she'll suckle."

John handed the little bundle swaddled in a small flannel blanket to his wife, and she presented the baby with supper.

"How much did she weigh," Ida asked.

> **I SEE BY THE PAPER...**
>
> **Woodstock's Population.**
> That Woodstock is growing at a rapid rate is shown by comparing the figures of the school census for 1902 and those for 1903. While there is a decrease in the number of persons of school age to the number of 52, there is shown an increase in the population of 266 over the year 1902. Total population in 1902 was 3146 and in 1903 is 3413.
>
> *Woodstock Sentinel,* July 2, 1903.

"Just over eight pounds. About as much as a good pork roast," John, always the future grocer answered.

"Oh, mercy, John! She's a baby not a meatloaf," cajoled Ida, but she was smiling. "So, is it Helen Frances or Frances Helen?" she asked.

"Helen is a good first name, I think," said John.

"Helen Frances Wienke," Ida proclaimed. "So be it."

July 3, 1903
Racine, Wisconsin

Dear Ida,

Oh, goodness we are so surprised by Helen Frances' arrival a month early. She must be a tiny baby and we are so glad to hear that both baby and you are doing fine. Mama practically shrieked when she heard the news. She so wanted to be there with you when Helen made her appearance, but that was not to be.

> **I SEE BY THE PAPER...**
>
> **Local Intelligence.**
> Next horse sale, July 8.
> Rev. N. A. Sunderlin's subject for Sunday morning will be: *Hurrah!* And for the evening service: *Which Kingdom?*
> Report of Woodstock Public library for week ending June 28, 1903: Number of visitors, 301; number of books loaned, 138.
> Mrs. C. M. Curtis, Librarian.
> We are requested to remind all of an ordinance regulating the size of firecrackers that can be shot off in this city, which is not to exceed three inches in length. The use of toy pistols, revolvers and guns of all kinds is absolutely prohibited.
> The attention of the parents of a number of boys living on Washington street is called on to the fact that said boys must stop their play at the new houses being erected for Holz, Connors and Wienke. They are destroying property and unless they are compelled to stop, some of them will get into trouble.
>
> *Woodstock Sentinel,* July 2, 1903.

Thank John for his phone call yesterday to inform us of your happy and healthy baby.

We will come Saturday on the noon train. I can only stay the weekend, but Mama will, I believe, be with you until you kick her out. I jest, but she is packing quite a large trunk for the trip. Better bring the buckboard to meet us.

We assume that her baptism will be this weekend or next and I can't wait to give you the dress that I made with my own hands, working my fingers to the bone for my newest niece. So, don't buy one if you thought to.

I want to get this in the mailbox before the postman picks up so you will get it tomorrow or Friday. I can't wait to meet Helen, and of course, to see you and John also.

Love,
Clara

"Oh Ida, she is just precious. Hello, little Helen Frances," Lena nuzzled the top of the fuzzy head of the baby she was holding.

"Well, you have a precious one here, too," Ida interjected looking down at the tiny three-month-old in her arms. "Just think Bertha, you are going to grow up with a friend named Helen."

Lena smiled, "I'm not sure how long Theo will be able to do without her. He was very thankful that Mama and I stepped in to help, but I know he is just brokenhearted and misses her so much. It's good that the weather is improved. He says he will come down every week to see her, and I believe him."

"And how are you holding up with little Evie pulling at your apron strings and Berty at your breast and another baby on the way," asked Ida. "You haven't promised too much, have you?"

"I'm lucky that Evie just stopped breastfeeding and was insistent on going on food just when Berty needed help. You know Berty had stopped gaining weight on that cow's milk and was promising to be a sickly child, if not worse. But she has gained three pounds since coming home with us, so we are hopeful that no permanent damage was done. How has your first month of motherhood gone?"

"Fine, she is a happy baby so far and keeps me right on a schedule of two to three hours between feedings. John groans when she cries at night, but I love getting up with her, letting her eat and then falling asleep in the rocker with her until the next feeding. Is that wrong to do?"

"Ida, however, you can get your sleep in, do it. I spent several nights when Berty first came sitting in the rocker next to her bassinet, just so she wouldn't be alone if she woke up. It seemed to work, and she is much less fussy now. Mother's do what they must."

"Thank you, my dear friend. You have taught me so much about being a mother."

I SEE BY THE PAPER...

New Regulations for Pitchers, Fielders, and Men at Bat.

At a conference in Washington, D. C. between President Pulliam and his staff of the National league umpires, held at Old Point Comfort, radical measures were taken to enforce rules against kicking and rowdyism. The following important construction was placed on rule 29, relative to the pitcher's position: It is construed as meaning that the pitcher, in taking his position, shall place no part of either foot back of the rubber, nor shall he take more than one step in delivering the ball to the batsman. The enforcement of this rule will do away with all preliminary steps, either to the rear or side of the pitcher's rubber.

A stricter interpretation of rules prohibiting the batsman from balking the catcher and that of the fielders interfering with base runners when caught between the bases was agreed on. No batsman hereafter will be allowed to take first base when hit by a slowly delivered ball, the umpire to be the judge of such speed. Emphasis is laid on the rule requiring runners to keep within the three-foot lines in going to first, and, in general, notice is given of the literal enforcement of playing rules.

Chicago Tribune.

I SEE BY THE PAPER...

Olivers Are Again Declared Victor.

Wow! What? Another? It was indeed a nice game. Four shutouts in the last five games played. The Olivers should get an incubation and hatch out a few of those goose eggs. Hill pitched a superb game. The visitors, who undoubtedly know how to bat, couldn't do a thing with his zigzaggers, pollywaggers, and twisters. When they did hit the ball, they went straight up in pop flies, easily handled by the infield. Saturday the Olivers play the Union-Giants, the crack colored aggregation. Will it be a goose egg? If so, will the fruit go into Farmer Ryan's market basket?

Woodstock Sentinel, July 23, 1903.

"Oh no, it's I who should be thanking you. Where would I be without Pickles and Olives?"

They laughed and then noticed that both babies were fast asleep in their arms.

August 5, 1903
365 Lincoln Avenue
Woodstock, Illinois

Dear Mama and Clara,

Oh, little Helen misses you so much, Mama! And so do I. Thank you for coming to help with our move and taking care of the little one. She is sweet and good-natured and smart. I do believe that she knows you are no longer here. And Clara, thanks for bringing Mama down. I hope two round trips in less than a month didn't wear you out so much you had to miss work. You are a sweet sister.

> **I SEE BY THE PAPER...**
>
> **Opened a New Addition.**
>
> John J. Murphy has opened a new addition in the west end. It is known as the Bellevue addition and comprises eighteen lots. Already eight have been sold, the purchasers being as follows: Will Glazier, 2; Geroge Donnelley, 2; F. W. Doten, 1; Albert Wienke, 2; Benj. Anderson, 1.
>
> *Woodstock Sentinel,* July 30, 1903.

I was never so surprised in all my life...first by a month early baby and then with the new house. Isn't John sweet? When I think of all the complaining I've done over the last few months about sharing a house with Mother Wienke, well...my face turns red just thinking about it.

> **Lazy Liver.**
>
> For a lazy liver try Chamberlain's Stomach and Liver Tablets. They invigorate the liver, aid the digestion, regulate the bowels, and prevent bilious attacks.

I got the curtains hung last night, with my fine husband's help, and they make all the difference. One hardly notices the unpainted walls. Al has promised to make time to paint in the next month or so, but he is so busy it might be later. I suppose I should have put off moving until he could do the painting, but I couldn't wait a moment longer. My own new house.

Clara, the baptismal dress was just beautiful. I think Helen looked like a little angel in it. You have become quite the seamstress. I pride myself to think that I have had a hand in that. And the bonnet from you, Mama, made quite the ensemble. I also loved that she cried when the water hit her forehead. Do you think she will actually be a singer?

Mother Wienke has been very sweet this week since you've gone. Each day, she has brought over food for dinner and has sat and rocked Helen to sleep for her afternoon nap, so I could rest. I feel I may not have had Christian thoughts about her or maybe it's true that distance makes the heart grow fonder, even if the distance is blocks instead of miles.

Well, Helen says it is time to eat so I must go. John will take this to the station this evening so that you will get it before the weekend. Again, thank you for all your help. I hope Papa Stoffel was well cared for by Clara during your absence, Mama. It's good practice for her. Ha!

Love,
Ida

"John, Frank, Charles," called out Bob seeing his brothers walking toward home. "Do you want a piece of this action?"

"Bob," they sang out in unison.

I SEE BY THE PAPER...

Mr. and Mrs. Charles Wienke of Beloit arrived Sunday for a visit with Woodstock relatives.

Woodstock Sentinel, August 6, 1903.

"I'm taking some action on the game tomorrow. Win, loss odds are stacked against the Olivers, but how about the point split or the number of strike-outs or Moriarity's putouts or runs?"

Charles shook his head, "Not me. I'm an out-of-towner. I only bet on the Beloiters."

"You think Moriarity is going to score runs? Plural?" laughed Frank.

"Of course, I do…or don't…it depends on which way you are leaning."

"OK, what are the odds of a shut out by the Cubs?" asked John.

"Five to one," answered Bob.

"I'll take that," said John. He forked over a quarter-dollar.

"Two bits? Two bits? Can you afford it? Don't let me take food out of your mouth! How about a dollar?" Bob said.

"Nope, a quarter-dollar will do. I'm a father now and must be conservative in my gambling," said John.

"Frank?"

"Hm. Well, I'll bet a dollar that the point split will be ten or more. What kind of odds can you give me on that?" asked Frank.

"How about three to one? Are you sure only a dollar? If you give me five dollars, you'll get fifteen dollars back if you win."

"OK, five dollars! Why not?" Frank agreed.

"Ha-ha! Gotcha both! No way Moriarity is going to let the National Leaguers shut out the Olivers…and ten points or more? I just won your money!" chortled Bob.

"We'll see. We'll be there…and don't you tell ANYONE we bet against the Olivers," Frank warned.

I SEE BY THE PAPER…

Selee's Cubs Play Woodstock Friday.

Tomorrow lovers of the great national sport in Woodstock will have the first opportunity of seeing a major league team in action on the home grounds when the Chicago national leaguers, various nick-named, the cubs, the microbes, the colts and the Selleeites, do the battle royal with the Olivers.

It is confidentially expected by the local management that fully 2,000 spectators or more will see the game, as advices from the neighboring towns and cities indicate large delegations. Reports from some of the country districts show that every farm wagon and team in the county will be in use and special provisions are to be made to take care of those that patronize the game

Having the leaguers here seems to indicate that the Olivers find the average amateur and small league team about the country too easy picking and want to tackle something that will prove more interesting. While there are few of even the warmest supporters, who are willing to back their opinions with collateral, that are coming out and saying that the Olivers will come out victorious, still there are many that are willing to wager a considerable amount that the locals will not be shutout.

Selee's team stands second in the per centage column and is a warm contestant for first place with Pittsburg.

Woodstock Sentinel, August 6, 1903.

"Don't worry, I won't. See you there, Frank and Mr. Cheapskate! See you later, Charles." Bob said as he noticed two more men coming down the walk. "Hey Clayt, Phil, want some action on the game tomorrow?"

Charles shook his head. "I wish he'd get a real job."

"He will. He's gotta settle down sometime," Frank said. "If the Cubs don't win the championship, it will be a sign."

"Of what?" asked John. "That he hasn't lost everything to the bookies?"

"That would be a start, wouldn't it? He's having too much fun with it. He'll never stop if he's always winning."

Sophia looked up from the eggs she was scrambling. A bit of milk in the eggs made them fluffy and then frying them in bacon grease added flavor just the way Carl had liked them. Carl...her hand stopped stirring. Carl...How long now? Almost twenty years he's gone, she thought.

> **I SEE BY THE PAPER...**
>
> **SEELEE'S CUBS SHUT OUT THE CRACK OLIVERS.**
>
> Selee and his microbes have come and gone, and they so thoroughly infected the Olivers with the germ of defeat, no matter how Dr. Ashmore and his bunch labored, he could not find an anti-toxin that would stop the progress of the disease, although he did hold it in check for six straight innings.
>
> The germs of defeat permeated the systems of the local lads to the tune of 12 and 0, which geometrically speaking along base ball lines, means that a shutout was scored.
>
> *Woodstock Sentinel*, August 13, 1903.

I will soon be joining him. Already she was sixty-seven last birthday, but so far so good. She had her boys nearby, and Albert had put in one of those new telephones, although she had used it but a few times. It was probably a waste of good money. The telephone was a large wooden box mounted on the wall in the kitchen. He had shown her how to use it. How to double click the lever on the side that held the listening part to get the hello-girl downtown. Then all she had to do was ask for him, and he would soon be at the other end, talking and listening. The box was mounted a bit too high for her; she wasn't a tall woman. Carl had been tall. He would have been able to talk into it without yelling. She was afraid she would have to find a short stool to stand on to reach it and get close enough to the talking part.

She went back to mixing the eggs, added the grease to the frying pan, and poured the mixture in. The eggs sizzled in the cast iron skillet that had cooked many meals for her children over the years. Not fancy, but it still did the job and would for some years to come.

As she watched the eggs cook, she thought back to Germany, to meeting Carl for the first time, and it made her smile. He was so young, they both were, and he was so shy. Why are men always so shy, she wondered? Carl took years to court her and then had to be pushed to even consider marriage saying he didn't want to drag her into his problems. But those years in Germany had been nothing but problems.

> **I SEE BY THE PAPER...**
>
> **Moriarty Plays with Chicago.**
>
> Last Sunday George Moriarty, the crack third baseman of the Oliver Typewriter baseball team of this city, played that position with Selee's Cubs of the National league at Chicago. That he made good is evident by the nice things said of him by the Chicago papers. The Chicago Daily News of Saturday evening had the following to offer:
> A well-known local baseball manager said today.
>
> "Watch that Moriarty that Selee has signed for a utility man I watched him on the Spaldings and I watched his work, both in the Three I league, where he was with Springfield, and again at Woodstock, where Selee picked him up. He is young, about 19 or so, and big and plays the third bag as if he was made for it."
>
> *Woodstock Sentinel.*

Carl had been drafted into the navy in 1850, during the period of the Prussian Revolution when he was eighteen years old. After five years, he said he just couldn't take it anymore and walked away from the ship when it was docked at Bremen. Instead of going home, where he was sure the authorities would find him, he went to Brandenburg and started calling himself Charles. It was there Sophia met him and fell in love.

Those years were not a happy time in Germany with "wars and rumors of wars" as the Bible said, but they had each other and a plan to come to America. Of course, the plan took longer than the courtship. They married to make travel easier, but that was swiftly followed by the birth of two boys Wilhelm and

August. Then finally, right under the noses of the authorities who were busy with another upcoming war, they went to Bremen in the dark of the night and boarded a ship for America.

They bet on the idea that the Regierungsbeamten, the government officials, would never believe that a deserter would have enough money for passage to America let alone for passage of himself, his wife and two children. After a few stressful minutes of looking at papers, all of them were safely onboard and soon across the ocean to America.

That was 1866, thought Sophia. We were young and ready for hard work. But the babies just kept coming… one boy after another. And then one evening Carl had come home with a cough, and a week later, he was gone. Germs took him, the doctor said. After the shock had worn off, there were all those boys to care for. They had become her life.

> **I SEE BY THE PAPER...**
>
> **O. T. Factory Notes.**
> Frank Wienke moved into his new house in Dacy's addition Saturday. Chas. Bier will move into the Glennon house, which Wienke vacated and Chas. Schmidt and wife (nee. Hobe) will begin housekeeping in the Stuffel house Bier vacated.
>
> *Woodstock Sentinel,* October 15, 1903.

> **I SEE BY THE PAPER...**
>
> **Court House Notes.**
> **Real Estate Transfers.**
> J Wienke and w to A Wienke, pt lt 8, blk 7 Wicher's ad Woodstock -- $1.00
> A Wienke and w to J Wienke, pt lt 7, blk 7, same -- $1.00
> J J Murphy and w to A Wienke, lts 6 and 7, blk 1, Murphy's ad Woodstock -- $1000.00
>
> *Woodstock Sentinel,* October 15, 1903.

While she was musing about the past, Sophia had finished the eggs, cut two thick slices of fresh-baked bread and made a sandwich, which she was now eating along with a cup of reheated coffee from breakfast. It was strange to be cooking for one person. Most of her daughters-in-law were good cooks, and she was rarely called on for help anymore. She was glad to have this house, so warm compared to the one on the edge of town and close to downtown she could even walk if the weather was good.

Sophia decided that life was finally being good to her and that she could just sit back and enjoy it, at least for a little while, couldn't she? She would get caught up on all her sewing and continue to make dinner for the various families once a week, but otherwise, it was time to just enjoy being a grandmother. Who knew how long she'd last, but she was going to make these last years happy ones. What else can I do? she thought.

BIG YACHT IS LAUNCHED
By Clara Doering

The day that the whole city of Racine has been waiting for came today. The launch of John W. Gates $50,000 yacht built by the Racine Boat Works. This day was especially poignant because this was the last launch of any boat by the Racine company as they are moving their boat works to Muskegon, Michigan, taking with it a number of upstanding Racine citizens who shall be missed.

By the two o'clock published launch time, a large crowd had gathered for the auspicious occasion only to be disappointed as the afternoon passed with a large force of men working to get the ship ready to roll majestically down into the Root River. There seemed to be quite a discussion going on regarding the safety of sending such a tall boat down the rollers, the culmination of which was the removal of the pilothouse that was placed aground to be added later.

As the afternoon reached the three o'clock quit time and beyond, workmen on their way home swelled the crowd on both sides of the river waiting patiently for the event to unfold. As 4:30 p.m. approached, the crew commenced knocking the blocking away cautiously trying to knock the same block on either side at the same time. While the crowd had hoped to see Mr. Gates watch his "baby" fall into the sea, he did not make an appearance, although a few officers of his company were sightseers. No society belle broke champagne over the bow, although this reporter did offer her services for same.

At around five o'clock, the last piece of wood holding the boat was liberated and the boat began to move toward the river. "She's off!" cried the crowd as the yacht slid into the water, the stern diving deep.

There was a tremendous splash and then the bow came up and the boat rested erectly on the water. Applause was heard signifying the success of the venture they had watched and soon the crowd was gone, and the crew was left with the work of reassembling the pieces removed.

I SEE BY THE PAPER...

Personal Mention.

Harry Cross, F. G. Arnold, Joe Connors and Robt. Wienke drove over to Elgin Monday evening in automobiles and attended a meeting of the Elks lodge.

Woodstock Sentinel, October 29, 2903

The yacht will be taken in a few days, after it is deemed shipshape, to LaSalle to be presented to the great man himself, and thereafter it will be sailed down the Mississippi to Arthur, Texas for the millionaire's pleasure and pastime over the winter. Fare thee well, Racine Boat Works. Ye shall be missed.

October 20, 1903
Racine Wisconsin

Dear Ida, John, and Helen,

Just a quick note to go with this article from last week. I'm sending a copy of what I sent to them rather than the edited down piece. It was edited and published in the paper, and they even paid me for it! I am so excited. Maybe I can be a reporter after all. Being a performer is getting pretty old already. Write soon and tell me what you think. The editor especially liked the line where I said I volunteered to break the champagne over the bow. I actually did that. I had a front-row seat to the whole spectacle. What fun! The crew was very nice and beautifully strong…oh, I shouldn't say such things when John might read this.

Now that I have "real credentials" I hope to do more reporting on more than buggy crashes. Wish me luck!

Love,
Clara

John rushed up the steps of his new house. He paused just a moment to look at the beautiful oak door newly stained. The house was small with only two bedrooms, but it was large enough for his small family at present, and he was drawing up plans for a more prominent situation to begin in the spring, he hoped. Still, the door looked stunning. He pushed it open and called out, "Ida?"

"In here, John." John turned toward the parlor and took in the scene of motherly bliss. The baby and mama were happily playing with rag dolls on the floor. Helen looked up and smiled. He swept her up into his arms, and she giggled as he kissed her and twirled her around.

"John, a bit less enthusiasm. She just ate," Ida warned. And with that, he set her gently back aground. She lay on her tummy with arms and feet excitedly punching the air. "Da, da, da, pmmm," she chortled.

"See she knows her da da," said John.

> **I SEE BY THE PAPER…**
>
> **Local Intelligence.**
>
> Hallowe'en pranks were very tame comparatively speaking in Woodstock, Saturday night.
>
> Mrs. Medlar has made arrangements with a fine greenhouse to furnish fresh cut flowers on short notice. Telephone No. 29.
>
> A large audience greeted Dr. Driver at the Woodstock opera house the lst evening, his lecture, *The Anglo-Saxon and the Future Rulership of the World*, being the second of the lyceum course. Dr. Driver is a profound student, a magnificent orator and electrifies his hearers. His lecture was one of the best ever heard in Woodstock.
>
> *Woodstock Sentinel*, November 5, 1903.

Ida rolled her eyes. "Here we were quietly having a conversation before nap and now she's all worked up again. Doesn't she look like she's a grounded turtle trying to get purchase to crawl away?"

"Well, you should be excited, my little turtle! Guess what I just heard."

"I don't know. Um…the Cubs took the pennant after all?"

"No…sad to say, no. Did you should have seen Bob's face when it became clear that the Pirates were going to take the league and Cubs would be third? A lot of pints were lifted that night, for sure. Guess again."

"Let's see, Mother Wienke has decided to stop feeding us so much because we are getting fat on her cooking."

John laughed, "Good try, no. Successful Germans are supposed to be fat."

"Well, then I don't know. I suppose the only thing left is politics. Who won this time?"

"You guessed it…we'll not exactly it, but close. Judge Donnelly is looking at a run for Governor!"

"Wow," said Ida, nonplussed. "I'll get lunch while you tell me. OK, little Helen, you just play here for a while. Mama will be right back."

"Dap," Helen said.

"The thing is that no one likes the other candidates, and there are a lot of them…but none looks like the cream that will rise to the top. So, we are going to keep a close watch on them and if after a bit there is still not a front runner, Judge Donnelly will be encouraged to throw his hat into the race. You know what that means, right?"

BATHS! BATHS! BATHS! Woodstock City Bath Rooms. South Side Public Square. Ready for Business. Tubular, Needle and Shampoo Combination Shower. The most exhilarating, Sanitary and Thoroughly Cleansing Bath Given in this City. Open Sunday Mornings from 7 to 12 o'clock.

Ida looked blank-faced at John. "What?"

"There will be jobs, lots of them, on the campaign and then after he's in at the Capitol. How would you like to live in Springfield?"

"Springfield?" John didn't notice that Ida's color had come up. "Might as well be Washington, D.C."

"Maybe later, but this is a wonderful opportunity…for the Judge, that is. Who knows who he'll hire as aides. But the campaign will be great! Traveling with the Judge and convincing people all over Illinois that he is the man for the job."

"That's wonderful," Ida said, trying to be a supportive wife. "What about us while you are out traveling."

John paused in his reverie. "You can come too. You like to travel, right? Trains, automobiles, streetcars. It will be fun."

"And the baby?"

"Ma can watch over her. We aren't talking about right this minute. We'll start planning now but the campaigning will be next summer and fall. She'll be big enough to be without us for a while."

Ida turned away so that John couldn't see the tears that had sprung up in her eyes, more from anger than hurt. Leave her baby? Was he crazy? No sense in fighting about it now. There would be time enough to make her position known. She busied herself making sandwiches from leftover pork roast, a real treat, shared by Mother Wienke midweek. Tomorrow they would join the Wienke's at Mother's house for Sunday dinner after church. Ida was taking German potato salad with its hot vinegary dressing, a recipe passed down from her mother brought from the old country. It was quiet in the room.

> ### I SEE BY THE PAPER...
>
> **Items of Interest.**
> Next horse sale, Dec. 9.
> This is the season of the deadly corn husker.
> Albert Wienke has moved into his new house.
> Be sure to read the news on the second page.
> Crystal Lake has been frozen over since Nov. 20.
> Candidates are beginning to show up all over the county.
> Judge Donnelly is now holding court at home after a bad bout of flu and will complete the term.
>
> *Woodstock Sentinel*, November 26, 1903.

"Ida?" John asked softly. "Are you mad?"

Ida turned to find him standing close behind her. Her anger melted. "No, John, but talk of leaving the baby is upsetting just now. Let's see what the future brings before we make plans for such an occurrence."

He took her in his arms. "OK. I was just excited by the possibility. We don't have to leave Helen anywhere you don't want to. We'll work it out."

Such a nice, gentle man, but with such dreams of grandeur. She must check with Herman about any plans they had made to come and look at possibilities in Woodstock. That might take John's mind off politics. Maybe a trip to Racine for Thanksgiving was in order.

She pushed back away from him, so she could see his blue eyes, much like Helen's, "Can we go to Racine for Thanksgiving?"

"Of course, we can. Helen would love the train ride."

There was a pounding at the door. Just back from their visit to Racine, John, Ida, and Helen were upstairs readying themselves for bed. Helen was tired and fussy and was demanding time with Ida while John took on the task of unpacking the suitcase. They looked at each other. Who would be at the door on a Sunday night at 10:00 p.m.? John headed for the stairs. For some reason, Ida called out, "Be careful, John."

As he approached the door, he left the lights off and peeked out between the curtains covering the central window. What he beheld was horrifying. He threw the door open. "Bob! What happened?"

"Oh good. I sought m'be you wert home n I'd hafta hide on da porch," Bob said, and he fell forward into John's arms. John took a furtive look around and then dragged him in through the door and bolted it. Bob had been beaten and was bloodied around the face and his hands were skinned and swollen. He seemed to be guarding his right side. John let him slump to the floor on the entrance rug.

Ida padded down the stairs and turned on the entrance light. "She is already asleep. Who was at the— Oh my!" Ida looked down at Bob, bleeding on her painted pine floor. "What has happened?"

"I'm not sure. Let's see if we can get him up and calculate the damage. He's drunk, so that's one thing. I assume someone has beaten him. He seems to be breathing alright although he could have a broken rib or two. He might just need some bandaging and a good night's sleep."

"OK, I'll go boil water for cleaning and coffee," Ida said. She bustled into the kitchen.

John got down on his knees beside his brother whose beautiful face was misshapen and bleeding. "Bob? Hey, Bob? Can you hear me?"

"Yesh," said Bob, without opening his eyes. John suspected that opening them was going to be a challenge for a few days.

"Can you tell me what happened? Who did this to you?"

"Beat sup, no money, all bets off," slurred Bob.

Oh no, thought John. "Are you saying that someone wasn't paid off fast enough from a bet?"

"Yesh, shtupid, shtupid, shtupid!" Bob hitting the floor with his left hand with each 'shtupid.'

"OK, let's see if we can get you over to the davenport. Ida's brought a blanket and let's see what damage has been done. Does anything seem broken?"

"Yesh, teeth, nose, hand, face…" Bob's list went on.

After they had cleaned off the blood and dirt, washed the cuts and splits, bandaged his head which was still oozing blood, wrapped his hands, and tried to get him to drink a little coffee, Bob dropped into a fitful sleep.

"You go on to bed, Mama. Your little bear will be up before dawn. I'll stay down here and sleep in the chair just in case he wakes up and doesn't remember what is going on. Or seems to be having trouble. Do you think I should call the doctor?"

Ida considered this. "I think you should be watchful. Wake him every so often and assess. But if it will make you feel better, go ahead and call the doctor now before it gets any later."

"I think if he was bleeding inside, it would be coming out of his nose or mouth or ears. I don't see that. I'll keep my eye on him overnight. Tomorrow, I'll get him over to Ma's. She'll be glad to care for him."

"OK, Papa. I hope he just sleeps through the night like Helen will." She pecked him on the cheek. "You are a good brother."

"Oh, there's time enough to be angry tomorrow. Wouldn't have done any good tonight. Sleep well."

Ida made her way upstairs, and John settled in the big chair next to the davenport. Bob moaned as he tried to move a bit.

John shook his head. "Stupid, stupid, stupid."

Ida sat by a west window us a meager beam of sunlight reading the newspaper on Christmas Eve afternoon. Helen was taking a nap and the house was quiet. The paper was full of interesting articles today.

Banker Hoy had broken a hip in a fall and at eighty-three years it was doubtful that he would recover. A bad train wreck had injured four in Harvard. A man in Cleveland killed himself and his whole family "due to despondency over the impoverished condition of the family purse and the near approach of Christmas." So sad.

A cartoon on page six showed Santa tucked neatly into a small roadster next to his bag of toys with the headline "Santa Claus Up-To-Date." Ida laughed and tried to imagine how Santa could be more efficient in an automobile than in a sleigh.

Mead and Charles advertised "Turkish layer figs and hollower dates." Maybe Figgy Pudding would be good for a Sunday dinner. She'd have to ask Ma Wienke.

Ida's favorite page by far was page eight where inspirational readings, poems and stories were found. Ida felt tears rise as she read Henry Van Dyke's "Keeping Christmas." She thought of all the bad thoughts and deeds she had had during the past year. How would she ever make up for them? Maybe by "Keeping Christmas" all year long.

KEEPING CHRISTMAS
By Henry Van Dyke in Youth's Companion
It is a good thing to observe Christmas Day. The mere marking of times and seasons when men agree to stop work and make merry together is a wise and wholesome custom. It helps one to feel the supremacy of the common life over the individual life. It reminds a man to set his own little watch, now until then, by the great clock of humanity.

But there is a better thing than observance of Christmas Day, and that is, *keeping Christmas.*

Are you willing to forget what you have done for other people and to remember what other people have done for you; to ignore what the world owes you and to think what you owe the world; to put your rights in the background and your duties in the middle distance and your chances to do a little more than your duty in the foreground; to see that your fellow men are just as real as you are, and try to look behind their faces to their hearts, hungry for joy; to own that probably the only good reason for your existence is not what you are going to get out of life, but what you are going to give to life; to close your book of complaints against the management of the universe and look around you for a place where you can sow a few seeds of happiness. Are you willing to do these things even for a day?

    Then you can keep Christmas.

    Are you willing to stoop down and consider the needs and the desires of little children; to remember the weakness and loneliness of people who are growing old; to stop asking how much your friends love you and ask yourself whether you love them enough; to bear in mind the things that other people have to bear in their hearts; to try to understand what those who live in the same house with you really want, without waiting for them to tell you; to trim your lamp so that it will give more light and less smoke, and to carry it in front so that your shadow will fall behind you; to make a grave for your ugly thoughts and a garden for your kindly feelings, with the gate open. Are you willing to do these things even for a day?

    Then you can keep Christmas.

    Are you willing to believe that love is the strongest thing in the world; stronger than hate, stronger than evil, stronger than death, and that the blessed life which began in Bethlehem nineteen hundred years ago is the image and brightness of the Eternal love?

    Then you can keep Christmas.

And if you keep it for a day, why not always?

John opened his eyes. All was black. Had something awakened him. A noise? Helen? He waited for it to repeat. Could have just been the house creaking. It was bitter cold outside. Who knew what might be popping and snapping. But then, he heard three distinct, evenly spaced raps. It was the door. Bob again? Come calling in the middle of the night in a drunken stupor to ask forgiveness? If it was Bob, he'd be sent packing.

John rose and felt for his robe, trying not to wake Ida and Helen. He had taken to pushing the slide lock on the doors at night, so whoever was knocking could not get in. He moved stealthily down the stairs; only a few steps squeaked. Without turning on any lights, he looked out the window to the front porch. A man, bundled against the cold, stood on the front porch. He raised his hand again. Rap, rap, rap! A bit harder this time. A thief wouldn't rap at the door multiple times. He went to the door and slid the bolt back, cracking it just enough to speak through, his toes giving some security pressed against the bottom of the door.

"Yes," he said.

"Oh good, John! It's Frank," said the stranger.

John threw open the door. "Frank? Come in. What's wrong? Ma? Anna? The children?"

"No Ma's fine. My family is fine, but there is a search going on for some kids that ran away from the Home."

John closed the door to the icy wind, and they made their way to the kitchen where the stove still allowed for a little heat. John turned on the overhead light and began stoking the stove to warm the room.

"They ran away two days ago when they were supposed to be walking to school," continued Frank. "Yesterday, Austin saw them in the shop trying to filch food. He gave them a loaf of bread and some peanut butter and sent them on their way."

"Just like him."

"But he also called the sheriff, who said they were missing from the Home. They

> **I SEE BY THE PAPER...**
>
> **German Lutheran Holds Annual Meeting.**
>
> The annual meeting of the German Lutheran church was held last Sunday. Officers for the coming year were elected as follows: President, F. G. Schuett; secretary, Frank Beth; treasurer, Louis Kirkman; elders, Frank Wienke, Louis Kneibusch and Herman Hallier; collectors, William Scharnau and Frank Vogt.
>
> **First Methodist**
>
> Sunday morning the pastor will preach a special sermon to old people and an invitation is extended to all those who are growing old. In the evening there will be a sermon or lecture on the close of the old year, *The Ruins of Time.*
>
> *Woodstock Sentinel,* December 24, 1903.

> **I SEE BY THE PAPER...**
>
> **Below Zero Weather.**
>
> Sunday morning found the mercury in the thermometers seeking the bottom of the tubes. Many of these weather gauges registered twenty-four below zero. Monday it was still cold enough to nip an ear or any exposed surface. By Wednesday the weather moderated a little.
>
> *Woodstock Sentinel,* December 24, 1903.

told him that they were going to Rockford to be home for Christmas."

"How old are we talking?"

"Youngest is eight; oldest is ten. I guess they are from Rockford originally."

"Mm."

"The administrator has gone up to Rockford to look, thinking they jumped a train, but the sheriff thinks they might still be local, and he called the various groups that donate to the Home for help. I got the call because I'm a church elder."

"OK, what do you need? Food, hot coffee, feet on the ground?"

"A group is going northwest toward Rockford and looking in ditches a few miles out of town. They asked me and this other sled to head toward McHenry. I have the sled out in front and wondered if you could join the search for a few hours."

"What time is it?"

"About three. Tomorrow is Christmas so you don't have to work. Just church. I promise to get you back for that."

"OK, let me go get on some warm clothes and tell Ida so she doesn't worry about where I've disappeared to. Make yourself at home. I'll be with you as quick as I can."

Frank unbuttoned his coat and removed his ear-flapper cap. He didn't want to overheat and then go back outside and be cold.

John took the stairs two at a time. He turned on the hall light and then opened the bedroom door wide so he could see to dress.

When he was dressed, he leaned close to the bed. He could just leave a note, but he decided to wake Ida to give her the story before he left.

"Ida?" he whispered. Her eyes flew open, and she sat straight up in bed and began to bring her feet out over the side.

"Helen!" she said.

"No, no. It's OK. Helen is fine. Just stay in bed. Here, lie back down."

"What's happened, John?" Her voice was shaky. A note might have been better.

"Some children from the Home are lost. Frank is here, and we are going to go look for them."

"Alone?"

"No, many are out looking."

"On Christmas Eve?"

"Yes. I will be back for church. OK?"

"I suppose. Be careful."

He kissed her, "I will."

The moon was a slim crescent against the black, star-filled sky, adding virtually no light to the ground below. There had been a little snow overnight, which blended the ditches with the road, but anything dark in the ditch would stand out. The lantern was not effective, and they eventually doused it, allowing their eyes to do their best in the dimness. Frank's horse Nick walked along until up ahead they could see the shape of another sled. Nick nickered a greeting that was returned. They pulled up beside the other sled.

"Any luck?" said John. "Oh sorry, stupid question. You wouldn't be out here if you'd had any luck."

"Right so," said the other man. John didn't recognize him. "Glad you're here. You take that ditch and will take this one. It will go faster than trying to see both at one time."

"Sounds good."

They made their way along slowly, side by side, searching the ditch their eyes looking for dark against the snowbanks or any kind of movement. After a long while, the other man spoke again, "How far out should we go, you think?"

John deferred to Frank who was driving the horse. "Well, let's see. They were seen in town, late afternoon. Got some food and if they hightailed it out right then they could have walked about three miles in an hour until they got hungry or tired, let's say five hours so about fifteen miles."

"OK. We are almost to McHenry. That is twelve miles. I'm sure they are searching the town there just like we are at home."

"We'll go to the city and then turn around and go back, in case they saw us coming and hid. We might be able to catch them as the sky lightens."

"Good plan!"

Several hours later, they were almost back to Woodstock, near the Children's Home on the edge of town. John now had the reigns and Frank scanned the ditch. One of the men in the other sled said, "Hey, look up dar!" They saw a figure silhouetted against the white of snow ahead. It was running toward them and screaming. John clapped the reigns and Nick quickened the pace. The other horse followed suit.

Soon they could discern that it was a woman in a light coat, screaming, what sounded like "It's a child! It's a child!" As they got abreast the spot where she stood, she said again, "It's a child crawling out of the cornfield."

Frank was out and to her before the others. She turned before he reached her and ran back up the road a bit and into the ditch bordering a cornfield. He followed. John brought Nick to a stop next to the ditch. Frank quickly scooped up the boy, not even half-grown, and carried him to the sled. He pulled out a few blankets to cover him. John took off his warm wool scarf and tied it gently around the boy's head covering his ears and lower face, so only his closed eyes were showing.

"John, go as quick as you can to Dr. Windmueller's. I'll stay here and help the search for the other two."

"G'dap!" John called to Nick, urging him into a quick trot which they maintained back into Woodstock. John looked back at the boy and was not sure if he was breathing. He alit from the sled and banged on the doctor's door. It was opened at once, and the good doctor emerged. Both men ran to the sled. John picked the boy up and brought him into the warmth of the office laying him on an examination bed. So light, he thought, so thin. The boy looked frozen with frost on his forehead and cheeks.

"How long?" asked the doctor.

"I don't know. Probably many hours. We found him in a ditch about a mile past the Children's Home. Can you believe it? So close. Frank and the others are searching the area for the other boys."

"OK. I'll do what I can. You go tell the sheriff if you can find him. I think he's running the town search."

"OK." John hurried back to the sled and began his search for the sheriff by going to the jail, which was where he found the sheriff and several deputies. On hearing the news, they jumped on their horses and took off toward McHenry Road.

John looked around the quiet town. There was a dull light in the eastern sky although it was still an hour before sunup. He decided he wouldn't go back out along the road, but rather gave Nick his head, and the horse went straight to the stable at Frank's. He brought the tired horse into the barn still attached to the sled. Nick went without comment to a bucket standing ready in the aisle and got a long drink while John closed the big doors to the cold. John took off the harness hanging it from the empty wooden pegs along the back wall. As soon as he was free, Nick went to his stall and lay down, rolling in the deep bed of straw which John was glad to see Frank had furnished earlier in the day.

"Good boy, Nick," praised John. The horse stood and shook, got another drink and began munching on a leaf of hay. John closed and latched the stall door and made his way back out into the yard. The windows of Frank's house were dark, so John began the three-block walk home. As he walked, he said a little prayer for the two boys still out on the cold McHenry Road.

The news that the boys had been found and that two of them had succumbed to the cold spread fast, and every church service, mass, or other gatherings from Christmas Day to New Year's Eve mentioned the tragedy. The matron of the

Children's Home and her husband took it very hard that these boys had died on their watch. The boys, they said, had been unhappy and undisciplined, claiming their actions were uncontrollable. They had done all that they could. Woodstock defended the Chicago Industrial Home for Children as a necessary and moral way to handle orphans and delinquents, although some said that they didn't know that the home even took in delinquents.

> ### I SEE BY THE PAPER...
>
> #### Thanks from the Poor.
>
> In the name of all the inmates of the poorhouse of McHenry county, I wish you a Merry Christmas and a Happy New Year. And to all the taxpayers of this poorhouse and particularly to the officers from this institution as the supervisors and to the superintendent G. K. Mills and wife, and we give our sincere gratitude to the Harvard ladies for the Christmas presents which we received through Santa Claus himself.
>
> I hope and wish the Lord will give you all the blessings and rewards for it and we will extend through the press or in any other way you think best our sincere gratitude.
>
> With sincerest of Christmas greetings, I am earnestly one of the paupers. L. K.
>
> *Woodstock Sentinel.*

Ida held John's hand tightly when the minister announced at the beginning of the Christmas service that the boys had been found dead. The congregation had prayed, not for the boys who were beyond human intervention, but for their families and for the Children's Home. John had said that it was a miracle that searchers had found even one boy alive.

"It's so sad," said Ida a week later, hands flying as she knit a scarf to replace one that John had lost on that trying night. "I suppose this scarf is going to remind you of the boys every time you put it on, isn't it?"

"That's fine. I was part of saving one rather than finding the others. I will wear it like a badge of honor."

"How's Frank?"

"OK. He was pretty upset that I didn't go back out to pick him up, but I explained that the horse was tired, and they seemed to have an excess of searchers at that point."

"How did he get back?"

"He walked back. It was that or ride in the sled with the corpses of two little boys."

"Oh, now I'll have that image in my head forever. How far was it?"

"A mile at most. He was fine."

"You could have said that he walked back because he needed the exercise. Or because he needed fresh air. Or because it was faster than waiting for the other sled."

"Sorry. I suppose any of those might be true. At any rate, he had to walk back, and I doubt he'll let me live down leaving him for a while."

"I guess, on this auspicious night, we have a lot to be thankful for."

John rose and came to sit next to her on the davenport. He stopped her hands with his own and looked into her eyes. "Last New Year's Eve we weren't even together."

"You're right. That was when I was so scared and acting crazy. I'm sorry."

"No need to apologize again. We are very lucky that we are here together and that our little one has both parents to furnish a good home. In truth, thinking about all those orphans got to me. Maybe we should consider going out there to have a look at them once Helen is a little older."

Ida looked down at her hands, clutched in his, and back up at his very serious eyes. She didn't know what to say. It wasn't often that he left her speechless.

"They do sometimes get babies who wouldn't have been damaged by running with hooligans or having barely survived bad families," he continued.

Ida cleared her throat, eyes back on their hands, but said nothing.

"Ida?"

"John…I…I…I'm not against the idea. I don't want Helen to be our only child, and certainly, a child from the Home needs a good family, but.…"

"But what?"

Ida thought about how she had, just a week earlier, promised to *Keep Christmas* all year long. She needed, right now, to put her own feelings aside and open her heart and home to…no, she couldn't do it. Not yet.

"But what?" John repeated.

"But not right now. Let's see what God provides first."

John loosened his grip and let his eyes stray from hers.

"I only thought—"

"I know, and it was a good thought. Let's think about it more, and we'll see what the future brings."

"So that's a definite maybe," said John, his eyes coming back.

Ida smiled. "A definite maybe."

John smiled also, holding her gaze. And then they heard Helen crying.

"Oh my, what is she doing awake at this time of night?"

"Have we been too loud?"

"I'll go get her. She might be a bit hungry. She didn't eat much at supper."

> **I SEE BY THE PAPER…**
>
> **Prosperous Year About to Close.**
>
> Woodstock points with pride to the achievements of the past twelve months. The measure of a city's prosperity is not found so much in the clearings of the banks or the volume of business done, as it is in the money expended in the construction of homes for the people.
>
> Over one hundred resident houses have been erected during the year commencing with May. By these figures it was shown that nearly $200,000 was expended alone in the erection of a large, handsome and expensive machine shop for the Oliver Typewriter factory and a large and commodious set of buildings for the Borden Condensing works, a substantial addition to the city power house and other industrial improvements.
>
> *Woodstock Sentinel,* December 31, 1903.

Before she went to the baby, she reached out and hugged her loving husband. "I love you, John. I will think about it, I promise." Then she stood and was away.

John repaired to his chair. It had been a somewhat a spur of the moment request. He didn't want to see that boy's frozen face in his dreams. He didn't want any of the children to face that awful death. But Ida was right. They needed to think about it more. He shook his head. I bet every home in Woodstock with two loving parents is having this conversation. He'd have to wait and see what the new year brought.

Ida walked in with Helen, wide-awake and still sniffling a little. John rose to greet them. "Well, hi there, little Helen. Did you get up to ring in the New Year?"

Helen put her fingers to her mouth and uttered a shaky sigh.

"She says she's hungry. Do you mind if I feed her right here?"

"Not at all. My girls know what they want. I'm just along for the ride."

Ida smiled, "And what a ride it's been so far. We are so glad you brought us home to Woodstock, aren't we Helen." She stood on tiptoe and placed a proper kiss on John's lips, and Helen giggled.

She sat and opened her multi-button bodice, and Helen eagerly began to suckle.

"My Madonna and child," John said. He meant it, but his look was wistful. It was, after all, New Year's Eve.

"Oh, for heaven's sake, John! Sit down and read the paper," Ida said, but there was a little upturn at the corners of her mouth, and she blushed slightly. "Don't worry. She'll be asleep in no time."

And she was.

Helen Frances Wienke
Five months old.
Born: July 2, 1903.

A Fine Grocer from Woodstock.

Coming in Summer 2020.

John is made an offer he can hardly resist from Ida's brother, Herman Doering. But Ida is with child and since the new house will break ground at any time, John is hesitant to put more on his plate. Ida encourages him to fulfill his dream of being a fine grocer from Woodstock.

But events become more challenging when Ida develops dangerous complications with her pregnancy, and John sells their house. Now eight months pregnant and homeless, will John and Ida be forced to return to Ma Wienke's boarding house?

A Fine Grocer from Woodstock continues the story of the Wienke and Doering families. John and Ida must meet the challenge of providing for their growing family and nourishing their relationship even in the face of mounting responsibility during the years 1904 to 1907.

Dear Reader

September 2019

Thank you for your interest in *Take Me Home to Woodstock,* the first book in *The Woodstock Tales.* The next in this series, *A Fine Grocer from Woodstock,* will be coming in the Summer of 2020 with a third book to follow at the beginning of 2021. I am excited to share the next adventures of the Wienke and Doering clans with you.

If you want to know more about when the next book will be available or upcoming events, please follow me at sallycissna@wordpress.com, where you'll find other stories featuring the Wienkes and Doerings. You can also follow *The Woodstock Tales* series at SuLu Press on Facebook for updates.

If you want to send me a message or question regarding the book or the series, please do so at sallycissna@sulupress.org. I look forward to hearing from you.

Ida, John, Helen, Clara, Bob and all the characters of *Take Me Home to Woodstock* are looking forward to seeing you again. And so am I.

Sally Cissna

www.ingramcontent.com/pod-product-compliance
Lightning Source LLC
Chambersburg PA
CBHW032021050726

47590CB00006B/2251